Dick Merriwell's Day

Iron Nerve

BURT L. STANDISH

Author of the celebrated "Merriwell" stories, which are the favorite reading of over half a million up-to-date (1904) American boys.

BOOKS FOR ATHLETICS

LONDON
IBOO PRESS HOUSE
86-90 PAUL STREET

Dick Merriwell's Day
Iron Nerve

BURT L. STANDISH
Author of the famous Merriwell Stories.

BOOKS FOR ATHLETICS

Layout & Cover © Copyright 2020 iBooPress, London

Published by
iBoo Press House

3rd Floor
86-90 Paul Street
London, EC2A4NE UK

t: +44 20 3695 0809
info@iboo.com II iBoo.com

ISBNs
978-1-64181-926-8 (h)
978-1-64181-927-5 (p)

We care about the environment. This paper used in this
publication is both acid free and totally chlorine-free (TCF).
It meets the minumum requirements of ANSI / NISO z39-
49-1992 (r 1997)

Printed in the United States

Dick Merriwell's Day

Iron Nerve

BURT L. STANDISH

Author of the celebrated "Merriwell" stories, which are the favorite reading of over half a million up-to-date (1904) American boys.

BOOKS FOR ATHLETICS

MERRIWELL SERIES
Stories of Frank and Dick Merriwell
Fascinating Stories of Athletics

A half million enthusiastic followers of the Merriwell brothers will attest the unfailing interest and wholesomeness of these adventures of two lads of high ideals, who play fair with themselves, as well as with the rest of the world.

These stories are rich in fun and thrills in all branches of sports and athletics. They are extremely high in moral tone, and cannot fail to be of immense benefit to every boy who reads them.

They have the splendid quality of firing a boy's ambition to become a good athlete, in order that he may develop into a strong, vigorous, right-thinking man.

Contents

DICK MERRIWELL'S DAY.

CHAPTER I

THE GREAT CRISIS.

Fairhaven had fought desperately for the game at Sea-slope, and three extra innings had been necessary to decide the contest; but the home club had won in the twelfth, the final score being four to three.

"I told you before the game began that we were going into second place to-day!" cried Sam Hyde, addressing Dick Merriwell, captain of the Fairhavens. "Hard luck for you, but we're out for the pennant."

"You're not out of reach yet, are you?" retorted Dick, as he prepared to pull on his sweater. "We still have a small show, haven't we?"

"Perhaps you may finish in third position if you can hold Maplewood down," said the Seaslope captain. "We're going to finish at the top, and I fancy Rockford will be in second place. It's now a fight between you and Maplewood to see which of you escape being tail-ender."

"Evidently you have it all settled—in your mind," smiled Dick. "These things don't always pan out the way they are planned."

"Just look over our record when you get a chance," invited Hyde. "When you've considered what we've done, it ought to satisfy you that we're going to swipe the pennant."

Having drawn on his sweater, Dick observed that Ray Garrett, the manager of the Fairhaven team, was looking blue and downcast. Merriwell clapped him on the shoulder and advised him to cheer up.

"It's tough!" muttered Garrett. "This game pushed us down from second position and let Seaslope head us. If Seaslope keeps up the pace it has set, Hyde is right in thinking it will win the pennant."

"You talk like a funeral!" exclaimed Dick. "Wait till we reach Rockford. We'll figure over the standing of the teams after we get there. I think you will see they are well bunched."

The recent victories of the Seaslope team had enthused its spectators, and the game this day had been witnessed by a wonderfully large crowd. Early in the season, when Seaslope was losing steadily, it had been difficult to get out a respectable gathering of spectators. Merriwell could not help thinking of the change as he watched the well-satisfied throng pouring out at the open gate of the inclosure. At last Seaslope was making money, and Jared Whitcomb, the manager of the team, was smiling and well satisfied.

"We've just about time enough to catch the next car for Rockford," said Garrett, looking at his watch. "Have you picked up all the stuff, fellows? Got all the bats? Where's the body protector? Don't leave anything."

Carrying their bat bags and other necessary luggage, the Fairhaven team hurried from the ground and cut across a field to reach the trolley line and intercept a car. In this manner they reached the car ahead of many who waited for it at a regular stopping place, and all the boys secured seats. It had been a hot day, and twelve hard innings had tired them to such an extent that they were glad to sit down.

"We must have that game to-morrow," said Garrett, who had taken pains to secure a seat beside Dick. "For that reason I'm not going to send you back to the island to-night. I don't want you to take that trip. If it should be rough to-morrow you might get shaken up coming over."

"That's a good idea," said Dick; "but I thought you intended to run an excursion to-morrow."

"I do. I'll run it just the same. More than that, I'm going to see if I can't stir up things on the island to-night. We must have a good big crowd of rooters with us in Rockford to-morrow. I will telephone the boys on the island and set them at work getting up a crowd. Dick, do you realize that the game to-morrow is going to be one of the hardest of the season?"

"Haven't a doubt of it," nodded Merriwell. "If Rockford won to-day from Maplewood, she'll be able to hold first place to-morrow whether she loses or not; but if Maplewood won——"

"It seems likely to me," interrupted Garrett. "Maplewood has been walloping almost everybody but us since getting her new team. A week ago I fancied Rockford might have the strongest team in the league. To-day I'm inclined to think she has the weakest."

"Time will tell. We'll find out how the teams stand as soon as we learn what happened in Maplewood."

Finding the boys were inclined to accept Garrett's rather gloomy view of the matter, Dick laughed at them and did his best to cheer them up.

"Don't you worry about us!" cried Obediah Tubbs. "We'll git into the game to-morrow, dern our picters! If Rockford takes a fall out of us she'll have to get up and hump herself."

On arriving in Rockford the boys eagerly looked over the bulletin of the Trolley League games displayed in front of the Star office.

"Great horn spoon!" cried Buckhart. "Just look at that! Maplewood lifted Rockford's scalp to-day! Nine to two! That was doing it some!"

"The standing is what interests me now," laughed Dick. "There it is, boys. Talk about teams being bunched! What do you think of that? Seaslope and Rockford are tied, having won twenty each and lost nineteen. Fairhaven and Maplewood are tied, having won nineteen each and lost twenty. That's the sort of baseball to make your hair curl. It keeps everybody guessing."

"Well, I'm bub-bub-bub-blamed glad Maplewood did beat Rockford to-day," chuckled Chip Jolliby. "I ain't gug-gug-gug-got no love for Maplewood, but it kinder makes things a little more even."

The boys left the car at the Corndike Hotel, where Garrett registered for them and secured rooms for the night.

By this time the various members of the Fairhaven team were well known in Rockford, and a number of persons lingering about the hotel office hailed them one after another by name.

Whitney, the clerk, shook hands with Dick.

"Too bad you dropped that game to-day, Merriwell," he said. "If you had won you would have been tied with us for first place. I keep a bulletin up, following the progress of the games. It was plain enough before the game at Maplewood was half finished that Rockford was going to lose, but you kept us guessing what the result would be at Seaslope. Seaslope's recent success led some of the boys to offer odds that she would take the game to-day. I dropped a five on it myself. I took the short end, and you fellows had me dancing after the ninth inning was finished and the report came in that the score was tied. Then came the white-wash in the tenth, and another in the eleventh. We heard that you finished your half of the twelfth without scoring, and I offered up a humble supplication for you to shut Seaslope out in her half. How did they get their run?"

"Nobody to blame," said Dick. "They earned it. Happened to have their best batters up and made a clean-earned run."

"No fault of the umpiring?"

"If anything," confessed Dick, "we got the best end of that."

"Well, that's good sporting talk!" exclaimed Whitney. "I am sick of hearing all the blame put on the umpiring. When a team loses, it generally blames the umpire. There'll be a hot time in Rock-ford to-morrow. We can't afford to let you have that game. We're obliged to hold first position, you know."

"Of course, you feel that way," retorted Dick. "We have ambi-tions, Mr. Whitney."

A Rockford man who had been standing near now stepped for-ward.

"You can find all the even money you want offered on Rock-ford," he said. "I'd like to bet ten dollars myself. Where are the sports that back your team? You're captain of it, and I suppose you'll bet something yourself, eh?"

"I don't make a practice of betting," said Dick.

The man laughed in an annoying manner.

"That's a good excuse for a weak heart," he said. "Here's your manager. I understand he made a heavy bet early in the season—something like five hundred dollars. He won, too. Perhaps he wants to peddle a little of that coin."

Garrett shook his head.

"There are reasons why I can't bet," he said, thinking of his promise to his mother.

Again the Rockford man laughed.

"Your judgment is better than your nerve," he declared. "Evi-dently you're going to hang onto that five hundred."

Ray flushed.

"I think you'll find plenty of men ready to accommodate you to-morrow," he said. "There will be an excursion from Fairhaven, and we expect a crowd."

"Tell your people to bring all the money they are anxious to lose."

A few moments later Garrett and Dick were alone in the room

assigned to them. Ray made some figures on a piece of paper and sat frowning over them. Finally his face cleared a little, and he began to laugh.

"What is it?" questioned Dick.

"I was just thinking of what might happen to-morrow. Fairhaven plays Rockford, while Maplewood goes against Seaslope. What if both Fairhaven and Maplewood win? Have you thought about that?"

"Haven't given it much thought yet," said Dick. "Let me see, both Fairhaven and Maplewood are one game behind at present. If they win to-morrow—why, every team in this league will be tied!"

"That's exactly what will happen," nodded Ray. "Wouldn't that be remarkable? If the two tail-end teams win to-morrow every team in this league will have won twenty games and lost twenty games. With the season so far advanced, I don't believe such a thing ever happened before in any league. Jingoes, wouldn't it kick up some excitement!"

"It would be the best thing that could happen for the league," said Dick. "But let's do a little more figuring. If we defeat Rockford and Seaslope wins from Maplewood, Seaslope will take first position, while we will be tied with Rockford for second."

"That's correct," said Garrett. "But if we lose and Maplewood wins, we go clean to the bottom. To-day we had a chance to be tied for first place and lost it. Another defeat may put us into last place. Dick, I confess I'm worried about that game to-morrow. Win it if you can."

"I promise you that every man on the team will do his level best," said Dick.

CHAPTER II

TOM FERNALD'S PROPOSITION.

om Fernald, the Rockford manager, returned home in anything but a pleasant frame of mind. He had counted on victory, and defeat had cost him some good money. Having heard of the result at Seaslope, he also figured over the standing of the teams, and his anxiousness increased as he fully realized the critical nature of the situation. He knew enough about baseball to understand that fortune had favored Rockford in many instances, and enabled her to retain first place. At one time he had encouraged Seaslope and rejoiced in her victories over Fairhaven and Maplewood, little dreaming the team was likely to become a dangerous antagonist for first position at the end of the season.

He had felt satisfied over the success of Maplewood with a new team, being confident that Rockford would not suffer through this success. Now the complexion of things had changed greatly. The loss of two more games might push Rockford down and make an opportunity for those who had previously criticised him and his management to say, "I told you so."

Fernald dropped off the car at the Corndike and came face to face with Brad Buckhart, of the Fairhavens, as he entered the hotel.

"How do you do, Buckhart?" he nodded. "So you had hard luck yourself, did you? It must have been a hot game. Twelve innings, was it?"

"Yes, twelve warm ones," nodded the Texan.

"You did well to hold Seaslope down in such a manner. Didn't think you could do it. Those fellows have a hard team to beat over there. How were the hits?"

"They made one more than we did."

"And the errors?"

"Neither team made an error to-day."

Fernald whistled.

"By Jove! that was a great game. What are you going to do to-morrow?"

Brad grinned.

"We're going to do our level best to make you hump yourself, Mr. Fernald," he replied. "We'll have my pard in the box to-morrow, and you know what that means."

"Then Merriwell didn't pitch to-day?"

"No."

"I'd like to have a little talk with you, Buckhart," said the Rockford manager, taking Brad by the arm. "Let's sit down over here."

The Texan wondered why Fernald should wish to talk with him, but walked over to some chairs in a corner of the office, where they sat down quite by themselves.

"You're a pretty good friend to Merriwell, aren't you?" asked Fernald.

"Sure thing," nodded Brad.

"And you're the only catcher on the Fairhaven team?"

"I opine I am. Some of the others might go under the bat, but they don't advertise themselves as catchers."

"There's no other man on the team who can hold Merriwell, is there?"

"I don't like to get swelled up in my statements, Mr. Fernald; but I will say that Dick and I are a whole lot familiar with each other, and work pretty well together."

The Rockford manager smiled.

"That's right," he confessed. "I have watched you, and you work together like machinery. Without a catcher behind the bat who knows him thoroughly and can hold him, Merriwell would not be particularly effective. Surely he couldn't use that so-called combination ball. It would fool a catcher just as much as it fools a batter. Whatever that combination ball is, it's a case of luck when a batter hits it fairly. Of course, I know it's no combination rise and drop, for that's impossible."

"You think so," laughed Brad. "I don't blame you any, Mr. Fernald; but I'll bet something some of your players will tell you it is a combined rise and drop."

Fernald shook his head.

"I know it's something mighty odd," was his acknowledgment; "but reason teaches me that a ball can't be thrown in such a manner that it will curve in one direction and reverse and curve in another. Merriwell apparently throws a rise to start with, but it's his style of delivery that makes the ball seem to rise. He throws it with a rotary movement that finally turns it into a drop."

"It certain appears that you've figured the thing out to your satisfaction; but what are you driving at?"

"It won't make any great difference with your team if we win to-morrow," said Fernald softly. "You will still be close enough on our heels to run us down before the season closes. It will make a big difference to me if we lose; I'll have all the cranks in this town on my back. How would you like to make a good thing out of the game to-morrow?"

The Texan started slightly, then turned slowly and stared at his companion.

"I sure would like to make a good thing out of it," he said, in a queer tone of voice. "That's natural."

"Perfectly," nodded Fernald, fancying he had deftly secured an opening, and likewise imagining that this sturdy boy was willing to listen to a proposition. "I want to give you a pointer Buckhart. I am going to bet on the game to-morrow. There'll be plenty of chaps ready to back your team. I am indifferent about making any money, but I don't want to lose any."

"It certain seems to me that you will either have to make some or lose some if you bet," said the Westerner.

"I may win my bets without making any money."

"I opine that's impossible, Mr. Fernald. How can you do it?"

"Well, for instance, supposing I had it fixed with some one on your team that whatever I won should go to him in case I did win. By this I mean that if Rockford took the game I would hand over my winnings to a member of the Fairhaven team. It's absolutely necessary, as I have explained to you, for us to stay in first position. That will be more valuable to me than any money I might win. If you can assure me that Rockford will hold her place by taking that game I will cover all the Fairhaven money that is pushed at me. You may send bettors to me and keep tabs on the amount posted. I don't care how much is put up, as long as I stand no chance of losing."

Brad's left hand was lowered at his side, and he quivered a little as his fingers closed into a hard, bony fist. Although the man was not aware of it, in that moment he was in danger of being smitten by that fist.

"I reckon I understand what you mean, Mr. Fernald," said the Texan. "You're proposing to me that I do something to give Rockford the game?"

"There's no need to put it thus plainly in words," said the manager. "You are sharp enough to understand. Here is your opportunity to make a big thing. In the most natural manner you can have a passed ball at a critical point in the game. You can make bad throws to head off men stealing bases. Such things are done by the best catchers in the business. They have their yellow days. No need to excite suspicion by it. Perhaps it might not even be necessary to do anything of the sort. If Rockford had a good lead, you could play your best game and still be sure you would get the boodle when the game was over. What do you say, Buckhart? Can I depend on you?"

"See here, Mr. Fernald," said the sturdy Texan, "I don't like to talk this thing over any more here. There are some people round who have looked at us right sharp already. We're attracting attention. If you will come up to room thirty-seven within ten minutes I'll give you an answer. I want a little time to think it over. I'll be waiting for you in that room. If you will notice, Whitney, the clerk, is watching us now. I opine I'll move."

Without waiting for Fernald to say whether he would come to room 37 or not, Brad rose and sauntered away.

As the Texan walked away he looked around the place searchingly. A shade of disappointment seemed to settle on his face.

"Where are the boys?" he muttered. "Some of them ought to be hanging round here."

For a moment he stepped out in front of the hotel. Chip Jolliby was standing out there with his hands in his pockets, watching the people on the street. Instantly Buckhart seized Jolliby by the arm and began speaking to him earnestly, in a low tone.

"Great juj-juj-juj-jingoes!" gasped the tall boy, as he listened.

"Here's the key to the door," said Brad, thrusting a key into Jolliby's hand. "Get a move on you. Must be plenty of witnesses."

Then the Western youth turned back into the hotel and ascended the stairs, whistling carelessly.

Barely had Buckhart disappeared when Jolliby observed a man passing on the street. With a spring Chip grasped this man's elbow.

"Hold on a mum-mum-mum-minute, Mr. Blackington," stuttered the tall lad. "I wish to sus-sus-see you on important bub-business."

"What's that?" asked Uriah Blackington, the former manager of the Rockford team. "Why, hello, Jolliby! You look excited. Losing that game to-day at Seaslope must have disturbed you somewhat."

"You're sus-sus-sus-still president of the Trolley League, aren't you?" asked Chip.

"I believe I am," nodded the Rockford man. "I wanted to resign, but they kept me in it."

"Have you gug-gug-got about twenty minutes to sus-sus-spare?" inquired Chip.

Blackington glanced at his handsome watch.

"Yes, forty minutes if it's anything interesting," he nodded. "What do you want?"

"Just cuc-cuc-come upstairs in a hurry," urged Chip. "There's something dud-dud-doing—something you ought to know about."

"What is it?"

"No tut-tut-time to explain now. Pup-pup-please come."

"Well," laughed Blackington good-naturedly, "you seem dreadfully anxious about it, and so I'll come. Go ahead."

They entered the hotel and Chip glanced around in apprehension, as they ascended the stairs, fearing they would be observed. To his relief no one paid any attention to them. Jolliby led the way to the door of a room on which he knocked.

"Come in," called a voice.

"Jingoes!" exclaimed Chip. "Didn't know there was anybub-bub-bub-body in there! Jest thought I'd knock and fuf-fuf-fuf-find out!"

He opened the door and stepped in, followed by Blackington, whose curiosity was greatly aroused by this time.

It was Merriwell's room they entered, and they found Dick and Ray Garrett still pondering over the figures representing the standing of the teams in the league.

"Is it you, Chip?" said Dick. "Why didn't you come in without stopping to knock? You don't have to knock on my door. Oh, hello! I see you have some one with you. How do you do, Mr. Blackington?"

Dick rose quickly and stepped forward to meet the president of the league, who shook hands with him cordially.

"Ain't gug-gug-gug-got no time to chin," said Jolliby, in a mysterious manner, holding up the key Buckhart had given him. "I want you fuf-fuf-folks to keep mighty still. Where's that dud-dud-door lead to, Dick?"

As he asked the question he pointed to a door at one side of the room.

"That leads into the next room," said Dick. "It's locked."

"Well, I think we'll tut-tut-try this key on it," whispered Jolliby, as he hurried toward the door.

His manner was so unusual that his companions watched him wonderingly. The key unlocked the door and Chip opened it a fraction, peering into the next room.

"All right," he said, with satisfaction, as he pulled the door softly to, but did not close it entirely.

"Tut-tut-turn out that light, Dick. Come over here, everybody. Get close to this door and kuk-kuk-kuk-keep all-fired still. You're gug-gug-going to hear something that'll interest you."

He checked their questions, and a few minutes later the quartette stood close by the door, silently waiting and listening.

Within three minutes some one entered the adjoining room. This person began to whistle, and Dick knew it was Brad Buckhart.

Less than three minutes after Brad entered that room, there came a knock on his door. On being invited to enter, the person who knocked cautiously opened the door and looked in.

It was Tom Fernald.

"Walk right in, Mr. Fernald," invited the Texan. "You see I'm all alone here. I'm waiting for you. Thought you might wish to talk to me up here where there's less danger of being observed or overheard."

Fernald came in and closed the door behind him.

"What if some one should come here and find us together in this room?" he asked.

The Westerner sauntered over to the door and turned the key in the lock.

"No danger anybody will git in that way," he smiled grimly. "Now we're alone here, Mr. Fernald, I'm ready to listen to your proposition. I want you to make it plain so I will understand. I don't propose to go into this thing any unless it's fixed so there will be not the slightest misunderstanding between us."

Brad then induced Fernald to again offer inducements to throw the game on the following day to Rockford.

"It's a great opportunity for you to make a big thing," said the tricky manager of the Rockford team.

"I should say so," nodded Brad. "Why, according to that offer, if I could induce people to bet five hundred dollars, or even a thousand, on Fairhaven, and Rockford won the game, I'd get all the boodle put up to back our team."

"I hardly think you could find five hundred dollars," said Fernald, "although it's possible you may. Of course, you will be able to discover people ready to bet anything from five to fifty dollars, and if you convince them it's a sure thing Fairhaven will win there may be one or two who will risk larger sums."

The Texan seemed to hesitate. He soberly shook his head.

"I confess I don't like to do it," he said. "It's a whole lot like stealing money. If any one ever finds it out it would cook my goose. All my friends would go back on me."

"How will any one ever find it out?" questioned Fernald. "There's no evidence that such a bargain was made between us."

"That sure is correct," nodded the Texan. "And for that same reason you may go back on me some and refuse to hand the money over after you get your paws on it. I can't make you give it up. If I tried that I'd be exposing myself. What assurance have I that you will be square with me?"

"My word!" cried Fernald. "I give you my word!"

Brad hunched his broad shoulders.

"Your word!" he exclaimed, with a short laugh. "Why, I don't opine the word of any galoot who will put up such a job is worth a great deal."

"Come, come, young man, don't be insolent!" exclaimed Fernald, in annoyance. "I can't afford to throw you down after a bargain of that sort. I have a standing to maintain here. I am taking more chances than you. If this thing should become known, and it could be proven that I entered into such a compact, I'd be dropped from the management of the Rockford team."

"Is that right?"

"Certainly it's right. Let me whisper something to you that I have never mentioned to any one before. Really I don't care a rap whether Rockford wins the pennant or not, but for the present I must keep my team at the head of the league. I must do it in order to satisfy the people here who have backed the team. If I can keep Rockford at the front up to within a few days of the finish I will be well satisfied. More than that, I will agree with you now to throw two of our last games in return for this one to-morrow."

"Why should you do that?" asked Brad, in a puzzled manner. "I don't see how that would benefit you."

"I will explain it. I am betting on my own team now, and I risk money for the purpose of making money. If I can keep Rockford ahead till near the finish of the season, there will be plenty of Rockford people ready to back us to win the pennant, and they'll back us good and heavy. I'll not let any of them suspect the game I'm playing, but I'll have some good men ready with my money to bet that Rockford does not win the pennant. I shall bet heavily, too. Then I'll throw the important games that will cause us to drop into second place. If your team can keep close onto our heels, you will go into first place and get the pennant. It will be a good thing for Fairhaven, as it will create enthusiasm over there and lead the islanders to put a team into the league next year. So you see, my boy, you're not damaging your own team by entering into this agreement with me about the game to-morrow. The loss of one game now will mean your final advancement."

Brad stood with his feet quite wide apart, and his hands on his hips, watching the crafty rascal all through this speech.

"Well, you're sure a first-class schemer!" exclaimed the Texan. "I've heard before that such things happen in professional baseball, but I didn't suppose there would be a chance for such a deal in a league like this. I opined every team in the league would be out for blood and ready to capture the pennant, if possible."

"That's the way it used to be in this league," retorted Fernald; "and it was a disadvantage to the league, for Rockford had a way of always winning the pennant, and the smaller places grew discouraged. If Rockford loses this year by a game or two she'll be right back in the league next year as fierce as ever. If Fairhaven loses, it's likely she'll be discouraged and won't try it another year. So you see I'm really willing to do a generous thing."

"Yes, a heap generous!" nodded Brad, with a touch of sarcasm he could not repress. "But do you consider it honest sport? Do you think it right to fool the backers of your team in such a manner? Without doubt some of those backers will bet their money that Rockford takes the pennant. Besides putting up their money to support the team, they'll lose their bets at the end of the season and be mighty sore over it."

"They are a lot of easy marks, anyhow!" snarled Fernald. "I don't see that you're called on to worry about them. The principal thing you care about is to come out on top, isn't it?"

"I certain should like to see Fairhaven come out on top," confessed Brad. "Still I am some afraid you're inclined to fool me. Without a witness to our agreement I can't be satisfied that you will stand by the whole of it. That being the case," he added, walking toward the door that opened into the adjoining room, "I will just call in a witness or two."

Having said this, he suddenly flung the door wide open.

Into the room stepped Dick Merriwell, followed by Ray Garrett.

"These yere gents are my witnesses," said the Texan. "They've heard our little agreement at my invitation." Then he paused, for Uriah Blackington followed Dick and Ray into the room, with Chip Jolliby at his heels.

The face of Blackington was like a thundercloud. He pointed an accusing finger at Fernald as he cried:

"So this is the kind of a man you are! I've always been inclined to think you a crook, although you've escaped detection until now!"

Fernald had turned pale, and for a moment or two he stood quite still, apparently thunderstruck and overcome. Suddenly he wheeled toward Buckhart, his fist clinched, and his teeth gleaming between his back-drawn lips. With the intention of striking the Texan, he made a single step.

In a twinkling Dick and Ray Garrett were between Brad and Fernald.

"Let him come! Let him come!" palpitated the Western lad. "I'll give him his medicine good and plenty."

"Better not raise a disturbance, Mr. Fernald," said Dick quietly. "It'll be a bad thing for you. A row here will cause this whole matter to come out, and if you're not ridden on a rail and tarred and feathered after that, it will surprise me."

CHAPTER III

A WORTHY PAIR.

hat's right," nodded Uriah Blackington. "If this thing gets out, you'll be driven out of Rockford, Fernald. There's only one thing for you to do."

"I hope you're not chump enough," said Fernald, "to think I meant it when I offered to throw the final games this season. I did that in order to lead this fellow into the bargain with me about the game to-morrow."

"I wouldn't believe you under oath!" retorted Blackington. "You're a thoroughly untrustworthy scoundrel! As president of this league, I demand your instant resignation from the position you hold."

"Oh, do you?"

"Yes, sir."

"I suppose you intend to become manager again?"

"Perhaps I do. You forced me out of it by your trickery, and if I'm asked to take the position again I may consent."

"Consent!" snarled Fernald. "You'll jump at it!"

"Sit down right here and now," commanded the president of the league sternly, "and write your resignation. I'll furnish the pen."

"And I'll furnish the paper," laughed Dick, stepping into his own room and returning in a moment with a sheet. "Here it is."

"That's bub-bub-bub-bub-business!" chattered Jolliby. "We'll gug-gug-gug-get rid of one crook! If we could catch old Hammerswell the same way it would be a mighty gug-gug-good thing for baseball in these parts!"

Fernald seemed undecided. He took a cigarette case from his pocket and extracted a cigarette, which he slowly rolled between his fingers. All the while he was thinking, but in vain he sought some loophole of escape. He had fallen into the trap, and the only way out of it was to assent to the demand made upon him.

"I want to tell you people one thing," he finally observed, having struck a match and lighted the cigarette. "No man up to date has ever played me a trick like this and not lived to repent it. This fool boy will repent it, too."

"Listen to the wind," chuckled Brad. "How it blows!"

Without another word Fernald sat down and wrote the resignation demanded by Blackington.

"There," he said, having signed his name, "now go ahead and blow on me, the whole of you. I want to tell you something more. You've put me in a bad hole. I have a few friends here who will stick by me. Some of them are bad men to have for enemies. I will find out who goes from this room and tells what has happened here. From the moment he opens his mouth to blow on me, the man who does so will be in constant danger. Night and day, asleep or awake, he'll be in danger."

"Better keep your threats to yourself, Fernald," advised Blackington. "If anything serious should happen your words will be remembered and will rise to accuse you."

Fernald laughed disdainfully as he turned toward the door.

"If any of you think I'm disposed of in this manner he will live to discover the mistake," declared the man, pausing with his hand on the knob. "You will still find me and my influence effectual in baseball in this league. Good night!"

"Well," said Brad, when the rascal had departed, "this is the first time any galoot ever tried to buy me. I sure reckon he didn't know who he was dealing with. Chip, you followed instructions a whole lot clever. I didn't expect you'd be able to get hold of Mr. Blackington, but I'm right glad you did. Only for the fact that Mr. Blackington heard the whole thing, Fernald would have made a fight before resigning as manager."

"He forced me to resign some time ago," said Blackington; "but the tables were turned on him to-night. I may not be reappointed as manager of the Rockford team. In fact, I am not anxious for the position, as it entails no end of worry and work. Nevertheless, it's pretty certain that whoever is now appointed to fill the place will be an honest man, and baseball will be benefited by it. With a man like Henry Duncan in Benton Hammerswell's place at Maplewood the patrons of this league would get a chance to see honest games."

"I don't suppose there's any way to fuf-fuf-fuf-force old Ham out, is there?" asked Chip, who was quite exultant over what had taken place.

"It's doubtful if he can be forced out," said Blackington. "He has everything in his hands up there. He's the sole backer of the team, and thus far it has cost him a fat little sum of money."

For a short time they talked over Fernald's trickery; but finally Blackington departed, having stated his intention of at once calling together the directors of the Rockford team in order that a new manager might be appointed. Although Tom Fernald had seemed to recover his nerve ere leaving room 37, he was quivering with rage as he descended the stairs. He hurried through the office and made his way directly to the small barroom in the basement of the Corndike.

Several persons were patronizing the bar, while in the corner sat a ragged young man, who seemed to be sleeping off the effects of too much drink. This chap had not purchased a drink since entering the place, but had slipped in quietly and apparently had fallen asleep on the chair almost as soon as he sat down.

"Whisky," growled Fernald, as he found a place at the bar.

"Hello!" exclaimed a man, whose elbow he happened to jostle. "Is it you, Tom? What's the matter? Sore because we took a fall out of you to-day?"

To Fernald's surprise he recognized Benton Hammerswell, the Maplewood manager.

"What are you doing down here, Hammerswell?" he inquired.

"Oh, I just run down to see how the baseball fans were feeling. Have been looking for you. Inquired at the office. They said you were around a short time ago, but I couldn't discover a sign of you. I thought it possible you might drift in here some time this evening. Taking whisky, are you? That's hardly hot-weather drink, and it's hot enough to-night."

"Yes, it's hot enough," nodded Fernald. "Too thundering hot! I've been given quite a sweat to-night."

Again Hammerswell eyed his companion closely.

"Dropping that game to us must have made you sore," he said, with a pantherish grin. "Never mind that, old boy. We'll take a fall out of Seaslope to-morrow. It's up to you to down Fairhaven and land the islanders at the bottom. That's where they belong. After we get Seaslope into third place and Fairhaven into fourth, we'll fight it out between us for the pennant. I've got the team to win games now. There's only one trouble with my bunch: Arlington is sore. I was compelled to promise that he should remain as captain of the team, but it wouldn't work.

"After getting my new men here a whole lot of them threatened to leave unless their regular captain was retained at their head. I had to agree to that. I have done my best to pacify Arlington by explaining that a man who pitches should not play in any game unless he is on the slab, and, therefore, it's not policy to keep him as captain of the team when he will play in no more than one-third of the games. I honestly believe the fellow'd rather be captain and not pitch at all. He's a good player, but has a mighty nasty disposition. Drink up, Tom. Here's luck for both of us to-morrow."

Fernald had poured a brimming glass of whisky, and he dashed it off at a gulp.

"There," he said, "perhaps that'll make me feel better. I'll tell you something that will surprise you, Benton."

"Go ahead! Surprises are coming thick lately."

"I am not manager of the Rockford team now."

Hammerswell was surprised indeed.

"What are you giving me?" he cried.

"Straight goods."

"You're not manager now?"

"No."

"Why not?"

"I resigned to-night."

"Resigned?"

"That's right."

"Well, why in blazes did you resign?"

"Step over here," invited Fernald, drawing the Maplewood man toward the corner where the tramp sat sleeping on his chair. "I'll tell you about it. Don't want to let every one hear."

"Go on!" urged Hammerswell. "They are paying no attention to us. This fellow is snoozing off a jag."

Fernald lowered his voice almost to a whisper. Swiftly he explained how he had attempted to clinch the coming game for Rockford by making a bargain with Brad Buckhart.

"Without Buckhart at his best," he said, "I was confident we could beat the islanders easily."

"Sure thing," nodded Hammerswell. "He's the only catcher they have, and the only man who can hold Dick Merriwell. Of course, they might get hold of Brodie, the fellow I let go when I engaged my new team; but Brodie can't handle Merriwell's combination ball. It would fool him just the same as it fools batters. You were right, Fernald; with Buckhart out of the game, or with him bought up, it would be a simple thing to down Fairhaven. One thing that led me down here to-night was to see you about this business. I wondered if there was no way it could be fixed so Rockford would have the game nailed to-morrow."

"It must be fixed," nodded Fernald. "Either that or I'll be compelled to hedge."

"Then you've bet on the game already?"

"Yes. I didn't tell this fellow, Buckhart, about it, but I've backed Rockford to win. I hate to hedge on this game. I'd almost as leave see Rockford beaten."

"No! no!" exclaimed Hammerswell, "not that! If Fairhaven loses she'll go to the bottom of the list. I know how you feel. I know you'd like to see Rockford lose her first game under another manager; but you can't have any friendly sentiment toward Fairhaven and this chap Buckhart, who trapped you."

The Rockford man shook his head.

"I am between two fires," he confessed. "I'd like to fix Buckhart, somehow. I'll do it, too! I don't know just how to get at him."

"A little dope in his coffee," whispered Hammerswell.

"He doesn't take coffee. Those chaps over there are temperance cranks. Every man on the team drinks water."

"Then a little dope in a glass of water—that'll do it."

"I believe I can get a drug into him all right," said Fernald. "I stand in with the head waiter here at the Corndike. He's a poker player, and I have divided winnings with him in more than one game we have played together. I did the crooked dealing and gave him the hands to win."

"Then it's a simple matter," whispered Hammerswell eagerly. "If you can fix it with the head waiter, I will provide the drug."

"What sort of a drug?" asked Fernald. "I don't like to monkey with stuff unless I know how it is going to work. I don't want to poison any one."

"Don't worry about that. I know a drug that will do the work, and it's perfectly tasteless."

"Where do you get it?"

"I'll get it. Leave that to me. If you will fix it with the head waiter, I'll provide the powder."

"Explain how the stuff works on a man who takes it," urged Fernald.

"It takes the life and judgment out of him. He loses his strength."

"Then it doesn't knock him flat? It doesn't put him down and out?"

"Not a bit of that. He'll keep on his feet, but he'll be useless as a ball player."

"Get me the dope," hissed Fernald. "I will guarantee to reach Buckhart. I'll soak that fellow, and I hope he makes a holy show of himself to-morrow."

"He will," chuckled Hammerswell.

"How long will it take you to get the powder?"

"There's plenty of time. I will find a man to purchase it here in Rockford at a drug store. Don't want to do it myself. Leave it all to me. You shall have it to-night, but you're not to use it until to-morrow noon. Understand that? If you use it before that time he might recover from the effect in time to play all right. He will feel it for four or five hours after taking the stuff."

"Then it's a go," said Fernald. "I'll make a big winning on Rockford to-morrow. After that I hope Rockford will get it in the neck regularly. Have another drink with me. Come on!"

They again stood up to the bar and called for drinks.

While they were drinking one of the bartenders noticed the sleeping fellow in the corner. Immediately he came from behind the bar and gave the sleeper a poke in the ribs.

"Here! here! what are you doing?" he demanded. "This is no lodging house."

Apparently the fellow was undisturbed. A second poke toppled him from his chair to the floor, where he sprawled awkwardly.

"Thunder and guns!" he muttered thickly; "that was an awful shock! Thought I was riding on the truck of a freight car. Lost my hold and fell off. The whole train went over me."

"This is no place for bums," said the bartender, surveying the fellow's ragged clothes. "When did you blow in here?"

"Beg your pardon, boss," said the young tramp, slowly and unsteadily rising to his feet. "Just arrived in your beautiful town. Came in my own parlor car. Brought an awful thirst with me, too. Open a bottle of Mumm's for me, and mark it down on a cake of ice."

The bartender called a boy.

"Open the basement door, Joe," he said. "Can't have this fellow strolling out through the office."

The basement door was quickly opened, and then, without a moment's delay, the bartender hustled the young tramp out and thrust him into the street, giving him a push that caused him to lose his feet and sit down heavily on the sidewalk.

"Too bad!" muttered the hobo, as he sat there and looked round over his shoulder at the door, which had closed behind him. "I didn't hear all of that. They whispered too low for me to catch the whole of it. They're up to something that interests me a great deal, as a chap by the name of Buckhart is concerned. I will keep my eyes open."

CHAPTER IV

ON PEACEFUL POINT.

After the ejectment of the hobo Fernald and Hammer-swell remained some little time before the bar, talking earnestly in low tones.

The whisky seemed to have a bad effect on Fernald. He grew flushed and excited. His indignation increased steadily as he thought of the trap into which he had fallen, and he repeatedly asserted his desire to square up with Buckhart.

"It's not enough to simply dope the fellow!" he growled.

"Be still," cautioned Hammerswell, touching his companion's wrist. "Don't let any one hear you speaking of that."

"I know what I'll do," said the Rockford sharp. "I'll have that fresh young fellow put out of business to-night unless he sticks close to this hotel."

"Put out of business?"

"Yes."

"How?"

"I know a way. I'd like to thump him myself, but I don't want to take part in it. I'll find the boys to do it. Let's have another drink."

After drinking again Fernald bade Hammerswell "so-long," promising to meet him within an hour at the same bar.

"That'll give me time to get the dope," whispered Hammer-swell. "I think I'll have it ready for you then."

Having left the hotel, Fernald turned down the street that led toward a part of the place known as Peaceful Point. This name was a misnomer, for Peaceful Point was anything but peaceful. In fact, it was the most dangerous and degraded section of Rockford. The most disreputable characters of the place lived on the point, where there were a number of low saloons, kitchen barrooms, gambling rooms, and other resorts of bad repute. Although it was said to be dangerous for a well-dressed man to venture onto the

Point after dark, Fernald proceeded thither unhesitatingly.

The street was crooked, the houses in need of repair and paint, and the neighborhood ill-smelling.

The night being warm, the doors and windows were open everywhere. There were men and women and a few ragged, shrill-voiced children on the street. Lights shone from the windows and the open doorways. Some carousing sailors went staggering and singing along the street ahead of Tom Fernald. Profanity and the smell of beer was in the air.

The appearance at that hour of a man dressed as well as Fernald was enough to cause the Pointers to survey him keenly. However, instead of creating surprise whenever he was recognized—and almost every one seemed to know him—his name was spoken and he was permitted to pass unmolested. Occasionally a man saluted him.

No one paid the slightest attention to the trampish-looking young man who slouched at a distance behind Fernald, carefully keeping track of the deposed manager of the Rockford team. This was the chap who had been thrown out of the Corndike barroom.

At last the hobo saw the man he was following pause a moment in front of a house from which came the sound of music, dancing, and bacchanalian laughter.

The pursuer reeled forward, as if finding it difficult to keep on his feet, and paused at the open doorway to look in. Beyond a short hall was another open door, and beyond that a room in which the dancing was taking place. Fernald had paused in the second doorway. He surveyed the disreputable throng searchingly, and soon singled out a strapping, big youth who was waltzing with a girl. Fernald lifted his arm and the man nodded. A moment later, without asking to be excused, the fellow abandoned his partner on the floor and joined the man in the doorway.

"Sorry to bother you, Bingo," said Fernald.

"No bother at all, boss," was the answer.

"Step over by this window," invited Fernald, who did not fancy the odor of the place. "Want to speak with you a moment, McCord."

They stopped by the open window, neither of them aware that outside that window a man was leaning against the side of the building.

"You know the Fairhaven catcher, don't you, Bingo?" asked Fernald.

"Sure t'ing," nodded the youth, wiping the perspiration from his face with his shirt sleeve. "I know all dem ball players in der whole league."

"Well, I suppose you took my pointer and bet something on the game to-morrow, didn't you?"

"Dat's what I did."

"I thought likely you would."

"Why, boss, I found some guys dat was bughouse. Dey have an idea dem kids is going to put it all over your team to-morrer. I borrowed ten plunks and shook it at um. De whole ten is up, and I count meself that much ahead. It's like finding money."

"It was a safe thing as long as I remained manager of the team here, Bingo; but I am out of it now."

"W'at?" gasped McCord, in astonishment. "What's dat you're giving us, Tom, old man? Out of it! Ain't you manager any more?"

"No."

"How's dat?" gasped the excited and astonished Bingo.

"It will take too much time to explain. But if you want to make it a sure thing that you gather in your bets it's up to you to do something."

"Tell me what, boss!"

"I want you to get after the Fairhaven catcher. The whole team is stopping at the Corndike. If you can run onto that fellow Buckhart on the street to-night and put him out of commission you'll fix the thing so your bets will be safe, as there is no other man who can fill his place to-morrow with Merriwell in the box."

"You want me to knock de block off dat chap, do yer?"

"If you can put him into the doctor's hands it will be a good job. Don't be satisfied to give him a thumping, but use him up so he'll be unable to play ball to-morrow. That's my advice."

"I'll do it if I get der chance, boss," nodded McCord. "Of course I don't want to be pinched for der job, and I can't jump him right out in public where dere'll be witnesses."

"Of course not. It's a warm evening, and I fancy the most of those fellows will walk out for a breath of air. If you could hang around and follow Buckhart until you get a good opportunity to light on him, it would be a fancy piece of work."

"I hate ter leave dis ball," confessed McCord; "but I can't afford to drop any good money on dat game."

"If you polish this Buckhart off in first-class shape, so he can't play to-morrow, I'll drop you a fiver out of my own pocket," promised Fernald.

"I'll get after dat guy right away, Tom," nodded the young thug.

"Better take two friends with you."

McCord looked surprised.

"What fer?" he demanded. "Don't you t'ink I can take care of him all by my lonesome? Why, I can eat dat chap! He's nutting but a boy."

"But he may have friends with him. You will need at least two or three companions to keep his friends off while you do him up. I suggest that you take not less than three. Then if you happen to run onto a bunch of them you will be all right."

"Mebbe dat's good advice," confessed Bingo. "I want to do der job in a hurry. I'd better have some good scrappers wid me."

"Any one here you can get?"

"None of my gang, but I guess I know where ter find der boys. Tapper Mullin is fingering the pasteboards down at Mike McGinnis' joint. He picked up a couple of sailor chaps what t'ought dey knew a lot about poker, and he's skinning dem of dere loose coin. I'll git him all right, and den I'll look after Skip Billings, anodder good man. You say der baseball chaps are at der Corndike? Well, you jest stroll back dere and hang around. If you see dis feller we're arter stroll out for a walk, jest watch which way he goes. I'll be along wid my pals in twenty or t'irty minutes."

Fernald left the place and retraced his steps toward the hotel. Instead of following him, the young hobo, who had listened outside the window, waited until Bingo McCord came out. He then trailed McCord.

Bingo had made no mistake in saying he knew where to find one of his pals. At McGinnis' place he was admitted to the room where the poker game was in progress, and he appeared just as one of the sailors vociferously announced that he had been cheated. There were five persons in the game, and three of them proceeded to jump on the two sailors without a moment's delay. The encounter that followed was decidedly brief, for McCord sailed into it and McGinnis himself took a hand. In less than two minutes the sailors, badly battered and minus their money, found themselves kicked into the street.

McCord tapped a tall, perspiring, red-headed chap on the shoulder.

"Seems ter me I dropped around jest in time, Mullin," he said.

"That's what!" growled Mullin, with a surly grin. "I saw you smash one of them chaps under the ear and drop him into the corner. They squealed over losing a little money. I've got some of it in my clothes. Come over to Pete Daley's and I'll blow you off."

"Over to Pete's it is," said McCord, in satisfaction. "I was jest going to invite you over dere meself. Dere's something doing, Tapper. I want ter find Skip Billings."

"Skip hangs around Pete's most of the time."

Together they proceeded to Daley's barroom, which was well filled with disreputable-looking and thirsty individuals. Neither of them noted that as they entered the young hobo followed at their heels, almost knocking against them.

Skip Billings, who had a broken nose and was thoroughly vicious in his appearance, was leaning against one end of the bar. McCord and Mullin joined him.

"This is on me," said Mullin, as he ordered beer.

"I beg your pardon, gents!" exclaimed the hobo, as he seemed to lose his balance and stumbled in among them. "Awful slippery floor! Don't waste your money. I will pay for the suds."

"Well, dat saves you a swipe on de jaw," said McCord. "You want ter be careful about butting inter dis bunch or you may git your block knocked off."

The hobo looked them over in an interesting manner.

"One, two, three," he counted, motioning toward each one of them with his finger. "Mebbe there's enough of you to do it."

"What's that?" the trio exclaimed in a breath, as they turned toward him.

"Wait a minute! wait a minute!" urged the tramp, holding up his hand. "After I pay for the suds you can try it if you want to. No use to fool yourself out of a drink in your haste."

McCord began to laugh.

"I guess dat's right, stranger," he admitted. "We'll drink on you and den we'll kick your face in."

The tramp did not appear to be frightened. Instead of that, standing in their midst, he coolly paid for the drinks from a small amount of loose change.

"The last of a misspent fortune," he said dolefully. "When that's gone I'll have to work—or steal. What's the use to quarrel, gents? Mebbe the three of you can put me out in short order, but I will go any one of you singly at any old thing. I will run, jump, wrastle, or fight any man in the place."

Now it happened that Skip Billings regarded himself as a clever wrestler, while as a fighter Tapper Mullin was known on the Point to be second only to Bingo McCord.

"Here's where we have a little sport!" exclaimed Bingo. "Clear der floor, gents, and see Skip pile this frisky chap up in a hurry."

The prospect of a wrestling match seemed to delight every one present, and without delay the space was cleared. Deliberately the young hobo removed his ragged coat and tossed it into a corner, flinging his battered hat after it.

"Better take your drink first," grinned McCord, motioning toward the single glass left standing on the bar.

"I'll take that later," said the hobo. "Had enough already. Mebbe I'll want it after I put this gent on his back."

"If you wait until you put me on my back," said Billings, "you'll never take another drink. Come on!"

A moment later they clinched.

If any one present expected to see Skip Billings down the stranger he was disappointed.

Although Billings seemed to obtain the best hold and made an effort to hurl the tramp over his hip, the strength and skill of the hobo enabled him to avoid a fall.

"Go on, Skip!" cried several. "Pile him up! Down him!"

"Down he goes!" panted Billings, as he back-locked his antagonist.

While they were falling the stranger seemed to fetch a remarkable writhing twist in the air, and when they struck heavily on the floor a shout of surprise went up, for Billings was underneath and flat on his back.

Billings himself was astounded, for until he landed on the floor he had fancied himself the victor. How he had been brought underneath while falling he could not conceive.

"What's dis?" shouted McCord, in great astonishment. "Did he t'row you, Skip? What's de matter wid yer?"

"Accident!" declared Billings savagely. "I had him going."

The tramp laughed.

"The secret of success," he observed, "is to keep a good thing up after you've started. You can't keep it up, me friend."

Being released, Billings scrambled to his feet, his face flushed and his eyes glaring.

"You'll never fool me another time that way!" he declared. "You can't throw me again in a hundred years!"

"Various opinions about that, me friend," chuckled the tramp. "But I guess this business is settled. One fall was to end it."

"One fall don't end it!" snarled Billings. "You will have to try it again."

"Now, hold on!" cried the stranger, holding up his hand. "I say it ain't fair—it ain't fair!"

"Make him take his medicine, Skip!" exclaimed several.

In spite of his protest, the tramp was compelled to meet Billings again.

The two men crouched at a little distance from each other, while McCord gave the word.

"Are you ready?" was his question.

"Sure!" growled Billings.

"All ready," said the stranger.

"Then fly at it!"

Round and round they circled, crouching low, their arms swinging, watching for an opening. Suddenly the tramp seemed to give Billings his chance. Skip rushed in and grabbed.

With a writhing twist, the tramp seemed to avoid the other man's hands, and an instant later he seized Billings about the body, flung the fellow's heels into the air, and hurled him fairly over his head.

The building shook and the glasses and bottles behind the bar rattled as Skip came down with a terrible thump, flat on his shoulder blades. The concussion stunned him for a moment, and he lay prone on his back, blinking at the smoky ceiling.

After a moment's silence the witnesses of this remarkable thing uttered a shout. Never had they seen a handsomer piece of work.

Slowly Billings sat up, looking around for his antagonist.

"Go for him!" he weakly muttered. "Knock the stuffing out of him!"

"Hold on, gents!" urged the tramp, once more holding up his hand. "I acknowledge you can do it if you all jump on me. There ain't no question about that. I'll take you one at a time; but I throw up the sponge if you're going to tackle me in a bunch."

"Let me git at him!" urged Tapper Mullin. "Mebbe he can wrastle, but when it comes to handling his dukes with me I think he'll be out of it. Where's the gloves, Pete? Bring out the mitts and I will pound him to a pulp!"

The prospect of a fistic encounter delighted the rough crowd and they burst into applause, wildly calling for the gloves.

"I acknowledge, gents," said the hobo, "that you've seen me at my best. As a wrastler I've made my reputation. When it comes to the gloves, I am nothing but a second-rater."

This seemed to increase Mullin's desire to get at the stranger.

"Be quiet as you can, gentlemen," said Daley, the proprietor, as he fished out a set of hard gloves from beneath the bar. "You know my place is strictly quiet and respectable."

"Where's my second?" inquired the tramp, as he inspected the gloves. "Ain't I got no one ter back me up? Is this whole bunch agin' me?"

To the surprise of all, Skip Billings immediately stepped forward.

"I'm behind you, pal," he said. "A man that can throw me over his head is pretty nifty, and I'm goin' to prophesy that you make it lively for Tapper."

"Thanks!" grinned the hobo, his dark eyes flashing. "Jest you watch out that I git fair play. Help me tie these mitts on, will you?"

Billings aided in tying the gloves onto the stranger's hands. In the meantime, McCord attended to Mullin, who had stripped down for the encounter.

"Don't let him touch you, Tapper," urged Bingo.

"Don't worry about that," retorted Mullin. "You're the only gent around this town that can put me out of business."

The interest of the crowd in the stranger had been thoroughly aroused. They saw now that he was not a bad-looking fellow by any means; indeed, it was possible that, washed up and dressed in decent clothing, he would present a rather attractive appearance.

In a few moments both men were ready. The interested spectators were now back on either side against the walls, in order that the boxers might have plenty of room.

"I'll bet a round for the crowd that Tapper puts him down and out within three minutes!" cried one.

"I will go you!" instantly exclaimed Skip Billings.

Without any formality the contestants met and began to spar. The stranger assumed a correct position and easily warded off the leads of his opponent when Mullin started without delay to press the contest. Round and round they went, ducking, dodging, and parrying.

"Get into him, Tapper!" urged the man who had offered to bet on him. "You're wasting time!"

Mullin heeded this adjuration and attempted to press his opponent. The tramp, however, was astonishingly catlike on his feet, and Tapper could not get in a telling blow.

At length the hobo broke through the other fellow's guard and gave him a severe jolt on the chin.

"That's it! that's it!" cried Billings, in satisfaction. "You reached him that time!"

This blow angered Mullin, who opened up furiously. Twice he touched the stranger, but the blows were too light to be effective. Then he received a thump in the ribs that brought a groan from his lips.

Faster and fiercer grew the contest. The spectators shouted their delight.

Suddenly the tramp landed on Tapper's mouth and split his lip, starting the blood.

Bingo McCord whistled his surprise.

"It's an even match," he declared. "Tapper will have to scratch gravel."

Mullin was intensely annoyed by his failure to get in an effective blow. This annoyance led him to give several openings, and finally he received a jolt that sent him to the floor.

Billings actually danced in delight.

"I told you!" he whooped.

Mullin scrambled up, his eyes glaring with fury. The moment he was on his feet he made a rush.

The stranger side-stepped and banged his opponent on the ribs. The blow seemed to stop Mullin in his tracks. His hands dropped a little, and an instant later he received a right-hander on the jaw that once more sent him flat.

This did not end the contest, however, for Tapper was not seriously hurt. He rose slowly, but rushed again as soon as he was on his feet. This time he swung twice and then attempted to clinch. His blows were avoided, and the stranger seized him about the waist and gave him a whirling flop into the air.

Mullin came down in the same heavy fashion as Billings had fallen.

"Foul! foul!" cried several.

"Excuse me!" exclaimed the stranger. "I didn't know any particular rules were mentioned."

A discussion arose that was stopped by McCord, who agreed with the hobo that no rules had been mentioned, and, therefore, no rules had been broken.

By this time Tapper was up once more. Although he had been jolted severely he would not quit.

"Give him all that's coming," urged Skip Billings, in the tramp's ear. "He won't crow over me after this."

The end of the match was not long postponed. Mullin had lost his head, and he quickly gave his opponent an opening that was accepted. A smashing blow on the jaw sent Tapper down and out. In fact, fully ten minutes elapsed before Mullin fully recovered.

During those ten minutes the stranger was congratulated by several witnesses, including Bingo McCord.

"You're a better man dan Mullin," confessed Bingo. "If I didn't have a little business on my hands to-night I'd try you a go myself. What's your name?"

"It's Hepworth Hoboson," was the answer. "I'm usually called Hep for short."

"Well, Hep, you're a rattler, and dat's straight goods. Are you going to stay round dese parts?"

"I may linger till I git restless," laughed Hoboson. "I can't stay very long in one place, for I adore traveling."

"Well, as long as you stay here dis is de gang for you to run wid," said McCord. "We'll take you in wid us. What do you say, Skip?"

"Why, sure," nodded Billings.

Mullin made no objection, and in this manner Hoboson was accepted as one of the tough set of Peaceful Point.

Although he did not call attention to the fact, Hep Hoboson was skillful in yet another manner. With the craft of a juggler he managed to spill the contents of every glass set before him, emptying the stuff into a sawdust-filled box that served as a cuspidor and stood close under the rail of the bar. Not even a swallow passed his lips. Once or twice he was seen lowering his empty glass, as if he had drunk the contents, and the suspicions of his companions were not aroused.

McCord seemed to take Hoboson into his confidence, for he asked the fellow to join them in going after Brad Buckhart.

"I've got good coin on der game to-morrer," said Bingo, "and I want to make it a sure t'ing dat Rockford wins. Wid dis catcher in der hospital, dem island chaps will be a cinch."

Thus it came about that the tramp was one of the party that left the Point in search of Buckhart.

Tom Fernald was smoking a cigarette in front of the Corndike Hotel when McCord and his companions passed. Fernald made a signal that caused McCord to step aside.

"Buckhart is out for a walk now," said the late manager of the Rockford team. "Merriwell is with him. They turned up Granite Street."

"All right," muttered Bingo. "We'll try to find him. Der four of us can put dem two guys out of business in about ten seconds."

Talking of baseball matters, Brad and Dick had turned to retrace their course to the hotel when they were met by McCord and his gang near the outskirts of the town. It happened that there was no street light in the immediate vicinity, and the spot was a favorable one for the purpose of the ruffians.

"Here dey are!" hissed McCord, as the unsuspecting boys appeared. "Git into dem and make a quick job, pals."

To the astonishment of McCord and his friends, Hoboson uttered a shout of warning.

"Look out, boys!" he cried. "They are going to slug you!"

"What's dat?" roared McCord furiously, as he wheeled on the

tramp.

Already Mullin and Billings had made a rush at Dick and Brad.

"Drat you!" grated Bingo. "What do you mean?"

"I always like to see fair play," declared Hoboson. "It ain't fair for four gents to jump on two boys."

Furious with rage, McCord tried to hit the hobo. He struck at Hep's face with his left, but the man dodged and Bingo's fist passed over his left shoulder. Quick as a flash, Hoboson reached up behind his neck with his right hand and grasped McCord's wrist. With a sweeping swing he sent Bingo McCord sailing through the air in a half circle, and flung him at least thirty feet away into some bushes by the roadside.

"I am with you, boys," cried the hobo, as he turned and sprang to the assistance of Dick and Brad, who were having their hands full.

In the bushes, with his shoulder twisted out of the socket, Bingo McCord rose, groaning, to his knees, and heard his companions shouting cries of dismay.

Merriwell and Buckhart were astounded by the manner in which Hoboson sailed into the two thugs. He struck Mullin and sent the fellow flying. Then he seized Billings and hurled him through the air.

After rising to his feet, Mullin lost no time in taking to his heels, and Billings was not slow in following him.

Already McCord had floundered out of the bushes, and, realizing his own helplessness, he dodged away into the darkness.

Hoboson stood with his hands on his hips, chuckling softly to himself.

"What does this mean?" asked Dick, in surprise.

"That's whatever I'd like to know," said Buckhart.

"It means," said the tramp, "that some tough characters planned to eat you up, but made a slight mistake by taking me into the game."

"Who are you?" asked Merriwell.

"I am a knight of the road. I am a preambulator of the highways. In other words, boys, I am what is disdainfully called a hobo."

"I don't understand it at all," again declared Dick.

"Then I will clear up the haze," said the tramp. "In this town there's a gent by the name of Fernald who has it in for Brad Buckhart."

"And I'm Brad Buckhart," muttered the Texan. "Was Fernald behind this business?"

"Sure as shooting. He put up the job and engaged the gang to do you dirt. By chance, while pretending to take a nap in the Corndike barroom, I heard him talking it over. It interested me, and I decided that I would have a finger in the fun. That explains why I am here."

"Well, we owe you thanks!" cried Dick, extending his hand. "What can we do for you?"

"If you git hard up for a rattling good ball player and a wizard behind the bat, don't forget Hep Hoboson," said the tramp.

"Are you a ball player?"

"Am I? You bet your wealth I am! I am a wonder!"

"Sorry," laughed Dick; "but we don't need any one just at present."

"Can't tell how soon you may," said Hoboson. "Things are always happening, you know. I'll be on hand to watch the game to-morrer, and if you need a substitute jest call on me. It would delight me to go behind the bat and handle the sphere in that position."

"Are you in need of money?" asked Dick, thrusting his hand into his pocket.

Hoboson held up his hand, at the same time shaking his head.

"A little money is sufficient for my passing wants," he said. "I couldn't think of accepting anything from you."

"Where are you stopping?"

"Any old place I hang my hat is home sweet home to me," was the answer.

"Have you enough to pay for your lodging to-night?"

"Sure thing. You can't reward me, my boy, for a little favor. I'll see you at the game to-morrer. Good night and pleasant dreams."

Then, although they called to him, the singular tramp hurried away and quickly disappeared in the darkness.

CHAPTER V

THE DOPE WORKS.

On Rockford the dinner hour came at midday, and the island boys ate heartily, all being in good spirits, for they believed, with Dick on the slab, there was an excellent prospect of defeating the locals that day. Being permitted to gorge himself with custard pie, Obediah Tubbs was unusually jolly and chipper.

An hour later, as Dick was donning his uniform in his room, Buckhart appeared, having already changed his clothes.

"Pard," said the Westerner, as he came in and dropped limply on a chair, "there sure is something the matter with me. Never before felt so blamed lifeless and inert in all my career."

"Perhaps you ate too much," suggested Dick.

"I don't opine it was that. Never had a square meal take the snap out of me this way before."

Merriwell now observed that his friend was unusually pale.

"I hope you're not sick, Brad!" he quickly exclaimed. "If you should fall sick now we'd be in a bad hole this afternoon."

"Oh, I'm not exactly sick," declared the Texan. "I'm jest weak and done up. Don't seem to care a rap whether I play ball or not. It's a mighty odd thing for me, and I don't know what to make of it."

Never before had Merriwell known his friend to be other than eager and enthusiastic in regard to a coming game, and this surprising change in Buckhart was quite enough to alarm the captain of the island team.

"Perhaps you need a little air," suggested Merriwell. "It's hot to-day. A good walk might brace you up."

"That's just what I don't want to take," said Buckhart. "I feel more like stretching out somewhere and keeping still."

Although he was not a little disturbed, Dick said nothing more until he had finished dressing for the ball field. When he was quite ready he tucked his favorite glove into his belt, looked around to make sure Garrett had sent all the bats to the field, and then called Brad to follow and started for the door.

With his hand on the knob, he paused and looked back.

Brad had not stirred. With a dreamy, far-away look in his eyes, he sat in a listless attitude, apparently quite unconscious of his surroundings or wrapped in deep thought.

"Come on, Buckhart!" impatiently cried Dick.

Still the other did not move.

Merriwell turned back and stepped quickly to his friend's side, seizing him by the shoulder and giving him a shake.

"Come out of that trance! What's the matter with you?"

Apparently with an effort, the Texan pulled himself together.

"What is it?" he inquired. "Was I asleep? Great horn spoon, I feel queer! Kind of numb all over!"

"Are you numb?" said Dick. "I should hate to see you go into a game in this condition. Brace up!"

Thus adjured, Buckhart rose with a great effort to his feet. He brushed a hand across his eyes, as if trying to wipe away a blurring mist.

"All right," he said grimly. "Go ahead, partner. I'm with you."

Although Dick flung the door open and stepped outside for his friend to follow, Buckhart made a strange miscalculation and ran full against the edge of the door, which caused him to recoil and very nearly upset him.

"Well, of all things!" gasped Merriwell, as he sprang back into the room and seized his companion by the arm. "Can't you see?"

"Sure," answered Brad; "but that door moved just as I arrived at it. It certain did, pard?"

"Have you been drinking?" inquired Dick.

"Hold on, Richard Merriwell!" growled the Texan resentfully. "You know I reside on the sprinkler. I never lap up ardent liquors."

"Well, this is the first time I ever saw a sober man in your condition."

Weakly Brad pushed Dick off.

"I am all right," he muttered grimly, evidently bracing up as much as possible. "I'll prove I'm all right."

He then walked out of the room, and Dick followed, closing and locking the door.

Once while descending the stairs the Texan stumbled and Dick caught hold of him, fearing he would lose his footing.

The boys were waiting below, and together the whole team left hurriedly.

In front of the hotel stood Tom Fernald, smoking a cigarette. He watched them as they came out, and his eyes surveyed Buckhart keenly. He noted Brad's pallor and faltering step. He also observed that Dick had hold of Buckhart's arm.

"All right," muttered Fernald to himself. "Ripley did the job. He told me he saw Buckhart drinking the glass of water into which the powder had been dropped, but I thought he might be lying. That wild and woolly young Texan is doped for fair. With him in that condition Fairhaven stands no show of winning."

Not one of the boys gave Fernald a glance. They started down the street, but paused at the first corner, for coming up another street that led to the water front was a large excursion party, headed by Brick McLane, of Fairhaven, who shouted at them and waved his hand.

"Here we are!" cried the husky lobsterman. "Here we are, a hundred and fifty of us right off the island. We're going to root for our team to-day."

It was the expected excursion party from Fairhaven, and at least fifty of the excursionists belonged to the fair sex.

Fairhaven had adopted Fardale's colors, red and black. The girls were bearing tiny red and black banners, while the men and boys had red and black ribbons knotted to the lapels of their coats. The crowd was strung out on the sidewalk until it looked to be nearly twice as large as it really was.

"He! he! he!" snickered Obediah Tubbs. "We're going ter have some backers to-day, by Jim! Rockford won't do all the hollering."

The face of Earl Gardner flushed with pleasure as he discovered Grace Garrett in the party.

Raymond Garrett now appeared, and, directed by him, the Fairhaven team marched toward the ball ground at the head of the excursionists.

"I've had a whole section of seats reserved for our crowd," he explained to Dick. "I'm going to keep them together to-day. We'll see if Rockford makes all the noise."

"With so many rooters to encourage us, we ought to win," declared Dick.

"Oh, we'll win!" laughed Ray. "I feel it in my bones. Lots of Rockfordites will be poorer and wiser to-night. They are betting all kinds of money that Rockford takes the game. I hear that Tom Fernald has put up two or three hundred dollars already, and is looking for bets now."

"He didn't seem to be looking with much eagerness when we left the hotel," retorted Dick. "Saw him standing in front of the Corndike all by himself."

Merriwell said nothing to Garrett of Buckhart's peculiar actions, but during the march to the ball ground he continued to watch Brad closely. To his relief, the Texan seemed to throw off some of the peculiar stupor that had attacked him.

When the field was reached and the islanders came pouring in at the gate, the Rockford spectators greeted them in various ways, some applauding and some uttering whistles and catcalls.

"They've come over to see their great team wiped off the map!" shouted a boy.

"That's right!" cried another. "There won't be anything but a grease spot left of Fairhaven after this game."

The local team was already practicing on the field. Dick and his players assembled at their bench, opening their bat bags and laying out the bats. Buckhart sat down, resting his elbows on his knees and his chin on his hands. In a hazy way he seemed to watch the practicing players.

"Get up here," commanded Dick, producing a ball and giving the Westerner a nudge. "I'm going to toss you a few."

Brad rose and walked out to catch the ball.

"Going to take them barehanded?" inquired Dick.

Brad glanced at his left hand with an expression of surprise.

"Forgot my mitt!" he muttered. "Where is it?"

One of the boys found the big catching mitt and tossed it to Brad, who failed to catch it and was struck in the stomach by it.

Dick walked briskly over to the Texan and spoke to him in a low tone.

"Shake yourself together!" he sharply commanded. "Get out of that trance!"

Evidently Buckhart tried to obey, for he pulled on the mitt and fastened it, and then made a pretense of liveliness as he got into position.

Dick threw him a few slow ones at first, and Brad handled them, although there was a deep frown on his face and he seemed under a constant strain. When Merriwell used more speed the Fairhaven catcher muffed the ball at intervals.

Tom Fernald had followed the islanders to the field, and he watched Merriwell and Buckhart a few moments. Having done this, he turned away and began to look after bets. When he could not find even money, he seemed willing to give odds, and in several instances he bet two to one on Rockford.

No one knew how much Dick Merriwell was worried. He sought to conceal his state of mind from his companions and succeeded in doing so. When he was seen talking earnestly in a low tone to Buckhart, it was supposed the two were discussing the signals and speaking of the weak points of the opposing batters.

Uriah Blackington was again on the ground as manager of the home team, and his appearance in that capacity apparently gave satisfaction to the better element in the Rockford crowd.

"It'll be a struggle of giants to-day—Garrett," he laughed, approaching the manager of the island team and placing a hand on his shoulder. "The critical point in the race for the pennant has been reached. We're compelled to take this game. Sorry for you, my boy."

"Perhaps you're wasting your sympathy," returned Ray smilingly. "I see you have some new men on your team. Evidently you picked up the best men you could get off Hammerswell's team which he released."

"Yes, I mittened onto Torrey and Morrisey. Torrey is in my opinion the fastest third baseman in this league, and Morrisey is a great outfielder."

"Those are not all your new men. I notice you have that Jersey City battery, Brodie and Kennedy."

"Sure thing! Going to put them against you to-day. Hammerswell didn't give those fellows a fair show. They are itching to demonstrate what they can do, and they'll work for their very lives this afternoon. Really, Garrett, I don't believe you have one chance in ten of taking this game. You know yourself that you've been lucky. Nothing but luck can explain the fact that a bunch of boys could keep up the pace in this league and make all the veterans hustle. Now don't you believe yourself that it was luck more than anything else?"

"I do not, Mr. Blackington. It was brains, team work, and determination to win, combined with remarkable playing on the part of those boys. I confess that without Merriwell it is quite likely Fairhaven would not be in her present position. His spirit dominates his team. He rules those boys with a hand of iron hidden in a glove of velvet."

Blackington laughed a little at this.

"I fail to see the hand of iron," he declared. "That's an excellent metaphor, Garrett, but I fancy it's all imagination."

Fairhaven now took the field for practice, which Dick made sharp and snappy, keeping every one, with the exception of Buckhart, on the move and on the qui vive the same as when playing in a game. Not more than ten minutes were spent in this practice. It began with a snap and ended with a snap, every player stopping and starting for the bench at a signal given by their captain.

The umpire walked onto the field and the home team trotted out.

The game was about to begin.

CHAPTER VI

BUCKHART'S BLUNDER.

As Earl Gardner, straight, handsome, and clear-eyed, walked out to the plate with his bat in his hand, Brick McLane suddenly rose in front of the Fairhaven crowd, lifted both hands above his head, and made a signal. To the jerking of the lobsterman's arms the islanders gave a cheer in concert that was surprisingly well done.

"What's that? What's that?" grinned big Bob Singleton. "They must have worked that thing up coming over. Sounds a little like Fardale, Dick."

"It sounds first-rate," nodded Merriwell. "It's the first time I've heard anything like a regular cheer since hitting this part of the country."

Gardner knew the eyes of Grace Garrett were on him, and, instead of making him nervous, this knowledge filled him with determination to lead off with a hit.

On the score books the two teams were recorded as follows:

Fairhaven.	Rockford.
Gardner, cf.	Spangler, cf.
Bold, ss.	Jenners, ss.
Bradley, 3d b.	Swarton, 1st b.
Singleton, 1st b.	Torrey, 3d b.
Buckhart, c.	Morrisey, lf.
Merriwell, p.	Stowe, 2d b.
Jolliby, lf.	Randolf, rf
Tubbs, 2d b.	Brodie, c.
Smart, rf.	Kennedy, p.

Blackington had spoken the truth when he stated to Garrett that he intended to put the Jersey City battery, Brodie and Kennedy, against Fairhaven. Kennedy was in the box, with Brodie crouching behind the bat.

Brodie opened with a high inshoot, and a strike was called as Earl missed the ball cleanly.

Back of third base at least half a hundred Rockford youngsters had gathered, and they whooped in shrill derision as Gardner missed.

"He'll never touch that pitcher!" shrieked one.

"Holes in his bat!" yelled another.

"He's got a crooked eye!" came from a third.

"Never could hit!" declared a fourth.

Kennedy grinned derisively at Earl.

"Too speedy for yer, kid?" he inquired. "I'll give yer an easy one."

But Gardner refused to reach for the wide out which followed, and a ball was called.

The pitcher then tried a drop, which was pronounced a ball, and Kennedy quickly decided to force him to swing on the next one.

Earl fouled it.

With two strikes and two balls called, the Jersey City pitcher again attempted to deceive Gardner, and again failed.

"Three balls!" called the umpire.

"Make him put it over, Earl," urged Dick. "If he does put it over give it a ride."

Kennedy did put it over, using all the speed he could command, without a curve.

Gardner snapped his bat round quickly and met the ball full and fair, sending it whistling over the head of the second baseman and bringing the island crowd up with a shout. It was a clean hit for Fairhaven's centre fielder.

"That's the way to soak 'em, dern their picters!" squealed Obediah Tubbs, as he danced with elephantine grace down the coaching line back of first.

"This is a regular three-ring circus!" cried a Rockford man sneeringly. "There goes the clown! Say, fatty, do you know how a fool looks?"

"Yep!" promptly answered Obed, turning and facing the speaker. "I noticed you when I first came onto the ground. I'll bring you a mirror so you can see for yourself."

"Right from the shoulder!" laughed Brick McLane. "How do you like it, man?"

The Fairhaven crowd laughed heartily, and, with a very red face, the would-be funny Rockfordite subsided.

Owen Bold was the second batter, and he held his bat in a certain position in his left hand as he walked to the plate. Gardner observed the signal and knew Bold would bunt the first ball that Kennedy pitched, in case it was over the plate. Being thus warned, Earl was on his toes and had a fair start when the batter dropped the ball down about four feet in front of the plate.

Bold dashed for first, but Torrey maintained his reputation for handling bunts cleverly, and secured the ball in time to make a beautiful throw to Swarton.

"Out at first!" shouted the umpire.

"Good sacrifice, Owen!" piped Obediah Tubbs. "That's the way to start her up!"

Bradley, the cockney lad from Fardale, was the next batter, and he held his bat straight up against his shoulder, gripping it with both hands, as he walked out. This told Gardner that Billy would try for a hit.

"Here's your victim, Kennedy!" called Brodie. "He can't touch you in a year."

"'Ow do you know so much?" inquired Bradley. "Your wisdom is hawful surprising!"

Kennedy was roused and he used all his skill in fooling Bradley. Billy fouled the first two balls, both of which were declared strikes.

"You're getting a pup-pup-pup-piece of it every time!" cried Jolliby. "Tut-tut-tut-take a good bite now!"

Fancying the batter was eager to hit, Kennedy tried to pull him on wide ones. Billy grinned at them and let them pass, with the result that three balls were swiftly called.

Brodie then signaled for a straight one.

As Billy swung to hit the next ball delivered the catcher swiftly touched the end of the bat and deflected it.

The ball plunked into Brodie's mitt, Bradley having missed it cleanly.

"Did you see 'im, umpire?" shouted Billy excitedly. "'E 'it my bat! 'E bothered me!"

"Oh, go lay down!" sneered Brodie. "Don't try that game! You're out! Quit your squealing!"

In spite of Billy's protest, the umpire persisted in declaring him out, having failed to observe Brodie's action.

"Watch that catcher, Mr. Umpire," urged Dick. "Don't let him do any of that!"

"I will watch him," promised the umpire.

Big Bob now stalked out to hit. As he took his position he glanced over his shoulder at Brodie.

"If you fool with my bat," he said, in a very low tone, "I'll land you a bunch of fives on the jaw!"

"Oh, you wouldn't hurt anybody!" retorted Brodie sneeringly. "You're nothing but a big baby! You can't get a hit off Kennedy if you try."

Singleton quickly convinced Brodie of his mistake by smashing the first ball along the ground so swiftly that Jenners was barely able to touch it with his fingers and deflect its course. Had Jenners failed to touch it at all Gardner would have scored. As it happened Stowe was able to get the ball in time to hold Earl at third, although big Bob reached first safely.

It was now Buckhart's turn to hit, but he sat on the bench without seeming aware of it.

"Get your batter out!" sharply ordered the umpire. "No delays!"

Dick gave Brad a punch.

"Come on, Buckhart!" he exclaimed. "It's your turn!"

The Texan rose slowly to his feet and walked toward the plate without picking up his bat. Those who saw him fancied he would secure the bat dropped by Bradley. This he did not do, but took his position to strike without a bat.

Quickly catching up Brad's pet stick, Dick went out and handed it to him.

"Get your eyes open, Buckhart!" he said, in a low tone. "Wake up, old man!"

Brad seemed to give himself a shake. He struck at the first ball delivered, missing it by more than a foot. However, it seemed that this swing of his bothered Brodie a little, for Singleton stole second without trouble, the Rockford catcher declining to throw down to the bag.

The next ball pitched was too high, but Buckhart again struck at it.

"What's the matter with him?" derisively cried the Rockford spectators.

Tom Fernald was watching everything closely, and a faint suggestion of a smile flitted over his face.

By the merest accident, it seemed, Buckhart hit the next ball a terrible crack and lined it far into the outfield. The hit seemed good for three bases at least, and it brought a shout of delight from the visiting islanders.

A moment later this shout turned to exclamations of surprise and dismay, for instead of running toward first, Buckhart turned in the wrong direction and ran toward third.

Gardner, who was trotting home and looking over his shoulder to see how far the ball went, did not observe the Texan until Brad collided with him.

Both were knocked down.

In astonishment Earl jumped up and seized Buckhart, dragging him to his feet.

"What's got into you?" he cried. "What are you trying to do? Where are you going?"

Brad made no answer, but endeavored to pass Earl and continue toward third.

By this time Dick Merriwell had reached the spot, and he seized Brad by the arm, turning him around.

"The other way, you crazy loon!" he exclaimed. "First base is on the other side!"

Realizing his blunder at last, Brad started across the diamond toward first.

"Get into the base line!" cried Dick.

Buckhart did not seem to hear this, for he continued toward first, without attempting to follow the base line.

Spangler had secured the ball at last, and he threw it to Stowe, who promptly lined it over to Bill Swarton. By the time the ball reached Swarton's hands, Buckhart was on first.

Swarton touched him with the ball and then called for the umpire to declare him out.

"Why, dern your picter!" cried Obediah Tubbs, "he's on the base! He can't be out!"

"He's out according to the rule covering base running to first," declared Swarton.

"What is that rule?" asked the umpire.

"It says a base runner is out if he runs more than three feet outside the line in the last half of the distance to first base, unless he does so to avoid a fielder attempting to field a batted ball," declared Swarton.

"That's correct!" nodded the umpire. "He was more than three feet outside the line! The man is out!"

At this some of the Fairhaven players raised a protest, but they were immediately silenced by Merriwell. "Swarton is right about the rule," admitted Dick. "The decision is just."

"Well, of all hard lul-lul-lul-luck that's the worst!" groaned Chip Jolliby. "It was a cuc-cuc-cuc-cuc-clean base hit. What in bub-bub-blazes is the mum-mum-mum-matter with Buckhart? He must be cuc-cuc-crazy!"

Brad seemed at last to realize what he had done. He walked in toward the Fairhaven bench, shaking his head and looking disgusted. He was still very pale.

"Pard," he said, in a low tone, as Dick hurried to him. "I sure am locoed. Things are a whole lot twisted. Never did such a fool thing before in my life. What do you suppose is the matter with me?"

"I don't know," confessed Dick; "but you cut us out of three runs, at least. If you can't brace up and come out of this trance, we're beaten at the very start."

"I will brace up, pard—I will brace up!" savagely declared Brad. "Just watch me now!"

CHAPTER VII

THE TRAMP STEPS IN.

he Texan went behind the bat, determined to arouse himself and do his level best.

But Dick had lost confidence in Brad, and others on the team were worried, realizing that something was wrong.

It is strange how the playing of one man on a team often affects the whole team, either for good or for bad. In this case Buckhart's blunder seemed to unman his companions.

Dick dared not let out his speed and use his best curves in the first inning, and as a result Spangler hit safely. Jenners drove one to Bradley, which Billy fumbled, and then Swarton lifted a long fly to left field.

"Just like batting it into a basket!" shrilly shouted Obediah Tubbs. "Gardner couldn't muff it if he tried."

To the astonishment of every one, Earl made a rank muff, and the bases were filled.

"Ha! ha! ha!" laughed Swarton, dancing up and down on first. "Got um going! They are up in the air!"

"They never could play ball!" shouted a Rockford man.

"You're another!" promptly retorted Brick McLane.

"Only for Fairhaven, you fellers would have the pennant nailed now! They've kept yer down!"

"You dreamed it!" was the retort. "Smoke up! Your pipe's going out!"

"Here's Torrey!" was the cry from the excited Rockford spectators. "Torrey will line it out! Just watch Torrey!"

While playing on the Maplewood team Torrey had demonstrated the fact that he was a remarkable batter. His hitting had been commented on a great deal by patrons of the games in the Trolley League.

Dick Merriwell had studied this chap's style of batting and discovered his weak spot. Regardless of Buckhart, Merriwell now began to whistle the ball over, using curves that he knew would bother the batter. This led Torrey to strike twice and miss.

"He'll hit it next time," asserted many. "He never strikes out."

After wasting two balls the captain of the Fairhaven team again sought Torrey's weak spot, and found it.

Brad's eyes had blurred, and he seemed uncertain as he put up his hands.

Torrey swung sharply, hit the ball on the under side of the bat, and seemed to drive it straight down to the ground. It struck like a piece of lead a foot in front of the plate and lay there.

"Fair hit!" cried the umpire.

Torrey dusted toward first, while Spangler, Jenners, and Swarton all moved up, Spangler making a dash for the plate.

In order to make a double play all Brad needed to do was to pick up the ball, touch the home plate, and throw to first.

Instead of doing this, Buckhart caught up the ball and threw toward first.

Spangler came romping home in safety, laughing in derisive satisfaction.

What added to the dismay of Dick and his companions was the fact that Buckhart threw over first, and before Smart could recover the ball and return it to the diamond, Torrey had reached the initial bag, while Jenners had followed Spangler to the plate and Swarton was well down the base line from second to third.

Fearing the boys would continue the bungling work by bad throwing, Dick shouted for Tubbs to hold the ball.

"Well, dern our picters!" shrilly cried the fat boy, as he stood with the ball in his hands, a look of disgust on his face. "We're a lot of lobsters!"

Merriwell quickly ran up to Brad.

"What's the matter with you, Buckhart? You're entirely out of gear, old man. You had a double play right in your hands. Every runner was forced. Had you stepped on the plate after picking up the ball you could have retired Spangler."

"That's right," nodded the Texan. "I know it now. Never did a thing like that before."

"Play ball! play ball!" cried the Rockford crowd, as Dick continued talking to Buckhart in a low tone, "Keep them at it, Swarton."

"They are delaying the game, Mr. Umpire!" cried Swarton. "Make them play!"

Dick returned to his position, while Buckhart again crouched behind the bat.

On the first ball pitched, Torrey darted toward second. Buckhart threw to Bold, who covered second base.

Swarton lost not a second in attempting to score.

Bold saw the Rockford captain tearing down the third-base line toward the plate, and therefore, without attempting to tag Torrey, he lined the ball back to Buckhart.

Brad had covered the home plate and would have stopped the score had he caught the ball. He muffed it and Swarton slid home safely.

The Rockford crowd roared its delight.

"The game is ours in the first inning," muttered Tom Fernald.

The excursionists from the island were silent now. Their faces expressed their consternation and dismay.

Morrisey danced out to the plate, eager to keep the good work up for Rockford.

His lack of confidence in Buckhart led Dick to pitch cautiously, and Morrisey hit the second ball delivered, driving it along the ground inside the first-base line.

Big Bob Singleton booted the ball into the diamond, then sprang back to first, as he saw Dick going after the sphere.

By sharp running Morrisey crossed first before Merriwell could throw him out.

"Is this a ball game?" laughed one of the Rockfordites. "It looks like a farce to me."

As Stowe seldom hit to left field, Smart moved over toward centre, playing in toward the diamond.

After missing one, Stowe hit the ball on a dead line to Smart. The little fellow added to the comedy of errors by muffing the liner and throwing poorly to Singleton, who was compelled to get off his sack in order to catch the ball.

Stowe crossed first before big Bob could get back to the bag.

Again the bases were filled.

Crouching under the bat, Buckhart peered through the wires of his cage, and to him those wires seemed as large as crowbars. Just as Dick delivered the first ball to Randolph the Fairhaven catcher snatched off his mask and flung it aside.

Randolph barely touched the ball with his bat. A second later Buckhart lay flat on his back, having been struck squarely between the eyes by a foul tip.

Immediately the umpire called time and several players gathered around Brad, while a boy brought a bucket of water.

The Texan started up a little the moment the water was dashed into his face. When he was lifted to his feet, however, he seemed blinded and dizzy.

"He's out of this game, Dick," said big Bob Singleton soberly. "He's off his feet now, and in less than three minutes he'll have a beautiful pair of eyes. What are we going to do for a catcher?"

Dick shook his head and looked around hopelessly.

"Can you catch, Bold?" he asked.

"Sorry," answered Owen Bold, "but I can't do a thing behind the bat."

By this time the spectators were aware that Buckhart had been knocked out of the game, and suddenly a man rose from the bleachers and attracted attention by calling in a loud voice to Dick:

"Howdy, Captain Merriwell! I am on hand to keep my promise! Told you you could depend on me if you needed me! I'll go under the bat and surprise the gaping multitude."

It was Hep Hoboson, the tramp. He descended from the bleachers and walked toward Dick, lazily dragging his feet.

The crowd shouted at him derisively and advised an officer to put him off the ground.

"Go back and sit down!" commanded the policeman. "If you don't I'll have to put you out."

"I want to speak with me friend, Richard Merriwell," said Hoboson, touching the brim of his dirty slouch hat. "Jest a word, please?"

Dick saw the tramp and was seized by a queer inclination to find out what Hoboson could do behind the bat. Immediately he approached the officer and said:

"It's all right, sir; I'm going to use him in the game."

"That's where your head's level," chuckled Hoboson, pulling his hat still farther over his left eye. "We'll paralyze this crowd with our remarkable battery work."

Having cast off his tattered coat, the hobo adjusted the body protector and mitt, pulled a mask on, and took his place under the bat. Already he had told Dick what signals he would use.

"This will be a great game!" sneered one of the Rockfordites. "They must be crazy to use that dirty bummer. Can't they get any one else?"

Evidently Hoboson heard these words, for he turned and wagged his mitt in the direction of the speaker.

"Wait a minute, me friend," he advised. "Don't judge by appearances. Appearances are often mighty deceiving."

He then signaled to Dick for a rise, and Randolph swung at the ball. Once more the batter touched it, but this time he put up a high foul.

Without removing the mask, Hoboson got under the ball and easily smothered it as it came down.

"Dern his picter, he done something, anyhow!" cried Obediah Tubbs, in relief.

"This is just the beginning," said Hoboson, as he tossed the ball back to Dick. "Don't be afraid of your wing, me boy. Let it out. Speed 'em over, and see me take care of this end of the diamond."

Still Dick was cautious, and he tried a slow bender on Brodie. The Rockford catcher hit the ball into the diamond and it took a high bound. Merriwell leaped into the air and caught it with his left hand, having plenty of time to throw to the plate, which put Torrey out, as he was forced. Like a flash, and with perfect accuracy, Hoboson lined the sphere into Singleton's hands for a double play, and Brodie was out at first, having failed to reach the sack in time.

For a moment the spectators seemed dazed, and then Brick McLane let out a wild roar of delight. Up he jumped and jerked his arms wildly as he led the cheering of the watching islanders.

"Jest as e—easy!" laughed Hoboson, bowing toward the applauding crowd. "Couldn't help it if I tried!"

As the Fairhaven team gathered at the bench, it was apparent that none of the boys cared about sitting down too close to Hoboson. Still they praised him for his work until he rather impolitely invited them to "shut up."

Although Merriwell led off with a clean two-bagger, Kennedy's skill proved too much for the three batters following, and Dick was left on second.

"Seems to me," said Hoboson, as he rose from the bench and stopped Dick, who had trotted in to secure his glove before going into the box—"seems ter me I've heard that you deliver a queer curve you call the combination ball. When I want you to t'row that one I'll give you this signal."

Saying which, he showed Dick the signal he would make.

"Better not try it," said Merriwell promptly. "You can't hold it. It would fool you just as it fools batters. When he's in condition Buckhart can handle it, but I don't dare use it with any one who is not accustomed to it."

"That's all right," said Hoboson. "Don't you worry. Jest hand it right up and see me do my duty."

For a pitcher Kennedy was a good hitter, and he opened Rockford's half of the seventh with a pretty single.

With Spangler at bat, two strikes and three balls were called.

Then Hoboson signaled for the combination ball.

Dick shook his head.

Hoboson repeated the signal, and again Dick shook his head. In apparent disgust, the tramp called for a straight ball. Spangler smashed it into right field, and Kennedy took third on the hit.

"You see what happens," said the tramp. "I tell yer not to be afraid, me boy. Jest deliver the goods and see me hold up my end."

On the first ball pitched to Jenners, Spangler started for second base, thinking that with Kennedy on third he had a fine opportunity to steal.

Apparently Hoboson was slow about throwing. To every one it seemed that Spangler had a start that would lead him safely down to second, when, after driving Kennedy back to third with a fake movement, the tramp lined the ball to Tubbs.

That ball fairly whizzed through the air, and it came straight into the hands of Obediah, who was a little to one side of second and in perfect position to tag the runner. Spangler slid and Obed put the ball on him.

"Out!" shouted the umpire.

Having seen this throw to second, Kennedy started off third once more and raced toward the home plate.

Tubbs sent the ball back to Hoboson, who covered the plate. It came straight into the hands of the tramp, and Kennedy stopped on the line, seeing he could not reach the home plate without being tagged. He turned and ran back toward third, expecting Hoboson would throw the ball. Instead of throwing to Bradley, the tramp ran after Kennedy with the ball in his hand.

Seeing Hoboson contemplated trying to run him down, Kennedy let himself out and did his best to get back to third. At every jump the tramp gained on the base runner, and just as Kennedy made his last leap to reach the bag the hobo struck him between the shoulder blades with the ball, using such force that the Rockford pitcher was hurled past third and sent sprawling on the ground four feet beyond the bag.

"Out!" shouted the umpire once more, but his decision was drowned by the wild roar from the delighted islanders. Brick McLane furiously waved his hat in the air and whooped at the top of his stentorian voice.

Laughing with satisfaction, Dick ran up to Hoboson and patted him on the shoulder.

"Well, you're certainly a sprinter, old boy," said Merriwell.

"T'anks," returned the tramp. "You're jest beginning to git onto me style. I tol' yer I was an all-round wizard, but you didn't believe me. Now, mebbe you'll try that combination when I call for it."

"The very next time," promised Dick.

The opportunity came very soon, for with two strikes and two balls called on Jenners, Hoboson signaled for Dick to use his most effective curve.

Merriwell sent in his combination, but did not get it over the plate.

Plunk!—the ball landed in the tramp's mitt and stuck there.

"Jest as e—easy!" he chuckled.

Again he called for this ball and again Dick used it. This time Jenners struck and missed, and once more the ball plunked into the catcher's mit and remained there.

Three Rockfordites were out.

"Well, I guess he can catch!" whooped McLane. "He's not a beaut, but he fills the bill!"

"Who in tut-tut-thunder is this fellow?" chattered Jolliby, as he reached the bench. "He's all right, Dick. I don't believe Rockford could have scored if we'd had him in the fuf-fuf-fuf-first place."

No one was more delighted than Dick at the work of the tramp catcher. He now sought to talk with Hoboson, but to his surprise the tramp seemed strangely shy and silent. Whenever Dick approached him the mysterious catcher edged off and evinced a disinclination to talk.

From that time to the finish of the game every witness was kept keyed to the highest pitch of excitement. Hoboson demonstrated that he was a batter and base runner as well as a wonderful catcher. Still Kennedy managed to keep the islanders down until the sixth inning. In the sixth Hoboson singled to right field.

A few moments later, on Dick's hit, Hoboson went racing over third with the speed of an express train and kept on to the plate.

Randolph threw to Brodie, but the tramp slid under and was declared safe, thus getting the first score for Fairhaven.

Dick took second on Randolph's throw, but again Kennedy mowed down Jolliby, Tubbs, and Smart in succession.

By this time the Rockfordites were aware that it was necessary to fight the thing through to the finish in order to secure the game. Try as they might, however, they could not bunch hits. With Hoboson handling the ball perfectly, Dick Merriwell pitched in a wonderful manner and prevented the enemy from making a further gain.

Ere the ninth inning began Merriwell found himself puzzling

over something familiar in Hoboson's style of catching. The Fairhaven captain began to fancy he had seen the tramp before, although he could not remember the occasion.

With one man out in the ninth, Singleton drove a hot one through Stowe and reached second by a daring run. Kennedy was afraid of Hoboson and tried to deceive him with curves. The tramp finally dropped the ball over the right-field fence for two bags, according to the ground rules, and Singleton scored.

With Hoboson on second, another run was needed to tie the score.

The island crowd was cheering wildly now, while the Rockfordites did their best to encourage Kennedy.

Merriwell picked out a good one and slammed it into the far extremity of centre field, sending Hoboson home and reaching third ere the ball was returned to the diamond. Some of the island spectators groaned as they saw Jolliby walk out to the plate. Not a hit had Chip made, and they feared what would happen now.

Chip hit the ball, but popped up a little fly to Torrey and was out. Tubbs lifted a foul a moment later, and Brodie caught it.

"That's the way ter do it!" cried Swarton. "Here's your next victim, Kennedy!"

It was Smart.

Fearing Smart would strike out, Dick edged off third and made a desperate dash for the plate as Brodie returned the ball to Kennedy after the first pitch.

Kennedy snapped the ball back to Brodie, who threw a little high, and Merriwell slid under safely, thus securing the run that put Fairhaven ahead. No wonder Brick McLane quite lost his voice from shouting. No wonder the islanders shrieked, and yelled, and waved the red and black.

"Got um now, pal!" said Hoboson, in satisfaction. "Let this feller strike out if he wants to. We'll hold 'em down."

Smart did strike out, but Fairhaven was one run ahead when Rockford went to bat for the last time.

Merriwell trusted fully to the tramp's skill as a back-stop, and his speed and curves actually dazzled the batters. He retired them in one-two-three order, and Brick McLane fell off the bleachers as the third man struck out and he realized Fairhaven had taken the game.

"Pretty well done, wasn't it, Dick?" said Hoboson, as he cast aside his battered old hat and seemed instantly to fling off a false wig at the same time. "Glad to get rid of those things. They are beastly hot."

"Wh—what!" gasped Dick, staring hard at the tramp. "Am I dreaming? Is it you?"

A second later Dick shouted to his companions.

"Come here, boys—come here! Take a look at our tramp! It's Bart Hodge, or I'm daffy!"

"Thought you'd tumble to me long before this," smiled Hodge, as he shook Dick's hand. "It was Frank's suggestion that I play this little trick. You can blame him. He sent me down here to see how you were getting along. Couldn't come himself."

"Well, I'm ashamed to be fooled in such a manner," confessed Dick. "If I'd ever looked you over closely in daylight I would have recognized you for all of your rags and dirt. Hodge, you're a dandy."

Then the watching crowd was amazed to see Dick Merriwell hug the ragged catcher.

CHAPTER VIII

BRAD LEARNS THE TRUTH.

hat's this—what's this, boys?" cried Dick, as they were passing the office of the Rockford Star, on their way to the hotel. "Just look at that bulletin board. Maplewood defeated Seaslope! Take a look at the standing of the teams! Did you ever before see anything like that?"

No wonder the boys uttered exclamations of surprise and astonishment as they stood in front of the bulletin board, for by the record there it was seen that every team in the Trolley League was tied. The four clubs had played forty games each, and all had won twenty and lost twenty.

"Now for the race to the finish!" exclaimed Merriwell. "It will be good and hot!"

No wonder the Fairhaven crowd was enthusiastic and delighted.

Bart Hodge was the hero of the day. Still wearing his ragged clothes, he marched at Dick's side with the ball players, his dark eyes gleaming and a smile on his face.

"Frank will enjoy the letter I'll write him," he declared. "I'll tell him how his plan worked. I didn't think I could fool you, Dick. It wasn't so difficult last night, for we met in the dark and you could not get a good look at me. To-day you were somewhat excited and wrought up over the game, which kept you from inspecting me closely."

"I thought you acted mighty queer," laughed Dick. "You kept that old hat on all the time and had it pulled down over your eyes. Besides that, you seemed disinclined to talk with me after we agreed on the signals we would use. Whenever I spoke you turned your head away and did not answer. Besides, I never dreamed of seeing Bart Hodge in rags and with his face and hands dirt-begrimed."

"It's good, clean dirt, Dick," retorted Hodge. "Still I confess I'm rather anxious to wash it off now. Hear that big chap whoop! He nearly broke his neck by falling off the bleachers when you struck out the last Rockford batter."

"That's McLane," said Dick. "He's one of our most enthusiastic supporters."

The big lobsterman was marching down the street, waving his hat in the air and occasionally letting out a yell that sounded like a steam calliope.

In the island crowd was Grace Garrett. Without attracting the attention of his companions, Earl Gardner dropped back and walked at Grace's side.

"Oh, I'm so glad you won the game to-day, Earl!" she exclaimed, placing her hand on his arm.

"I didn't win it," he laughed. "Dick and Bart Hodge deserve all the credit."

"Not all the credit," she denied. "But who is this Bart Hodge? Is he really a tramp?"

"Hardly that!" smiled Gardner. "He's a chum and comrade of Dick Merriwell's brother, Frank."

"Well, how does he happen to be here now?"

"Frank Merriwell sent him. He couldn't come himself, and so he sent Hodge. It was a mighty lucky thing for us that Hodge turned up just when he did. No other man could have gone behind the bat and handled Dick's pitching to-day."

"What was the matter with Brad Buckhart? He actually seemed crazy."

Earl shook his head.

"That was something mighty queer," he said. "Buckhart was ill—he's ill now, and he has two bad-looking eyes. That ball struck him between the eyes, and they are nearly closed up."

"It was dreadful!" said Grace. "It frightened all the girls. I thought he was killed."

"It takes something harder than a baseball to kill that Texan," declared Gardner. "Dick tried to induce him to go to a doctor, but he remained through the game and kept a wet handkerchief over his bruise."

With a handkerchief tied round his head, Buckhart was plodding along at the rear of the ball players. The Western lad was doing some thinking now. Gradually his head seemed getting clearer, and he was trying to devise some explanation for his own remarkable actions on the ball field. He remembered very well the singular feeling of lassitude and weakness that came upon him a short time after eating dinner at the Corndike Hotel that day. Over and over to himself Buckhart put this question:

"What did I eat that knocked me out?"

As the ball players were passing the Corndike, Uriah Blackington hurried out of the hotel, and called to Ray Garrett.

"Come here a moment, Garrett," he urged. "Bring Merriwell with you."

Ray and Dick joined the Rockford manager.

"I've just received a telephone message from Hammerswell and Whitcomb," said Blackington. "They urged me to call a meeting right away for the purpose of making certain changes in the schedule."

"Why should there be any changes made?" asked Garrett. "Isn't the schedule satisfactory to Rockford?"

"Not exactly," answered Blackington. "We wish to make one or two changes ourselves."

"Ten to one," cut in Dick, "this is some sort of a trick on the part of Hammerswell. Don't help him out in his schemes, Mr. Blackington."

In a frank manner the Rockford man placed a hand on Dick's shoulder.

"Don't you worry about that, my boy," he said. "I have no particular use for Benton Hammerswell. Still, as two of the managers in the league have called for this meeting, one must be held. They demand it at once, saying they will be here within an hour and ready to transact business. Mr. Garrett can stop off and attend the meeting, while the rest of you may return to the island."

"If I stop," said Ray, "I want you to remain with me, Dick. I may need your advice. We'll not go back to Fairhaven on the Lady May to-night, for, according to our agreement with the captain, that boat leaves here as soon as possible after the game."

"Wait a minute," said Merriwell. "Perhaps Captain Jennings might be induced to wait a while if we pay him. There'll be a moon to-night, and there are no signs of fog."

"The excursionists might object."

"Let's go down to the boat and talk it over."

As they started off, Blackington called to them:

"Under any circumstances one of you must stay if you wish to have a finger in the alteration of the schedule."

When the Lady May was reached Garrett gathered the excursionists and told them it was necessary for Dick and himself to remain in Rockford two hours at least.

"If you people say so," said Ray, "the Lady May will swing off at once with you; but if you're in no haste we'll see if the captain can be induced to wait for us."

"Oh, say!" cried Brick McLane, "we want to take everybody back with us. There'll be a warm time on the island when we git there."

"That's right! that's right!" cried several of the others. "If the captain will wait we'll wait."

There was not a dissenting voice, and therefore Ray and Dick talked with Captain Jennings at once. He agreed to wait until nine o'clock if they desired, in case he received ten dollars extra for the delay. This amount was promised him and the excursionists were notified.

"I'm glad of that," said Hodge. "It will give me a chance to change my clothes and cross to the island with you. I had my luggage forwarded to the Corndike, and it's there now, I suppose."

The baggage belonging to the ball players had been sent from the hotel to the steamer, and the boys were now given an opportunity to change their clothes in the cabin. As they were making this change it was discovered that Buckhart was not with them.

Immediately Dick became alarmed.

"Where is that fellow?" he exclaimed. "Has any one seen him?"

Some remembered Brad had marched down the street with them, but still he could not be found on the steamer.

"First thing," said Dick, as he hurriedly finished dressing, "is to look him up. What the dickens can be the matter with him?"

While Dick and Ray were talking with Blackington, Buckhart had walked into the Corndike quite unobserved and taken a seat in the office near an open window at the front of the hotel. He was still puzzling over his own condition and seemed quite unaware that his friends and the excursionists proceeded to the steamer without noticing he was missing.

For at least thirty minutes the Texan sat in a big chair by the open window. Finally he shook himself a little and started to get up. As he did so he glanced through the window and saw Tom Fernald standing just outside. The look on Fernald's face was one of bitter disappointment.

"He's some sore," thought Brad. "I opine he lost a dollar or two to-day."

A slender young chap approached Fernald and spoke to him. This slender fellow the Texan recognized as Pete Knox, head waiter at the Corndike.

"I need that money now," said Knox, in a low tone, "and I need it mighty bad, too."

Fernald frowned.

"You'll have to wait," he retorted. "I can't pay you."

"But you promised it to me right after the game. I've been discharged here."

"Discharged?"

"Yes."

"Why? How's that?"

"I don't know. I was fired this afternoon, and I'm out of a job. Haven't a dollar, either. So you see the twenty-five you agreed to pay me will come in handy."

"You're no worse off than I am," said Fernald. "I am broke. Lost my good money on this beastly ball game."

"That wasn't my fault," said Knox. "I thought you were sure of winning if you could get that stuff into the Fairhaven catcher."

Buckhart grasped the arms of his chair and every muscle grew tense.

"I should have won," growled Fernald. "That ragged bummer upset my calculations. He's as good a catcher as Buckhart—or better."

"You can't blame me if your game miscarried," said Knox. "I followed directions, and I saw Buckhart drink the water, which I brought him myself. I want my money now. I can't help how much you lost, you'll settle with me."

"And you'll both settle with me!" roared the Texan, as he leaped like a panther through the open window and lighted on the sidewalk outside.

"Here's one for you!"

Saying which he struck Knox a blow that sent the fellow spinning, wheeling instantly on Fernald, who seemed electrified by the occurrence.

"Had me drugged, did you?" snarled the Westerner. "You get yours next!"

Fernald was not exactly a weak man, but his astonishment prevented him from meeting the assault of the enraged boy. Brad's hard fist landed on the man's chin and sent him backward a step. The Texan would have followed up this blow with another, but at that juncture Dick and Ray Garrett came round the corner, having returned from the steamer. Merriwell seized his excited friend by the wrist and held him, while Garrett promptly stepped between the man and boy.

"Let go, pard—let go!" grated the Texan. "Let me smash that cur!"

"Where are the police?" exclaimed Fernald. "I'll have him arrested!"

"You're crazy, Brad!" said Dick. "What ails you?"

"I know what ailed me to-day!" panted the Fairhaven catcher. "I was drugged! This low-down coyote paid the waiter here to get the stuff into me! Stand back, pard, and let me square up the score!"

It required all of Merriwell's strength to hold the furious lad back.

"How do you know this, Brad?" demanded Dick.

"Just heard them talking right here by this window."

"That's a lie!" asserted Fernald. "Where's Knox? He'll say it's a lie!"

But the fellow who had been knocked down by Buckhart was not to be found. He had picked himself up and hurried away as he saw the people gather in front of the hotel.

Finding Knox had fled, Fernald became still more bold.

"Somebody call the police," he said. "We'll have this crazy chap locked up."

"Let them lock me up!" hissed Buckhart. "I am ready to tell the judge why I jumped on Fernald."

"All right," nodded Dick, "go ahead and call your policemen."

Then he turned to the crowd that had gathered.

"Gentlemen," he said, "some of you were present at the ball game to-day, I fancy. You must remember the singular behavior of our catcher here. He complained of feeling wrong directly after dinner. Yesterday Tom Fernald tried to bribe him—tried to induce him to throw the game to-day. Deny it if you want to, Mr. Fernald; we have proof of it. Buckhart induced Fernald to make the offer in a room of this hotel, and several of us heard all the talk. If you doubt my word, ask Uriah Blackington; I fancy you won't doubt him. He was present and heard it all. That's why Fernald was compelled to resign as manager of your team. Evidently he has been looking for revenge. It's my belief that no man who makes a living as a professional gambler can be on the square. I doubted the squareness of Fernald from the first. He has been proved a crook. I mean it, Fernald—you're a crook!"

The deposed manager of the Rockford team was pale, but he forced a sneering laugh.

"You will find I have some friends in this town," he declared. "You think yourself very smart, young chap, but in time you will get what's coming to you."

This speech was promptly hissed by some one in the crowd, and as if that hiss was a signal, a storm of hisses followed it.

Fernald shrugged his shoulders and snapped his fingers defiantly.

"You go to blazes, the whole of you!" he exclaimed.

Then he turned and walked away, paying no attention to the scornful remarks of the crowd.

"Let him go, Brad," urged Dick, restraining the Texan. "It's my opinion he lost enough money to-day to punish him for his dirty work."

CHAPTER IX

CHANGING THE SCHEDULE.

ick and Ray Garrett were waiting in Uriah Blackington's office when Hammerswell and Jared Whitcomb
entered. The Maplewood manager carried himself
with an air of self-satisfaction and importance.

"Well, gentlemen," he said, "it seems that the Trolley League is
ready to start afresh on a level footing. No team has an advantage
now, and that's a good thing for the league. I have the boys to
make you hustle, and Maplewood proposes to walk off with the
pennant."

"What's this business about changing the schedule?" asked Garrett. "Fairhaven is satisfied with the schedule as it stands."

"Maplewood and Seaslope are not," retorted Hammerswell. "I
also understand that Rockford would like to make one or two
changes. Is that right, Mr. Blackington?"

"If these changes can be made without stirring up hard feelings
I favor it," nodded Uriah Blackington. "I don't want to kick up
strife. There's been enough of that."

"You see, Garrett," said Hammerswell, "three of us wish to
make some changes. If you object, you will stand alone."

"What are the changes you wish to make?" inquired Ray.

"I have the thing all jotted down here," said Hammerswell, producing a sheet of paper. "Mr. Whitcomb and myself have agreed
on it. Just look it over, Mr. Blackington."

Uriah Blackington glanced over the altered schedule and nodded.

"That's satisfactory to me," he said. "You have given us two Friday games in place of a game Thursday and a game Wednesday.
Friday is the best day for Rockford."

Garrett waited quietly until the others had examined the newly
outlined schedule. He then took it and inspected it with Dick.

"What do you think about the changes?" he asked, in a low tone.

"See here," said Dick, pointing at the schedule, "Hammerswell has shifted the game to-morrow so that it is to be in Maplewood instead of Fairhaven. Do you see his object?"

"I don't know."

"It's plain enough. His team is winning now. With all the teams tied, he fancies he can gain an advantage by playing the next game at home. Two teams must lose to-morrow. That will place them both tied for last position. The two teams that win will be tied for first position. Hammerswell is looking for first position. If he secures an advantage by winning to-morrow, he'll have a fairly good hold on the place."

"Then you object to that change, do you?"

"Wait a minute," said Dick. "Let me run this thing over. You see he has it fixed so our final game of the season is to be played in Maplewood. I object to that. If he has this game in Maplewood to-morrow, Fairhaven must have the last two games at home. Stand firm on that, Ray. If they agree to it we can afford to accept these other changes."

"That's right," nodded Garrett, and immediately he announced to the meeting Fairhaven's position in the matter.

Hammerswell raised an objection, and was feebly backed by Whitcomb. The Maplewood man turned in appeal to Uriah Blackington.

"You see there are two of us against one, Mr. Blackington. That ought to decide the matter."

"But it doesn't," declared the Rockford manager grimly.

"Why not?"

"Because we've agreed on a schedule, and unless all managers are satisfied with any changes made there can be no changes. If you want this game to-morrow at Maplewood, Mr. Hammerswell, you will have to accept Fairhaven's terms and give them the last two games on the island."

In vain Hammerswell argued and pleaded. With difficulty he repressed his annoyance and anger. For once he found it impossible to carry things his own way, and in the end he was compelled to acquiesce to Garrett's terms. When this final agreement was made, the altered schedule was accepted by vote in the regular manner.

"We got the best of that, Garrett," smiled Dick, as they left Blackington's office together. "The two last games on the island should be rousers for us. If we are in position to fight for first place, we will have big crowds and make a fat thing out of it."

"That's right, Dick," nodded Ray. "You were long-headed in demanding that change. I am sorry we have to return to Fairhaven to-night. That trip across always shakes the team up some and puts it out of condition. We'll have to return as early as possible to-morrow in order to rest up on the mainland before the game."

"Why not remain here?" suggested Dick. "Hammerswell counts on our making the trip to-morrow, and without doubt he expects his players to be in first-class condition, while we should be somewhat shaken up. Let's fool him."

"A good suggestion!" cried Garrett. "If they celebrate on the island to-night they will have to do so without us. We'll stay right here."

Thus it came about that the Lady May returned to Fairhaven without the ball team.

That night Dick Merriwell and Bart Hodge sat up until a late hour talking. Of course, Dick was anxious to hear all about his brother, and therefore he plied Hodge with questions.

"Why didn't Frank come himself?" he asked for the third time.

"He wanted to," said Hodge, "but he felt that he couldn't spare the time just now. His mining interests have kept him busy during the last few weeks."

"Where did you leave him—in Denver?"

"No; in Chicago."

"Chicago?" exclaimed Dick. "Why? How was that? I didn't suppose——"

"It was business that took us both to Chicago. We have been negotiating with a syndicate that wants to buy the Phantom Mine in the Mazatzals. They sent an expert to examine the property, and we know he made a favorable report, for they offered us a price on it. We wired our terms, and they urged us to come on to Chicago. When we arrived there, however, they attempted to cut down on us, and the whole deal hung up. Had we put it through, it was our intention to come on here together in time to witness the final games in this league. I have left everything in Frank's hands. He wished me to come on, and we agreed on our rock-bottom price before I pulled out of Chicago. If the syndicate comes to terms, all right; if they don't accept our figures, the deal is off."

"Are you anxious to sell your interest in the mine?" asked Dick.

"Not exactly anxious," answered Hodge; "but I have a wish to go into business in the East, and the money I should receive would be enough to set me up. Frank has his other mines to look after, and he's willing to let go of the Phantom. Still, we know it's valuable property, and we're not going to sell it for anything under a fair price."

"I thought," said Dick, "that there still might be some trouble over that mine, and that possibly you were willing to dispose of it for that reason."

"Not a bit of trouble," smiled Hodge. "All that thing seems settled. Frank has downed his enemies in the West, and things are moving swimmingly. His San Pablo Mine, in Mexico, is the richest property, but the expense of packing ore a long distance to the railroad, and shipping it north to a smelter, cuts down his profits. He has a scheme now of organizing a company to build a railroad that will give him an outlet to the north. It's likely he'll try to push this project along while he is in Chicago. If the railroad is ever constructed, it is likely he'll be actively engaged in the work. Dick, your brother is a hustler."

Dick's eyes gleamed and his face wore an expression of pride.

"Frank's all right," he declared. "Not many fellows have a brother like him."

Bart smiled and nodded.

"Those are nearly the words he used about you the night before I left Chicago. We were talking of old times at Fardale, and finally he fell to speaking of you. He's pretty proud of you, Dick."

"I don't know of anything I have ever done to make him proud of me," said the boy.

"Well, I rather fancy you've demonstrated that you have the right stuff in you. He feels certain you'll make a good record at Yale if you get there."

"Bart," said Dick soberly, "the knowledge that my brother expects so much of me will be enough to always keep me at my best. Not only does this keep me at my best, but I fancy, at times, it causes me to rise above myself. Whatever I become, whatever successes I achieve, I shall owe everything to Frank."

Bart rose quickly and seized Dick's hand. His own face was glowing now.

"My own sentiments, my boy," he cried. "Only for the influence and friendship of Frank Merriwell I might have gone to the dogs. I was well started on a bad road. When we first met I took a positive dislike to him, which rapidly developed into hatred. I was not above mean things at that time, and I lost no opportunity to injure him. Almost any other fellow having such an enemy would have sought revenge for those injuries. Instead of that, when I got into serious trouble Frank gave me a helping hand. At first I thought he feared me, but after a while events demonstrated that he feared no one, and I realized that his actions came through his natural generosity and nobility.

"Then I compared myself with him, and the result filled me with shame. At first I was resentful because I realized he was so much my superior. I tried to pull off by myself and keep away from him. Fate would not have it so. The course of events flung us together, and it seems to me now that in a single moment all my hatred and jealousy vanished, and I came to respect and admire him, even though I fancied he could never regard me as a friend. I had a nasty disposition, and whenever anything went wrong I was inclined to take a slump and forget whatever good resolutions I had made. Time after time he lifted me over bad places and set me on the right road. Ninety-nine persons out of a thousand would have lost patience with me. He proved to be one in a thousand, and his patience never failed. He fancied he saw the making of a man in me, and therefore he forgave all my slips and failings. Do you wonder I swear by him, Dick?

"There came a time when my loyalty was taxed. I think I was smitten on Elsie Bellwood the first time I saw her; but I knew Frank cared for her, and I fancied I would prove myself contemptibly disloyal if I betrayed him by showing the slightest regard for Elsie. Thus it was that for two or three years, at least, I smothered and repressed my feelings toward her. Not until I knew beyond doubt that Frank cared more for Inza Burrage than for Elsie did I give way to my feelings. Even then I didn't dream Elsie could care for me. But it has turned out all right at last."

A strange look came to the boy's face.

"If I tell you something, Bart," he said impulsively, "you mustn't ever give it away. Promise you won't."

"All right," nodded Hodge. "I promise."

"Well, had I been in Frank's place I'm sure I would have chosen Elsie. Don't misunderstand me. I like Inza, I admire Inza."

Hodge laughed outright.

"Dick," he said, "you and I are much alike. I recognized that fact long ago. Now tell me all about yourself and your experiences down here. I am going to write Frank to-night in order to let him know how our little plan worked. He suggested the tramp business in imitation of a tramp we once met while making a tour with a ball team composed of Yale men. The fellow called himself Willie Walker, or something of that sort, and he was a genuine hobo. I was knocked out and couldn't go behind the bat. Walker appeared on the field during practice and demonstrated that he could catch. Merry put him into a game, and he proved to be a wizard. Strangest part of it all was that he was a Yale graduate who had once played on the varsity team. We never found out his real name. While Frank and I were talking things over the night before I started East, he suggested that I should try the trick. I was certain I couldn't make it work, but finally agreed to try it. It was lucky I did."

"Lucky!" cried Dick. "I should say so! Only for you we'd lost that game."

"But the real luck came about when I heard Fernald and this Maplewood man, Hammerswell, plotting downstairs in this hotel. I pretended to be asleep, but I was pretty wide-awake. All the time I was straining my ears to catch what they were saying. They kept muttering and whispering, and I could not hear much of it. However, I decided to watch Fernald, and in that manner it came about that I got in with those toughs engaged by Fernald to knock you and Brad out. That upset Fernald's calculations somewhat, but he succeeded in drugging Buckhart. Fernald did not originate that plan; Hammerswell was responsible for it."

"That miserable scoundrel has been at the bottom of all the crookedness in this league!" cried Dick. "He's a thoroughbred rascal, and he's bound to get his just deserts in time."

Dick then told Bart all about his adventures since arriving in Maplewood with his baseball team. Naturally, Hodge was very indignant as he listened to the recounting of Benton Hammerswell's plots.

"I congratulate you, Dick!" he cried when the boy had finished. "You have done amazingly well to hold your own in this league. It's evident all the crookedness has been aimed at you. With the teams tied as they are, and Fernald dropped from the management of the Rockford team, you have a chance to land in first place. It's going to be a hard game at Maplewood to-morrow."

"That's right," nodded Dick. "Hammerswell means to take that game, somehow."

"Better go to bed now," advised Hodge. "The rest of the boys are snoozing ere this. I shall sit up a while to write."

Long after Dick had fallen asleep Hodge sat writing to Frank. He told how the tramp trick had worked, and all about Dick's gallant fight in the Trolley League.

"It's evident, Frank," he wrote, in conclusion, "that you have a brother with the real Merriwell blood in his veins. He never quits. I wish you might be here to witness the final games in this league, for, unless Fairhaven is beaten by treachery and plotting, I am confident Dick will land his team on top at the finish."

CHAPTER X

AT THE CLUBHOUSE.

he following morning, shortly after breakfast, Dick received a call over the telephone. It proved to be Henry Duncan, of Maplewood, and after talking a few moments Merriwell told his companions that they had been invited to Maplewood as guests of the Maplewood Canoe Club.

"I think we'd better go, fellows," he said. "Mr. Duncan wants us to come. He says the sympathy of the summer visitors at Maplewood is with us, and they hope we'll win the game to-day."

"Where be we going to eat?" questioned Obediah Tubbs anxiously. "We was put out of the Maple Heights Hotel, you know, and the only place up there where we can git anything is at that dirty little restaurant. I s'pose you might git plenty of pie there, such as it is."

"Don't worry about that," laughed Dick. "Mr. Duncan says he'll have a spread at the clubhouse."

"Then lul-lul-lul-let's go!" cried Jolliby.

"Yes, let's go!" exclaimed the others.

Thus it came about that Henry Duncan's invitation was accepted and the boys left Rockford on the nine-o'clock car. They were in good spirits, every one of them, Buckhart having fully recovered his former condition. As the car passed Uriah Blackington's office, the lawyer thrust his head out of the window and waved his hand at them, crying:

"Do your best to-day, boys. We'll take one off Seaslope, and if you beat Maplewood there'll be fun the next time we meet."

It was a beautiful morning, and the boys sang and joked as the trolley car bore them toward the Maplewood hills.

Perhaps two-thirds of the journey had been made when the car stopped to let a passenger off. It started up and proceeded slowly onto a curve of the track, where there was a high embankment on one side.

Suddenly, without warning, the car left the track, but the motorman instantly shut off the power.

They stopped with one corner of the car lurching over the embankment.

Already some of the boys had leaped off, and there was a general scramble when the car stopped.

"Pretty near a bad accident," said Hodge, shaking his head.

"Pretty near it!" exclaimed the pale-faced motorman. "I should say so! If I hadn't stopped to let that passenger off, I should have been driving this car at usual speed round the curve here, and we must have gone down the embankment."

"I'd like to know how it happened, anyway," declared the conductor. "There was no reason why we should jump the track. We were apparently creeping along."

Together with the motorman he made an examination, and in a few moments both men betrayed consternation and excitement. They called the passengers to look at one of the rails.

"See here," said the motorman, "this rail has been monkeyed with! It is loose. The rails are spread here. This was no accident! Some one did the job with the deliberate intention of running this car off the track!"

"What do you think of that, Dick?" asked Hodge, in young Merriwell's ear.

"I may be mistaken," muttered the boy; "but it looks to me like more of Benton Hammerswell's work."

"But it doesn't seem possible," said Bart, shaking his head. "Why, many of us might have been killed had the car gone off this bank. It's certain some of us would have been severely injured."

"In which case," said Dick, "Maplewood would have had an easy thing this afternoon."

"It doesn't seem possible," continued Hodge; "that man Hammerswell must be a scoundrel of the worst type."

"Didn't I tell you so?"

"But he's the limit! He's not only a scoundrel, but he's crazy to try such things."

"You can bet he had no direct hand in it himself. I believe he was the instructor, and some of his tools did the work."

There was a long delay, but finally a car from Maplewood picked up the passengers and carried them on to their destination.

As they came in sight of the Maple Heights Hotel, Hodge betrayed his keen interest in the surroundings.

"It was through me that Frank came here to play baseball long ago," he said. "I induced him to come. Those were hot times, and it appears that they are just as warm nowadays. I remember old Artemus Hammerswell and his son Herbert. Artemus had money, and Herbert thought himself a thoroughbred. There's bad blood in these Hammerswells. They got the worst of it in the old days, and I fancy Benton Hammerswell will get the worst of it now."

"There he is!" exclaimed Brad Buckhart, pointing toward the veranda of the hotel. "He's there on the steps talking to another man. Yes, by the great horn spoon, the man he's talking with is Tom Fernald!"

The Texan was somewhat excited. Dick clutched Brad's shoulder to prevent him from getting off the car at once.

"What do you think you're going to do, Buckhart?" he demanded.

"I'd just like to prance up there and put my brand on both those varmints!" declared the Westerner.

"But they're men, and you're only a boy," said Hodge. "They would be two to one against you."

"I certain don't opine that would hold me up any. I reckon Fernald got something from me last night."

The excited Texan was restrained until the car stopped at the platform built for the passengers who wished to get off at the hotel.

On that platform were a number of summer visitors, both ladies and gentlemen. Three men stepped forward as the boys left the car. They were Henry Duncan, William Drake, and Eustace Smiley. Duncan clasped Dick's hand.

"Good morning, my boy!" he exclaimed heartily. "I'm glad you accepted our invitation. Hammerswell found out about it, and he's hot under the collar. I don't know what he's been doing, but he made a great hustle when he learned you were coming."

"I think we know what he was doing," declared Dick. "We're lucky to arrive uninjured, Mr. Duncan."

He then told of their narrow escape from a serious accident.

"Do you think it possible any one actually tampered with those rails?" gasped William Drake, in horror.

"My goodness! my goodness!" cried Eustace Smiley, his pudgy hands uplifted. "It must have been an accident."

"It will be investigated," said Dick. "Both motorman and conductor declared the rails had been loosened and spread."

"Dreadful! dreadful!" said Smiley.

Bart Hodge now stepped forward and made himself known to Duncan, who remembered him well and welcomed him once more to Maplewood.

"In order to avoid trouble with Hammerswell," said Duncan, "we decided to entertain you at the clubhouse instead of at the hotel. Hammerswell has been keeping his team at the hotel, and he has some sort of a pull there."

"We're well aware of that," nodded Dick, smiling grimly. "He had a pull sufficient to push us from the place the day we first arrived in this town."

"A most disgraceful piece of business," said Smiley.

Dick refrained from mentioning the fact that on the occasion spoken of Eustace Smiley had supinely agreed to anything Hammerswell proposed.

Led by Duncan and his two companions, the boys marched down the winding road to a small, cleared grove on the shore of the lake, and there they found the cool and comfortable home of the Maplewood Canoe Club.

The clubhouse was built at the water's edge, and dozens of canoes were to be seen. Some were floating in the water, several were drawn up on shore, while still others were found in a part of the clubhouse built for the purpose of storing them. Five or six club members were sitting on the veranda, smoking and chatting. Out on the mirror-like surface of the lake a few were paddling around in canoes.

It was a peaceful spot, and the boys eagerly sniffed the agreeable odor of the pines which grew in that vicinity.

"Well, dern my picter!" chuckled Obediah Tubbs. "I'd just like to come right down here and loaf through the rest of the warm weather!"

"Make yourselves at home, boys," said Mr. Duncan. "Everything about the place is yours as long as you stay here. Use any of the canoes you wish to use."

There were plenty of comfortable chairs, and the boys promptly accepted the invitation to make themselves at home.

"Hey!" cried Jolliby, as he discovered a set of boxing gloves hanging on the wall inside the clubhouse. "Here are the articles to have fuf-fuf-fun with. Come on, Tubbs. I'll just gug-gug-gug-gug-go you one."

"I am too tired," said Obediah, who was comfortably fanning himself in the big chair he had appropriated. "I don't want to hit you either."

"Dud-dud-dud-don't you?" sneered Chip, as he brought out the gloves. "You dud-dud-don't want to hit me, hey? Don't worry about that. Just juj-juj-juj-jump right up and hit me as much as you can."

"Go away from me," advised Obediah, with an attempt at sternness. "If I ever did hit you once I'd knock a lung out of you."

"Gug-gug-gug-get up," cried Chip immediately, as he began putting on one pair of gloves. "Come right ahead and tut-tut-tut-try it."

The boys laughed and applauded, urging Obediah to get up and show what he could do.

In vain Chip urged him, and at last, walking over to Obediah, he began to tap him with the gloves.

"Get up!" cried Jolliby. "If you dud-dud-don't I'll fuf-fuf-flatten that nose of yours all over your fuf-fuf-fuf-fuf-face!"

"Dern your picter," squeaked Obediah immediately, "if you hit me again I'll soak you on the bugle!"

"That's the talk!" said Earl Gardner. "Go for him, Obediah!"

"I jest hate to see anything like this!" said Ted Smart, as he forced the other pair of gloves onto Tubbs. "It fills me with the utmost distress! Put them on quick, Obed, and sail into him. You'll break my heart if you do it, but I think you'd better do it!"

While Tubbs was hesitating Jolliby gave him a tap on the nose that brought tears into his eyes. With a wild squeal, the fat boy leaped into the air and began putting on the gloves. With difficulty he was repressed while they were tied at the wrists, and when everything was ready the two boys squared away.

"Now if you want to see science," said the fat boy, flourishing his hands wildly, "jest you keep your optics on me. I'll show you some kinks that will make you wink."

It was indeed a comical spectacle to see the tall, thin chap and the fat, rotund lad get at it. Instantly at the word they made a jump at each other. Jolliby shut his eyes and thrust out his long left arm. Tubbs ran plumb against it and sat down heavily.

"Hold on, dern your picter!" exclaimed Obed. "That ain't fair! That ain't no way to box! Why don't you do it right?"

"I guess that was gug-gug-gug-good enough for you," laughed Chip, dancing around his antagonist and making some curious flourishes with his hands. "Hope you ain't going to quit as sus-soon as this."

"You hold on!" said Tubbs, slowly getting onto his hands and knees and rolling up his eyes at Jolliby. "Don't you do a thing till I straighten up. I'm going to swat you in the solar system."

Having risen to his feet, Tubbs began to prance round with the grace of a baby elephant. Jolliby followed him up and struck at him repeatedly, but Obediah managed to keep out of reach every time.

Finally the tall boy grew weary and disgusted.

"This is no running mum-mum-mum-mum-match!" he panted, as he lowered his hands and stood glaring resentfully at Obediah. "I can't chase you all over the county."

"Got enough?" asked Obed, insinuatingly, as he approached Chip.

"Not by a juj-juj-juj-jugful!"

"Then take that!" cried the fat boy, as he delivered a swinging blow that landed in the pit of Jolliby's stomach.

Chip was doubled up like a jackknife. As he remained clasping his stomach and gasping, Obediah once more danced round, waving his hands in the air and crying:

"I guess that jarred you some!"

"That was fuf-fuf-fuf-foul!" came quickly from Jolliby.

"Didn't nobody call time that I heard," said Obed. "I asked you if you had enough and you said you didn't. I thought I'd give yer some more."

"Oh, you dud-dud-dud-did, hey?" cried the tall boy fiercely, as he straightened up. "That's the way you dud-dud-dud-do it, hey? Well, just dud-dud-dud-do it some more!"

The encounter that followed convulsed every witness with laughter. Both lads seemed to close their eyes whenever they got into close connection, and at least nine out of ten of their blows were wasted on the empty air. Indeed, at one time they were actually back to back and still punching away with their eyes tightly closed. Finally Jolliby caught Obediah's head under his arm and held it thus, while he threatened to smash the fat boy with his free hand.

"Break away!" laughed Dick, as he forced them apart, being compelled to drag Obediah from Jolliby's clutch by main force.

"Here!" squealed the fat boy, holding out his hand to Chip, "give me my ear! You raked it off! I want it!"

"Got enough?" again demanded Chip.

"Not if anybody will furnish me with a custard pie and you will wait for me to eat it. I'm hungry."

"You're both pretty well used up," said Dick. "Perhaps you'd better finish this after you've had a little rest."

"All right," said both Chip and Obediah in a breath, for they were glad to stop.

"Gentlemen!" said Ted Smart, rising and making a sweeping gesture toward the contestants, "I wish to call your attention to the most marvelous boxers of modern times."

Unobserved by the boys, a tall, awkward, sandy-whiskered man and a raw-boned, muscular-looking youth had approached the clubhouse while Chip and Obediah were engaged. They were now standing a few feet away, and the men laughed sneeringly at Smart's words.

"Was that what you fellers call boxing?" he derisively inquired. "Why, my boy, Jack, here, can put on the gloves and knock the stuffing out of any of your crowd."

The speaker was John Cole.

The boys recognized him instantly, for Cole had been on the original athletic committee at Maplewood when Dick and his friends arrived at that place. He had backed Benton Hammerswell in all Hammerswell's moves.

Jack Cole was really an athlete of no mean ability. He was also a good baseball player, and had been retained on the Maplewood team by Hammerswell up to the time that the Maplewood manager had engaged a new team throughout.

"I tell yer," said John Cole, looking the boys over and letting his eyes rest on Dick Merriwell, "when Jack and I heerd you fellers had come down here, we jest decided to walk over and see yer. Mebbe you remember the fu'st day you came into Maplewood?"

"Yes, we remember it very well," replied Dick.

"Do yer? I'm glad yer do! Mebbe you remember that there was a baseball game started and that it ended in a row?"

"Yes; we remember that."

"Do yer? Well, I am glad yer do! My boy pitched in that game, and he was in the fight. He got hurt in that fight and had a black eye for a week afterward."

"Too bad!" said Ted Smart. "I am so sorry for poor Jack! Did he really have a black eye? It's a shame he didn't have two black eyes."

"Now, don't you try ter git funny with me, you little runt!" snapped John Cole. "Jack ain't looking fer no trouble with you. You ain't wurth noticing."

"Thanks for the compliment," said Ted.

"There's one feller here," pursued Cole, thrusting his fingers into his sandy beard and scratching his chin, "that my boy, Jack, says he'd like to have a little settlement with."

"I opine I'm the party," said Buckhart, rising.

"No, you ain't," denied Cole. "That's the feller right there."

He pointed straight at Dick.

"He's the feller!" palpitated Cole. "You've got the boxing gloves right here. Now, jest let him put them on with my boy, and I'll bet ten cents that Jack will knock the stuffing out of him inside of two minutes."

"That's right, dad," said Jack. "If he ain't afraid of me he'll put 'em on."

"Step right up," invited Dick. "I can't refuse to accept such a challenge, even if you knock me out in less than one minute. I'll have to put the gloves on with you."

CHAPTER XI

THE BOXING BOUT.

In Maplewood Jack Cole had a reputation as a fighter. In fact, the village boys regarded him as a wonder. At one time he had whipped three of them in a square fight, and it was said that nothing ever hurt him. He seemed to be able to stand punishment without feeling it.

Although old John Cole was a man of some means, he was ignorant and extremely offensive in his ways. Old John believed his son a wonder. It was his conviction that no one of Jack's age could get the best of him.

This being the case, the old man had fretted and fumed over the result of his son's early encounter with the Merriwell crowd in Maplewood. The fact that Jack had come from that encounter with a beautiful black eye, and that neither Dick nor any of his friends had shown visible marks of the conflict, was quite enough to cause the boy's father to long for a time when his son could obtain revenge. He had repeatedly said that some day Jack would "take the starch out of that Merriwell feller."

The man looked grimly confident as Jack donned the gloves.

"Sail right in, boy," he said in a low tone, as he fastened the gloves on young Cole's hands. "Jest knock him silly. If you ever land good and fair with your left, he'll know something has struck him, you bate!"

Jack was full of confidence as he stepped out to face Dick. He put up his hands after his own fashion, yet the guard was not a bad one.

"They're off!" cried Ted Smart. "Will some one please lend me a handkerchief to dry my tears!"

At first Dick worked cautiously, with the object of finding out just how skillful his antagonist really was. He came forward lightly, feinted, moved swiftly to the right, and thus circled round young Cole.

Cole was quick enough in his movements; but kept his face toward Dick and gave no good opening for a blow. At the same time he followed young Merriwell up in a deliberate manner, evidently watching for an opening himself.

"Don't fool with him, Jack!" cried old John. "Jest pitch right in and soak him hard!"

"Yes; pitch right in, Jack!" urged Ted Smart. "I'd love to see you soak him hard! It would do me no end of good to see you soak him hard! Please soak him hard!"

"Dern his picter! he'll get all that's coming to him when he tries it!" declared Obediah Tubbs. "He'll find Dick ain't no easy mark same as Jolliby is."

"Who's an easy mum-mum-mum-mark?" exclaimed Jolliby hotly. "You didn't fuf-fuf-fuf-find it so easy."

"Shut up, both of you!" growled big Bob Singleton. "You've played your part as clowns; now watch the heavy men."

After a few moments Cole began to press Dick harder and harder. The fact that young Merriwell continued to avoid him by swift footwork convinced Jack that his antagonist was afraid.

"Why don't yer stand up and spar right?" he demanded, at last. "Be you trying to wind me? Is that your game? Well, I guess I can stand it as long as you can. I'll git at yer before I'm done."

"That's the talk, my boy!" cried old John. "When you do git at him jest let him know it."

"Oh, he'll know it, all right," grinned the Maplewood boy.

Then, to his surprise, Dick suddenly came in on him, feinted with his right, jabbed quick with his left, and got away.

The blow had landed on Cole's chin, knocking his teeth together and setting his head back.

"Too bad! too bad!" sobbed Smart. "I hate to see it!"

"Don't let him hit yer that way!" shouted old John, in angered astonishment.

"He done it when I wasn't watching," asserted Jack. "He can't do it again."

Barely had he made this statement when Dick once more sprang forward, dodged to one side, ducked and avoided Cole's blow, ending by smashing the Maplewood lad full and hard in the short ribs. He was away like a flash, and had not been touched.

Now Jack Cole was aroused in earnest. He followed Merriwell up and struck two or three blows, which would have been decidedly effective had they landed. They were either dodged or parried by Dick.

"If he ever plants one of them it'll be all over," asserted the boy's father.

When Cole retreated he found Dick after him. There was an exchange of blows at short range, and Merriwell hit his antagonist at least three times. As he got away, Cole tapped him lightly on the cheek.

Although Merriwell's dark eyes were flashing, there was a smile on his lips.

"Why don't you corner him, Jack?" shouted the old man, as he clawed at his whiskers. "Git him inter a corner and then thump him."

Henry Duncan, together with some of the club members, watched the encounter. They knew Cole's reputation in Maplewood, and Duncan feared at the outset that he would prove too much for Merriwell.

"He's a strapping, raw-boned fellow," said Duncan. "If he ever lands a fair swing on Merriwell I'm afraid that will end the whole business."

"I understand that Cole encourages his son in his fighting inclinations," said William Drake.

"Quite true! quite true!" nodded Eustace Smiley. "It's reported around Maplewood that Jack Cole aspires to become a pugilist. He thinks he can make a record in the ring when he gets old enough."

"I am almost sorry we permitted this," said Duncan in a low tone. "When I told the boys to make themselves at home I hardly fancied anything like this would occur. An ordinary boxing bout is harmless enough, but this seems to be an encounter for blood."

"Two to one," remarked Drake, "this is Hammerswell's work. It's my idea he put the Cole boy up to it, with the notion that Merriwell might be knocked out and injured so that he would be unable to do his best in the ball game to-day."

Brad Buckhart heard some of this talk, and at once he stepped over to the men.

"Don't you worry any at all about my pard," he said. "He's just fooling with that chap now. He hasn't tried to hit him yet. Dick has touched him a few times just to get him started."

"There he goes!" again palpitated Smiley. "My gracious! that boy's quick as a cat on his feet!"

Again Dick had closed in on Cole, struck him several light blows, and escaped without a return.

"He doesn't seem to have much force in his blows," observed William Drake. "Apparently he can hit Cole almost at will, but he can't hurt him."

"Wait some," advised Brad. "He hasn't made up his mind to do any damage yet. He's enjoying this little racket a whole lot."

"But while he fools with Cole," said Duncan, "he is exposing himself to a blow that might put him out. Those are hard gloves, and a good jolt with them will count almost as much as a blow with the bare fist."

Buckhart remained undisturbed and confident, repeating his assurance that Dick could take care of himself. At length Cole became exasperated at Dick's success in closing with him and getting away without harm.

"Now you're doing it, Jack!" shouted his father, as the Maplewood boy followed Merriwell up with a rush and succeeded in landing a spent blow. "Keep him going, son, keep him going!"

Of a sudden young Merriwell stopped and met his antagonist as the fellow came on. Parrying two blows, Dick struck once with a swinging upward movement that actually lifted Cole off his feet and dropped him to the floor.

Old John gave a gasp of astonishment. With the exception of Smart, Dick's friends laughed. Ted pretended to shed tears.

Jack Cole came up with a spring, and lost no time in getting at it again.

And now Henry Duncan noted that, although Cole was breathing quite heavily, Merriwell seemed perfectly fresh and unwinded.

"Your friend has the staying power," he remarked to Brad.

The Texan smiled.

"You bet your boots!" he nodded. "That's the way he wins out. He never quits."

By this time old John Cole was greatly excited. He pranced this way and that, calling to his son and urging him on.

"Never touched yer, boy!" he shouted. "He can't jar you that way!"

Faster and more furious became the encounter. Cole swung repeatedly with his left, trying to get in a telling blow. Once he brushed Dick's cheek, and once he landed on Merriwell's chest. In return he was hit repeatedly, but did not seem to mind it.

"I will git yer before I'm done!" he hissed. "I'll put yer out of business!"

Dick saw vindictiveness in his opponent's eyes, and detected hatred in the intonation of Cole's voice.

Up to this point Merriwell had shown his skill as a boxer, without attempting to do his enemy any serious injury. He now saw that Cole would not recognize the fact that he was outpointed unless compelled to do so by a fair knock-out.

Dick now played for Jack's wind, and several times he landed hard on the pit of his stomach.

Enraged by his failure to get in an effective blow, Cole grappled and sought to throw Merriwell. In a moment his feet were snapped into the air, and he was lifted and tossed across Dick's hip, being sent sprawling fifteen feet away.

"If he tries to turn this into a wrestling match, my pard will certain show him some tricks at that," laughed Buckhart.

With his eyes glaring and his teeth set, Jack Cole scrambled up and dashed at Merriwell.

Dick sidestepped and struck a blow that stopped the other lad in his tracks.

"Give him the grand coup, partner!" exclaimed Buckhart. "You can do it."

Indeed, Dick might have finished the encounter then and there, for Cole had dropped his hands and was quite unguarded. Merriwell did make a move to deliver the blow, but restrained himself.

"Perhaps he's going to call it off," he said.

"Not by a jugful!" roared old John. "Git ter going there, Jack!"

Seeming to recover in a moment, Cole accepted this advice, and again pitched into Dick.

During the next few moments the boxing was so swift that the eye followed the blows with difficulty. Once Dick was struck, but he recovered quickly, and a moment later delivered a blow that started the blood from his opponent's nose.

Cole did not mind a little blood. In fact, it seemed to make a fury of him, and he launched himself at Dick, striking right and left with sledge-hammer force.

"We ought to stop it, gentlemen—we ought to stop it!" palpitated Eustace Smiley.

"It will be all over in a minute," declared Buckhart. "Don't worry about it."

He was right, for Dick found his opening and gave Cole a solar-plexus blow that again stopped the fellow short. Then Merriwell swung on Jack's jaw and the boy went "down and out."

Old John could scarcely believe the evidence of his eyes. As he stooped over his son, he continued urging him to get up and resume the fighting.

Jack tried to rise, but his strength was gone, and everything seemed to swing about him.

"Git up, boy—git up!" snarled old John. "You can do him yit!"

"I—I can't!" weakly, whispered the defeated chap. "No—use—dad!"

Then he dropped back and lay sprawled out on the floor.

CHAPTER XII

AN IMPROMPTU CANOE RACE.

ater was dashed into Cole's face, and he was given a swallow or two. It was some minutes before he could sit on a chair without threatening to pitch off to the floor.

When he could sit up he looked around for Dick.

Merriwell was there, and, as he stepped forward, he said:

"I hope you're not badly hurt, Cole. I didn't mean to wind it up this way, but you forced me. I had to."

"That's all right," said Cole in a low tone. "It's not wound up yet!"

"Whatever does he want, pard?" exclaimed Buckhart. "Is he piggish enough to be itching for any more?"

"I hope not," said Dick. "He ought to be satisfied."

"I ain't satisfied!" grated Jack. "I never had nobody do me up before, and I won't forget this!"

"It's an outrage!" declared old John, flourishing his fists in the air and glaring around. "I say it's an outrage, Henry Duncan!"

"You brought it on your son, sir," said Duncan coldly. "You came here and forced the encounter. Merriwell was considerate with your son until he saw it was Jack's purpose to do him injury."

"He couldn't do up my boy again in a year!" snapped the old man. "It was jest an accident, anyhow!"

"You mulish old ignoramus!" exclaimed Duncan, in exasperation he could not repress. "Only for you at the outset we would have retained these boys here as the Maplewood baseball team. You joined Hammerswell and backed him up when he refused to accept them. He used you as his tool. Are you satisfied with the result? When he became tired of your boy he kicked him off the Maplewood team. You're a particularly offensive nuisance, John Cole. This clubhouse is on private grounds, and hereafter I wish you and your son to keep away from it. We don't want you here. Perhaps that's plain enough for you to understand."

"Oh, yes, it's plain enough!" snarled old John. "I understand all about you, Duncan! You think you're mighty fine and aristocratic because you happened to get in with the summer folk who come here. You think you're a lot better than us people who belong here."

"That will do!" said Duncan. "I think your son is able to use his feet now. Take him and walk."

Although old John seized Jack by the arm and they started away, he continued to splutter and snarl until he was quite out of hearing.

"I congratulate you, my boy," said Mr. Duncan, as he placed his hand on Dick's shoulder. "I confess I feared that strapping chap would be too much for you. You demonstrated that you knew more than he about the science of boxing, but until near the finish I didn't fancy you could put him out. Your forbearance is creditable."

"I thought he might quit," said Dick.

"He's not the kind to quit easily. I advise you to look out for him. It's my opinion he's revengeful and will try to square this thing up. It won't surprise me if you had trouble at the ball field this afternoon."

The boys spent the rest of the afternoon lazing about on the veranda of the clubhouse or swimming in the lake. Near midday one of the rooms of the clubhouse was closed and the boys heard the rattling of crockery within that room.

This interested Tubbs at once, and he immediately pricked up his ears, while a look of expectancy came to his face.

"Something doing in there," he piped. "Seems ter me I smell pie."

Within thirty minutes Mr. Duncan appeared on the veranda and invited the boys to come in.

The room had again been thrown open, and the sight they beheld caused them to gasp in astonishment. A long table was covered with a snowy cloth. This table was daintily set, and the display of food upon it made their mouths water.

But by far the most agreeable spectacle was presented by six young girls in white, three on one side of the table and three on the other, who evidently were there to act as waitresses.

Brad Buckhart stopped short and caught his breath.

"Oh, say," he muttered, "I can't do it! I certain can't plant myself there with them to wait on us. They are the real swell articles, and

I sure feel more like making a choice and inviting one to dine with me some."

The astonishment the boys could not conceal caused the girls to smile a little.

"Sit right down, boys," laughed Henry Duncan. "This is not the Maple Heights Hotel, but I fancy you will find enough here to satisfy you."

"To satisfy us!" said Obediah Tubbs, in his piping voice, which he tried to repress. "Well, if anybody in this crowd isn't satisfied with what there's here, he ought to go drown himself, by Jim!"

"Sus-sus-sus-sus-shut up!" whispered Jolliby. "Don't make a fool of yourself!"

"He couldn't do that," said Smart. "Nature got ahead of him on that job."

It was a jolly meal. The boys enjoyed themselves thoroughly, especially Tubbs, whose liking for pie was known by the pretty girl who waited on him. She had pie of all kinds for Obediah, and he sampled every variety placed before him.

"I bet I'll play the best game I ever played in my life this afternoon," he chuckled.

When the meal was finished Dick made a little speech of thanks, addressed to the girls, to Henry Duncan, and to the Maplewood Canoe Club.

"For some time," answered Mr. Duncan, "it has been my desire to show you in some manner that there are those in Maplewood who sincerely regret what took place here on your first arrival in the town. We wished to show our friendly feeling toward you and your companions of the Fairhaven baseball team. Baseball properly played is a clean, manly, wholesome sport. I am sorry to say that baseball as conducted by one or two teams in this league has been anything but clean, manly, and wholesome. It was my conviction from the first that Fairhaven had a team to be proud of, both as gentlemen and as ball players. Never yet, on the ball field or elsewhere, have I heard anything from a Fairhaven player that could offend the most sensitive and particular person. I wish to add that, with the single exception of Benton Hammerswell, the original Maplewood Baseball Association regrets exceedingly that you were not all retained in Maplewood to represent this town in the league. You have made a gallant struggle against seemingly overwhelming odds, and should you succeed in winning the pennant for Fairhaven, be sure that many persons in Maplewood will feel intensely satisfied over such a result."

He was heartily applauded, and again Dick uttered a few words of thanks.

The pretty waitresses smiled on the boys as they filed out of the room, and then the sliding door closed once more.

After dinner some of the boys tried the canoes. Brad was anxious to try one, and induced Dick to accompany him. They were given the use of Henry Duncan's own canoe, and in this they sped away over the smooth surface of the lake.

In the bottom of the canoe lay a coil of small rope, which Buckhart observed, wondering for what purpose it was generally used.

"Talk about flying!" laughed the Texan. "This is the next thing to it. I say, pard, did you hear them say anything about a fine echo that can be heard at the upper end of this lake? They say the hills yonder fling back the sounds and make them wonderfully distinct. Let's paddle over there and give the echo a try-out. What do you say?"

Dick readily agreed, and they headed toward the precipitous hills near the head of the lake. As they approached the locality for which they were heading, they passed close to a small and heavily wooded island.

Suddenly Dick ducked involuntarily, for over his head he heard the hum of a bullet almost simultaneously with the crack of a rifle somewhere on the island.

"That was a little too close!" he exclaimed. "Somebody is decidedly careless!"

Buckhart blazed his indignation.

"I should say so!" he exclaimed. "It must have been a right close call, partner."

"Don't think he missed me by more than a foot, at most," said Dick.

Brad had paused with his paddle uplifted. A strange expression settled on his rugged face.

"Look here, Dick," he said, in a low tone, "I don't more than half reckon that was accidental."

"What do you mean?"

"Somehow I fancy a whole lot that the bullet was intended for you."

"Impossible!" exclaimed Dick.

"All the same, I've got it into my head that way. I say, partner, let's land on that island and see who did the shooting."

Immediately Dick dipped his paddle into the water and headed the canoe toward the island.

Barely had they taken a stroke or two, before Merriwell saw another canoe move out from the opposite side of the island and swiftly glide away. There were two persons in it, and both were plying paddles.

"There they go, Buckhart!" said Dick. "One of them fired that shot."

"Hike up, partner!" exclaimed the Texan. "Let's get after the galoots good and lively."

Without delay the pursuit began. The occupants of the strange canoe glanced back and saw they were followed. Immediately they bent to their work, and this aroused both Brad and Dick.

"They are a heap anxious to get away, pard," breathed the Texan. "That looks a whole lot guilty."

"Do you know them?" asked Dick.

"Haven't taken a square squint at them yet."

"It's Jack Cole in the stern," Merriwell declared.

"That varmint!" grated Brad. "Then it's a plenty lucky the bullet missed you at all."

"I don't like to think Jack Cole would deliberately do a thing like that," said Dick.

"I judge I know the other gentleman," suddenly declared Brad. "If that bullet had come my way I'd bet all my loose collateral he fired at me."

Dick's keen eyes surveyed Cole's companion in the canoe.

"Brad," he said, "I believe that's Tom Fernald."

"Hit him first crack out of the box," said the Texan.

"They'll deny they fired at all."

"That's what they will. It's up to us to run them down and take a look into their canoe. If they have a gun with them, then they can do some explaining. Bend to it, partner. We're gaining."

Both canoes were merrily flying now. Cole and his companion were doing their best, but Fernald's skill with the paddle was not equal to that of the boy. Sometimes he missed a stroke and Cole was heard speaking sharply to him.

The excitement of the race took hold of Brad and Dick. With the steadiness of clockwork they swung their paddles and bent to the task.

Dip and lift! Dip and lift!

On either side the smooth water seemed flying backward, while the canoe raised a slight ripple and left a broadening wake behind it.

Cole and Fernald headed down the western shore of the lake, apparently looking for a good chance to run in and leave the canoe before their pursuers could come up. All along there the shore was rocky, and no favorable landing spot presented itself.

"We've got them, Brad!" laughed Dick exultantly.

The faces of the boys were flushed and their eyes gleaming. They felt the breeze rush past their ears.

Before long Fernald began to show signs of weariness. Once more Cole was heard speaking to him, and this time it was plain the boy urged him to keep at it and do his best.

"Wait some," invited Buckhart. "We want to chat with you a little."

"You go to thunder!" cried Cole, once more glancing back.

Still the pursuers continued. Fernald seemed inclined to give up, but Cole would not quit.

Foot by foot the canoe in the rear drew nearer to the one in advance. The distance that separated them was cut down swiftly, and Brad muttered:

"We'll be on top of them in less than two minutes."

Not more than ten feet lay between the canoes when Buckhart, giving an unusually heavy surge at the paddle, met with an accident.

The handle of the paddle snapped short off.

The Texan uttered an exclamation of dismay.

Glancing back, Cole saw what had happened, and again urged Fernald to exert himself.

"Now wouldn't that bump you some!" exclaimed Brad. "In four seconds more I could have placed my hand on his neck."

Dick had not ceased paddling. Instead of that, he seemed to put more force into his strokes, if such a thing were possible.

Although both Fernald and Cole pulled away as hard as they could, the distance between the boats increased with astonishing slowness. Plainly Merriwell was nearly equal to the task of keeping up alone.

Suddenly an idea occurred to Buckhart. He turned his body and reached backward for the coil of rope behind him.

"Keep it up, partner!" he palpitated. "Just hold her as she is a minute."

Then the Texan made a running noose in one end of the rope. He did this with the skill acquired from cowboy instructors on his father's ranch. Having accomplished his object, the Texan ran off some of the rope into loops, which he held in his left hand.

"She may not work, Dick," he said. "All the same, we'll give her a try."

Then, as he knelt in the canoe, he swung the loop of the rope once or twice round his head and sent it writhing through the air.

The cast was made with all the cleverness of a Mexican lariat thrower. The noose fell over Cole's head and shoulders, and Buckhart quickly drew it taut, pinning Jack's arms to his sides.

Had Cole been aware of Brad's purpose, he might have flung the noose off by quickly lifting his arms. Not being aware of it, he was taken by surprise and found himself unable to ply the paddle. Not only that, but the forward motion of his canoe was checked and a steady pull by the Texan drew the other canoe nearer.

In his excitement Cole made an effort to cast aside the noose. In doing this he partly rose to his feet, and a moment later the canoe shot out from beneath him, sending him with a loud splash into the water.

It happened at that very moment that Buckhart had relaxed his grip on the rope slightly as he moved forward toward the prow of the canoe, with the intention of grasping the one in advance. As Cole went down, the rope was snapped from Buckhart's fingers.

Although Cole had thus been projected into the lake, the canoe from which he plunged did not upset. It seemed to dart from beneath him.

Fernald turned a somewhat agitated face to look round and was amazed to find himself alone in the canoe. In a moment, nevertheless, he realized that his late companion had fallen overboard. He also saw that attention had been turned from him to Cole.

Immediately the man retreated toward the middle of the canoe in order to balance it evenly, and then, without offering to aid in the rescue of Jack Cole, he paddled hurriedly away.

"Hold on, Fernald!" cried Dick. "Wait and help your friend! Don't play the coward!"

The man made no retort, but continued to pull away.

Cole rose to the surface and attempted to swim. To his horror, he found he was entangled in the rope in such a manner that he could not take a stroke.

With a gurgling cry, he again disappeared from view.

Dick Merriwell wasted no time. Slipping off his shoes and speaking a word of warning to Brad in order that the Texan might not be taken by surprise and upset, he plunged from the canoe into the lake, thus promptly going to the assistance of his enemy.

CHAPTER XIII

COLE'S CHANGE OF HEART.

hen Cole again came to the surface Merriwell was near enough to make a quick, forward lunge and seized him. Fortunate indeed was this for the fellow entangled in the rope, as he could make no effective efforts to keep himself afloat, and his struggle to free his limbs was sufficient to cause him to sink again only for Dick's promptness in reaching him.

Fortunately for the would-be rescuer, Cole's hands were bound to his sides by the rope which had become wound about him, and, therefore, he could not clutch Merriwell.

Nevertheless, he struggled to free himself, at the same time choking and strangling as Dick sought to keep his mouth and nose above the surface.

"Be still!" ordered Dick. "Are you anxious to drown? If you keep still we'll get you out all right."

At first the helpless fellow did not seem to hear, but after a while Merriwell succeeded in impressing upon him the idea that he was hindering his own rescue by his efforts, and when Cole gave up struggling Dick found it no great task to keep him afloat.

By this time Buckhart had brought the canoe round close to them and cautiously reached over to grasp Cole by the shoulder.

"Don't let him catch hold and upset me, Dick," warned the Texan. "He's liable to do it."

"Not now," answered Merriwell. "Not until he can use his hands."

By the time Dick freed Cole from the rope, which he finally succeeded in doing, both he and Brad had impressed it upon the fellow that it would be fatal to catch hold of the side of the canoe. They induced him to wait until the stern of the canvas craft was swung round to him, and then, directed by Dick, he got hold of it.

"Paddle toward the shore, Buckhart!" cried Merriwell. "You will have to tow him into shallow water."

"Why can't I git into the canoe?" asked Cole. "I'm afraid I'll let go and sink."

"If you attempted to get into that canoe you'd upset it, and then you would have a chance to sink or swim," answered Dick. "If you keep the hold you have we'll get you close to shore so that you can wade out."

"What are you going to do?"

"I am going to stay with you," assured Dick. "Don't be afraid of that. I'll not try to get into that canoe."

"Could you do it without upsetting it?"

"Yes."

"Then why can't I?"

"You don't know the trick."

"Is it a trick?"

"Certainly it is. Not one man in a hundred who uses a canoe can do it."

In spite of his peril Cole's curiosity seemed to be aroused, and he asked:

"How did you know the trick?"

"It was taught me by an Indian," answered Merriwell.

In the meantime Buckhart was carefully and slowly paddling toward the near shore. As has been stated, this shore was very rocky, and when the prow of the canoe softly touched these rocks neither Cole nor Dick could reach bottom with his feet and still keep his head above the surface.

"Jingoes!" exclaimed Merriwell, "it must fall off almost perpendicular from the water's edge here; but we're close to the shore, and you can swim that far, Cole."

"I don't know," answered Jack doubtingly. "I'm afraid I can't do it now. My clothes are heavy as lead, and I can't swim much, anyhow."

"I opine it's a whole lot lucky for you that my pard went into the drink to give you a hand," said the Texan. "Just hang on and I'll swing the prow round close to the rocks."

This he finally did, and not until Jack Cole could almost touch the rocks did his feet reach bottom. Even then the bank seemed so precipitous that he was afraid to let go his hold on the canoe, and only with the assistance of Dick did he finally succeed in dragging himself out.

Merriwell followed him.

"There you are," he said. "You had a pretty good bath, and

you're fortunate to get out of it so well."

For the first time Cole seemed to think of his late companion.

"Where's Fernald?" he asked.

"Echo answers, 'where?'" said Dick.

"What became of him?"

"He scooted."

"Scooted?"

"Yes."

"You mean that he left me to drown?"

"He didn't linger long after you went overboard."

Slowly a look of anger came to Jack Cole's plain face.

"So that's the kind of a man he is!" exclaimed the Maplewood boy savagely. "Left me to drown when I was all tangled up in that rope, did he? Well, he'll hear from me!"

"In the future," suggested Buckhart, "I should advise you to be some particular in the choice of your side partners."

"Who fired that shot from the island?" demanded Dick.

"What shot?" asked Jack, in apparent surprise.

"Don't you know anything about it?"

"Not a thing."

"Pitch him into the drink again, partner, if he doesn't own up!" cried the Texan, in exasperation.

Cole scrambled back from the edge of the water quickly, snarling:

"Don't you try it! Don't you touch me!"

"Don't worry," retorted Dick. "If you haven't learned your lesson by this time you never will. You'd better own up about the shooting."

"Don't know nothing about no shooting," sullenly persisted the Maplewood boy.

"Didn't you hear the shot?"

"No."

"Now you know he's lying, Dick!" cried Buckhart. "Of course he heard it! I reckon he fired it himself!"

"That's a lie!" shouted Jack excitedly. "If any one says such a thing about me he lies!"

"It was fired from that island," said Merriwell, "and the bullet came pretty near me, too. Weren't you on the island with Fernald?"

"No."

"But we saw you leaving it."

"Never," denied Cole. "We just paddled past the island and saw you coming after us."

"What made you try to get away?"

Jack hesitated, and seemed to find it difficult to answer. After a time he muttered:

"That's none of your business! Perhaps we wanted to see if you could ketch us."

"Well, I certain judge you found out," said Buckhart.

"You came near drowning me!" grated Cole. "If that had happened you'd been to blame."

"You ought to be some ashamed to talk that fashion," said the Texan; "but I don't opine there's anything like shame in you. Come on, Dick, we'll go back and make out a complaint against him. We'll have him arrested for firing that shot."

"Go ahead," sneered Cole. "That's all the good it'll do you."

Deciding it was useless to waste further words on the fellow, Dick stepped into the canoe as Buckhart again swung the prow close to the shore.

"You'll have time to think it over while you're walking round the shore to Maplewood," said Merriwell. "Remember that Tom Fernald deserted you and left you to drown."

"And don't forget," suggested Buckhart, "that Dick Merriwell jumped in and pulled you out some."

The Texan then swung the canoe round and began paddling away.

Cole remained watching them some minutes, but finally turned and plodded off, soon disappearing from view.

Returning to the clubhouse, the boys told of their adventure, arousing the indignation of the listeners.

"It was sheer carelessness for any one to be shooting in such a manner," said William Drake.

"It was a whole lot more than carelessness," averred Buckhart. "I opine one of us was the target aimed at."

"Impossible!" exclaimed Drake. "I can't believe such a thing. No, no, my boy; you must be mistaken. No one round here would do such a thing."

"I'm not disputing with you, sir," retorted the Texan; "but I presume you will let me hold my own opinion on that point."

As the only change of clothing he had with him was a baseball suit, Dick soon got into that, while his wet garments were hung out to dry.

Less than an hour after the adventure on the lake the boys were surprised at the appearance of Jack Cole at the clubhouse. Cole's clothing still hung wet upon his limbs, and it seemed evident that he had come at once to the clubhouse after tramping round the shore of the lake.

"I'd like to speak with you, Dick Merriwell," he said.

"All right," said Dick, rising at once and approaching Cole. "Here I am. Go ahead."

"Won't you jest step out here alone with me?" invited Jack. "I'd rather talk to you where there won't nobody hear us."

"Keep your eyes open, pard," warned the Texan.

"Don't worry," said Dick, and he followed Cole, who walked away a short distance into the little grove.

The Maplewood boy seemed hesitating and downcast as he again turned to face Merriwell.

"I've been thinking about that business over t'other side of the lake," he said. "The more I thought about it the sorer I got. I ain't seen Tom Fernald sence. When I do he'll hear from me, and don't you forgit it! I'll tell him something he won't like. I've been thinking that it was up to me to thank you for jumping in and keeping me from drowning."

Dick was surprised, for gratitude from Cole had been the last thing expected by him.

"I couldn't leave you to drown after you were thrown into the water in that manner," he said.

"I guess you're not the kind of a feller to go off and leave anybody in such a situation. I've been thinking about you, too, while I was walking round here. You know I took a dislike to you the fust time I saw you. I thought your brother was coming here with a baseball team, and I was down on him even before I saw him. That was 'cause I wanted to play myself and I s'posed I wouldn't have no chance. Then when we challenged your fellers to play and you batted me out of the box it made me roaring ugly. Right on top of that we sailed into you, and you got the best of the fight, which didn't make me feel no better toward you. I kept saying I'd git even somehow, and I hoped I'd be able to do it while I was playing on the team here, but the chance never came round. Then when Hammerswell got his new team, he dropped me along with the others."

"What are you driving at?" asked Dick. "I hope you didn't fire that shot from the island, Cole."

"No, I didn't!" cried the Maplewood boy quickly. "I'm going to tell you the truth about that. It was Fernald who done it. He had a pistol. It wasn't no gun he used. I didn't know why he wanted to land on the island when he saw you coming over that way, but we landed and he watched until you was close. Fust thing I knew I see him pull out a pistol and cock it. Even then I didn't s'pose he was goin' ter shoot at nobody, but in a minute he lifted it, and I came near spitting my heart right out, for I saw he was pointing it at one of you fellers in the canoe. Jest as he shot I gave his arm a poke and that spoiled his aim. He was mad, too, I tell yer. When I asked him what he was trying ter do he said he could tell anybody it was an accident—that we was jest firing at a mark on the island. I was all-fired skat, and I wanted to git away. We hustled into our canoe, and you know the rest. I don't think he tried to shoot at you. It seemed to me that he was firing at the other feller. Mebbe the bullet went nearer you because I poked his arm."

"Look here, Cole," said Dick earnestly, "are you ready to swear to this in court?"

The Maplewood boy betrayed evident alarm.

"No, no!" he exclaimed. "I won't do that! Why, Fernald would lay it up agin' me, and I'd git soaked for it sometime."

"But if you were compelled to tell the story in court you wouldn't perjure yourself?"

"I don't know for sure that he really tried to shoot at either one of you," said Cole, a crafty look coming into his eyes. "If I had to tell anything in court I'd say I didn't know jest what he was tryin' to shoot at; but I saw you out there and knew the bullet was going to come pretty near you, and so I poked his arm. If he said he was firing at a mark or a bird I couldn't deny it."

Dick saw at once that any attempt to use Cole as a witness against Fernald would fail.

"I ain't going to be your enemy no more," declared Jack. "I decided on that while I was walking round the shore. If I can help you somehow I'll do it, too; but I won't go into court and git into no trouble that way."

"I suppose you know that the trolley car that was bringing us to Maplewood this afternoon jumped the track, and that the rails had been loosened and spread by some one?" questioned Dick.

"I heerd about it," nodded Cole.

"When did you hear—in advance, or after it occurred?"

"I ain't going to say nothing about that, either," declared the Maplewood lad, with a show of uneasiness. "I know lots of things I won't say nothing about."

Although Dick questioned him in the cleverest manner, Cole persisted in his determination to remain silent on the subject of the trolley-car affair.

"But I want to tell you something that may help you some," said Jack. "I want you to know it so you'll be prepared for what you're goin' against this afternoon. Hammerswell means to beat you somehow, and he's made plans to do it. He'll have a tough crowd on hand to rattle you and bulldoze you. He's got all the fellers around him to come to help him, and paid 'em, too. Then he sent for Fernald, and Fernald picked up a still tougher gang in Rockford. They'll all be here in a bunch, and you want to look out for a lot of trouble. I promised to help them, but I won't do it now. No, sir! Instead of helping them, I'm goin' to holler for you. If I can do anything more than holler I'll do it, you bet! But I'm afraid you're goin' ter lose the game. I'd like to see you win it now, but I don't believe you can."

"Well," said Dick, "I'm obliged for this warning, at least. If we get a fair deal on the field, the crowd may hoot and yell as much as it likes. I don't believe it can rattle the boys very much. We'll be ready for hoodlumism, and the chances are that sort of business will simply serve to make the boys play harder."

"I hope so, blamed if I don't!" nodded Cole. "Now I guess I'll go home and change my clothes. I wish I was goin' ter play this afternoon, but I'm glad I ain't going ter play agin' you."

A sudden idea came to Dick.

"Are you in earnest about wishing to play?" he asked. "Do you really want us to win?"

"Sure thing."

"Then put on your suit and come to the field. I've seen you pitch, and, with a catcher who knows his business under the bat, I am sure you can do a good turn. I pitched a hard game yesterday and another the day before that. Bold has rheumatism in the shoulder of his pitching arm, and he's afraid he'll not last through the game to-day. This climate with its fog has knocked his arm out. I shall start the game with Bold in the box. If he is batted hard some one will have to take his place. I don't wish to use my own arm up, and it's possible I might give you a chance to hand the ball up a few innings in case you were on our bench."

The eyes of Jack Cole actually gleamed. A strange look of eagerness came to his plain face.

"You don't mean it?" he cried. "You wouldn't really and truly use me to pitch for you? Why, I've thought a hundred times that if I could pitch just one game with your fellers behind me I'd show some of the folks round here what I could do. I never dreamed I'd have the chance."

"I'm not promising you the chance to-day," said Dick. "I am simply promising to try you a few innings in case you're absolutely needed; but I wish you to understand that you must say nothing of this to anybody. You're not to let a soul know you may play with us until you reach the field and sit on our bench. I don't want any one to get after you and make any talk to you."

"I will keep mum," promised Cole, "and I'll be there, Mr. Merriwell. You can depend on me, you bet!"

Saying which, he hastened away.

CHAPTER XIV

TRICKS COME THICK.

ever before had such a roaring crowd assembled on the Maplewood ball field. Special cars came rolling into town, loaded down with men and boys, who sprang off and went marching away toward the field. They were loud and boisterous in manner, and many of them announced repeatedly that they were there to see the home team win. That a great number of them were toughs could be seen at a glance. When the game began, however, not all the spectators assembled on the field were of this tough class. The summer visitors of Maplewood were on hand in an unusually large body, and even while practice was going on some of them complained to Benton Hammerswell that the language of the roughs present was offensive. They asked the Maplewood manager if he could not do something to keep these offensive persons quiet.

"I am afraid it's impossible," he answered. "I didn't expect such a crowd to-day or I would have had officers present. I am sorry if they are offensive in their conduct or talk, but I can't repress them without assistance."

In his heart he had no desire to repress them. Jack Cole had not spoken a falsehood when he told Dick that through Hammerswell the toughs had been gathered up and brought to the field.

No one seemed to observe Cole until he was noticed batting the ball while the Fairhaven team was practicing. Then there were numerous expressions of surprise over the fact that Jack was in a playing suit.

Hammerswell observed him and walked swiftly over to the home team's bench, on which sat Chester Arlington.

"What's that fellow, Cole, doing here?" inquired the Maplewood manager.

"You tell me," said Chester sourly. "I don't know."

"He has a suit on."

"My eyes are all right. I see he has."

"What's the matter with you? You're crusty."

"It's my turn to pitch to-day," said Chester. "Are you going to put me in?"

"Sit still," retorted Hammerswell. "We have to win this game to-day, and I'm taking no chances. Raymer is the best pitcher in this league, and he goes into the box."

Instantly Chester rose, savagely flinging down the ball he had been holding while sitting.

"Then I'm done!" he snarled. "This ends it for me! I quit you now, Hammerswell, and I hope your old team is wiped off the map!"

"Hold on!" commanded the manager sharply. "You've been paid in advance. You've received your salary for another week."

"Oh, forget it!" sneered Arlington. "That's all right! I'll keep it!"

Benton exposed his teeth beneath his small, dark mustache.

"You will cough it up if you quit," he asserted.

Arlington faced him unhesitatingly.

"Don't dream such a thing for a minute!" he snarled. "I'll cough up nothing. Instead of that, I may ask you to cough up a little. I know about some of the tricks arranged for this game. I know where certain balls are hidden in the outfield. Do you want me to talk?"

"You'd better keep still," answered Hammerswell, in a whisper.

Chet snapped his fingers.

"All right. Then don't talk to me about returning any money you've given me. I'm going up to the hotel to get into my other clothes. I will leave this suit outside your door, as I won't want it any more this year."

Without another word, he turned his back on Hammerswell and walked away.

Just before the game began Dick called his players around him and many of the spectators observed with surprise that Jack Cole was one of them. With Dick in their midst, they pressed close, getting their heads together and listening to him.

"Boys," said Merriwell, glancing from one to another, with his calm, dark eyes, "this is going to be a fierce old fight to-day. Over there by first base you can see a lot of toughs who have been brought here to rattle us and who will do so if possible. Just close your ears to howls and insults. Don't let them distract your attention from the game for a single moment. Let's go into this thing with the determination of winning out or leaving our carcasses right here on the field.

"If we can stick to it with the right spirit we'll stand a show of winning. It's spirit that tells, boys. I want you to get into the mood. Keep on your toes every instant. No matter where you're playing, keep alert and wide-awake. The outfielders need to be just as watchful and alert as the infielders. Seconds count in getting after the ball. The player who starts at the crack of the bat gains time. I know you want to win. If we should carry off this game we would be tied with one of the other teams for first place.

"From this day to the finish of the season it's going to be a fierce old struggle. Every game won counts heavily for final success. Every game lost will be a millstone to drag down the defeated team. Throughout all the yelling and howling of these hoodlums, don't forget that we've friends here. The summer people are with us, but it's not likely they'll make enough noise to be heard while the toughs are whooping it up. Now, fellows, let's get after that pitcher at the start. A good start counts, and we may worry Raymer if we connect with his delivery at the outset."

During this talk Merriwell's players seemed to feel the spirit of undying determination that he possessed. As his eyes turned from one to another, it seemed that he poured out upon them a little of his own spirit, and when the game began every one of them was filled with it.

The batting order of both teams follows:

Fairhavens.	Maplewood.
Gardner, rf.	Mole, cf.
Bold, p.	Hunston, 1st b.
Bradley, 3d b.	Connor, ss.
Buckhart, c.	Halligan, lf.
Merriwell, ss.	Lumley, 3d b.
Jolliby, cf.	Dillard, 2d b.
Singleton, 1st b.	Farrell, rf.
Tubbs, 2d b.	Garvin, c.
Smart, rf.	Raymer, p.

Gardner walked out with a springy step and took his position at the plate. Raymer whistled over a swift one, and Earl promptly drove it far into left field. As the ball bounded past the fielder, who was running after it, it seemed certain that Gardner would make three bases, and there was a possibility of his circling the diamond and scoring.

Some of those who watched the ball bound away to the fence were surprised to see Halligan pause in his pursuit of it, stoop quickly, and pick something up. Then the fellow turned and threw a ball to Connor, who had run out a little toward left field.

"How did that happen?" exclaimed William Drake. "That's not the ball!"

Connor snapped the ball he had received to Dillard at second, and Gardner's run was checked there.

"Wait a minute, Mr. Umpire!" cried Dick, starting out onto the diamond. "That's not the ball in play! That's not the ball Gardner hit!"

Immediately there was a terrific uproar from the crowd of hoodlums. They yelled at Dick, and hurled upon him all sorts of epithets. Some of them even started to follow him onto the field.

"Get off the field!" commanded the umpire. "If you crowd out here I'll stop the game! Get back behind the ropes!"

They retreated reluctantly, still howling at Dick.

The umpire thought the ball thrown in by Halligan was the one he had put in play, and therefore Dick's protest was passed over.

"I'll have Gardner look for the right ball when he takes the field," said Merriwell, as he retreated to he bench.

Bold was the next batter, and he took a signal from Dick, which led him to bunt the second ball pitched by Raymer. He cleverly sent it slowly rolling along the ground just inside the first-base line.

On this bunt Gardner easily took third, while Bold was thrown out at first. Earl crossed third base as if contemplating dashing home, and the ball was sent across to Lumley by Hunston. This forced Gardner to dive back to the bag: but he was off again in a twinkling as he saw the throw was a bad one.

Lumley jumped for the ball, thrust out his left hand, but barely touched it with his fingers.

Then Gardner raced home with the first run for Fairhaven.

"That's the right spirit," assured Dick, patting Earl on the back. "They spoiled your homer with a trick, but you led Hunston into a bad throw and scored just the same. I want you to look for that ball out there in left field. I think you will find it close to the fence."

"I wondered how he got it so soon and threw it in," said Earl.

This beginning by the visitors seemed to enrage the crowd of hoodlums. As Bradley strode out to hit they whooped and yelled at him as loudly as possible. Some of them made references to his personal appearance, and two or three called him foul names.

Again Dick started up and made a signal to the umpire.

There was a lull, and he was heard demanding that something should be done to stop the rowdyism.

"Where is Mr. Hammerswell?" cried the umpire, looking around for the Maplewood manager.

But Hammerswell was keeping under cover just then. He had decided to keep out of sight and could not be found.

The umpire warned the crowd, but his warning proved ineffective. They laughed at him and invited him to "go fall off the earth."

Bradley seemed deaf to all the racket. He missed a good one over the outside corner, then let two pass and struck under a sharp rise.

"You can't hit, you lobster!" whooped one of the thugs.

"Back to the fool house!" yelled another.

"Where did you get that face?" howled a third. "It's enough to frighten a Hottentot!"

But these things were mild beside some of the language used, and the ladies were shocked by what they were compelled to hear.

"This is the end of Hammerswell's baseball days in Maplewood," said Dick to Buckhart. "He may last through the season, but I'll guarantee he never again runs a team here."

"The varmint ought to be hanged!" snarled the Texan. "A rope and a limb is what's coming to him." Bradley finally cracked out a clean single and easily took first.

Then Buckhart walked to the plate and slammed the ball fairly against centre-field fence. It rebounded and was lost in some grass near the fence.

Nevertheless, Mole lost no time in searching for it. In the midst of a tuft of grass he found a ball snugly hidden, and this he sent back into the diamond.

Ted Smart was on the coaching line near third, and his signal sent Bradley across that bag and onward to the plate.

Mole's throw to Dillard was swift and accurate. Dillard wheeled and lined the ball to Garvin, who tagged Bradley the moment before Billy reached the plate. Buckhart had crossed second, and he made an attempt to reach third on Dillard's throw to Garvin.

The catcher snapped the ball over to Lumley, who tagged Brad as he was sliding, and in this manner two men were put out, which retired the islanders.

In fact, neither Bradley nor Buckhart had been legally put out, for the ball returned by Mole was not the one batted to the fence by the Texan. Dick suspected this, but was not sure of it.

By this time Bart Hodge, who had thus far restrained himself with difficulty, was thoroughly aroused. His fighting blood was up, and he longed to get into the game himself.

"This doesn't seem much like old Maplewood," he muttered. "In the old days this was the cleanest town in the league. Frank will hardly believe it when I write him about this game."

Bold went into the box for Fairhaven, and immediately the hoodlums began to yell at him. They piled on the insults thicker and thicker, but he seemed entirely unaware of their howling. At intervals he had felt a slight catch in his shoulder, but he fancied this might work out as the game progressed.

Mole was a good waiter, and in the end he secured a pass to first, as Bold could not seem to locate the plate. Hunston followed, and he bunted the second ball pitched, rolling it slowly down just inside the third-base line.

As Bradley came leaping in to handle this bunt, he was confused to see two balls rolling slowly along within a foot of each other.

Some one on the opposite side of the home plate had tossed out another ball, which thus rolled into the diamond beside the one hit.

Bradley caught up the wrong ball and snapped it to Singleton. Had it been the right ball Hunston should have been declared out, for it reached big Bob's hands before the runner touched first.

Then arose an argument over which ball was in play, and the umpire confessed that he did not know. For this very reason he refused to declare Hunston out.

Bart Hodge seemed inclined to seek the fellow who had thrown the ball out onto the diamond, but Jack Cole advised him against it.

"Better keep still," said Cole. "That gang will all jump any one who starts trouble to-day."

"It's about the dirtiest ball playing I ever witnessed," said Bart. "I have seen a few tricks in my day, but they are coming thick and fast here."

Connor followed up the successes attained by the men ahead of him by dropping a little fly just over the infield, and this filled the bases.

Bold now settled down to do his best, but whenever he threw a drop there was a snapping sensation in his shoulder and his entire arm received a twinge of pain. This prevented him from using his most effective ball, and in the end Halligan smashed a line drive far into the field, scoring three men and reaching second base himself.

"I am afraid the game is lost in the very first inning," muttered Hodge regretfully.

CHAPTER XV

McLANE AND HIS PEACEMAKERS.

he summer visitors present were fairly disgusted by the rowdyism of the tough gang. In vain they protested. They were mocked and derided and invited to "go chase themselves." At last, unable to stand it longer, ladies began to leave the field in large numbers, accompanied by many of the gentlemen.

"Is there anything like law and order in this town?" exclaimed Henry Duncan. "Are there no officers to stop such disgraceful conduct and arrest these ruffians?"

"Arrest nothing!" sneered one of the young toughs. "I'd like to see any officer try to pinch one of this gang! He'd get his head busted. You'd better take a sneak, mister, before something falls on you."

"It certainly is a shame," nodded William Drake. "Those Fairhaven lads will be given no show at all. Already the umpire is frightened, for he knows he'll be mobbed unless he gives everything to Hammerswell's team."

The departure of the summer visitors from the field left Dick and his friends almost wholly without sympathizers and supporters.

Bart Hodge stood near the Fairhaven bench, watching and listening, a heavy cloud on his face and slumbering fire in his eyes.

"I'd like to have Frank's Terrible Thirty here for about ten minutes," he thought. "I reckon they'd clean out this mob in less time than that. This isn't sport; it's robbery."

Henry Duncan touched him on the shoulder.

"It's no use," he said, soberly shaking his head. "The boys haven't a chance under such conditions. I should advise you to urge Dick to take his team off the field. Of course the umpire will be bulldozed into forfeiting the game to Maplewood, but Dick can quit under protest, and I believe the game will be thrown out and not counted in the series."

It was Bart's turn to shake his head.

"I don't believe Dick can be induced to leave the field," he said. "He knew well enough what he was going against to-day, and he'll fight it out to the finish. He has too much spirit to be a quitter."

"That won't be quitting," declared Duncan. "It would be a simple demand for fair play and justice."

"Still I'm certain Dick wouldn't hear to it."

"Well, I'm going out and look for an officer. I'm going to see if there's no way to keep the peace here."

"It would take twenty officers to quell this mob," said Hodge. "One man couldn't do a thing."

Nevertheless Henry Duncan went forth in search of the local deputy sheriff, only to find that the officer was not in town. Later it was learned that he had been advised to get out of Maplewood and remain away until after the game was over.

Lumley, the batter who followed Halligan, tried hard to imitate the example of his predecessor in hitting, but drove a grounder to Obediah Tubbs, who gathered it up cleanly and whistled it to Singleton for an "out" that could not be disputed. Nevertheless, the hoodlums howled at Obediah, big Bob, and the umpire. They climbed over the ropes and crowded close to the base line on both sides of the field. In vain the umpire ordered them back.

Dillard obtained a scratch hit and reached first while Halligan took third.

Farrell lifted a fly to Jolliby, on which Halligan scored. With two men out, Garvin put up a ball that big Bob easily got under near first base. Just as the ball struck in Singleton's hands two of the spectators rushed at him and upset him. They were not quick enough to keep him from making the catch, and the big first baseman held fast to the ball as he went down. He sprang up instantly and held the ball in his hand as he turned toward his assailant, who had retreated beyond the base line.

The umpire's decision that Garvin was out was greeted with howls of angry disapproval by the hoodlums.

Maplewood had secured four scores in the first inning through trickery and the disreputable behavior of the crowd.

As the islanders came into their bench they were mocked and jeered and insulted in a manner that infuriated Buckhart, who was restrained with difficulty from retorting.

Merriwell was the first batter, and he sent a hot one to Connor, who fumbled it and made a scramble to pick it up.

Dick might have crossed first in safely with perfect ease, but as he ran down the base line one of the thugs stepped forward, thrust out a foot and tripped him. Before the captain of the islanders could recover Connor had secured the ball and thrown it across the diamond to Hunston.

"I swear I'll stand no more of this!" snarled Buckhart, as he started up from the bench. "I'm going to put my brand on somebody if the whole herd stampedes over me!"

Dick seized him by the arm and checked him, pointing toward the gate.

"Who are those men?" he asked.

Through the gate came a broad-shouldered chap, and following him there appeared twenty more burly individuals. They were dressed in rough, working clothes, and every man had his coat off and his shirt sleeves rolled up.

The Texan uttered a cry of grim satisfaction and delight.

"Brick McLane, by all that's lucky!" he shouted. "Those men with him are stonecutters from the island. There'll be something doing now."

With McLane and his stonecutters Henry Duncan had also appeared. Already he had told McLane all about what was taking place, and the husky lobsterman now marched onto the field, with his backers at his heels. Straight out to the home plate strode those men, and there McLane halted them.

"Gents," cried the lobsterman, holding up one hand, "me and my friends is here to see a square deal. We understand Fairhaven isn't getting it. We understand there's some intimidating business taking place. I guess the most of you has heard of me. I generally make good any promise, and right here I want to promise them chaps that is kicking up a disturbance that we'll surely wade into them and give them all the fun they want unless they cool down directly. From this time on this ball game is going to be on the level. Mr. Umpire, you give the decisions jest as you think is correct, and I'll guarantee you protection when the game is finished. There shan't nobody put a finger onto yer."

In a surprising manner Benton Hammerswell had appeared from somewhere and was standing near the Maplewood bench as McLane made his announcement. The Maplewood manager felt a touch on his elbow, and turned to see Chester Arlington, in street clothes, at his side. Chester smiled scornfully into Hammerswell's face.

"Perhaps you've stolen the game already," said Arlington. "If not, you won't win it by your little plan. I knew last night that you intended to play crooked and keep me out of the box to-day, and I likewise heard you plan to bulldoze Fairhaven out of this game. I decided to spoil the trick for you, and therefore I telephoned Brick McLane and told him all about it. I advised him to bring over a fighting crowd with him, and he's here with twenty of the toughest scrappers to be found on Fairhaven Island. You can thank me."

With an exclamation of rage, Hammerswell wheeled and struck at Chester's face.

Arlington dodged like a flash and retreated, still laughing mockingly.

McLane's announcement had been received with a few cries of derision from the ruffians. Nevertheless, every one of them knew the lobsterman was there to back up his talk, and they realized he had brought fighters with him.

Having had his say, McLane marched his force to a position back of the Fairhaven bench and told the players to go on with the game.

For a short time the hoodlums were quieted, but, being far superior to the island crowd in numbers, they soon began to hoot and jeer once more.

When Jolliby reached first on a dropped third strike, and Singleton followed him on four balls, the thugs decided it was time to do something.

With his hands on his hips, McLane was watching. He saw one of the ruffians back of third base hurl a stone at Singleton. The stone struck big Bob in the back of the neck and knocked him to his hands and knees.

Then the lobsterman let out a roar like that of an enraged lion. He shouted an order to his companions, and they leaped forward and caught up the bats of the Fairhaven players.

"Charge!" thundered McLane.

Without a moment's delay, the stonecutters charged at the lobsterman's heels, and he led them into the mob of hoodlums back of the first-base line.

The bats began to rise and fall, and thudding blows were followed with howls of pain, while the ruffians fell over one another in their desperate attempt to get away.

"Out of the gate!" shouted McLane. "Get off the field or we'll annihilate every one of yer!"

The thugs offered little resistance. Some of them were beaten down and trampled on. Those who could fled toward the gate and lost no time in obeying the lobsterman's order. Like a lot of cattle the most of them were driven from the field. Some were badly injured, and two or three were dragged off by their friends.

The spectators who were not concerned in this encounter stood up and watched it breathlessly. The few ladies who remained on the field were badly frightened, and some of the men who accompanied them were alarmed.

It was all over in a surprisingly short time. Having driven the leaders of the mob off and warned them not to return unless they were seeking broken heads, McLane led his triumphant little band back to the Fairhaven bench.

"Ladies and gentlemen," he said, stepping forward a bit, "it's a shame anything like this should happen, but we jest had to do it. Don't you be scared any more. It's all over. There won't be any more trouble this afternoon. This game will go on all right, and it'll be on the level, too. Jest settle down and watch the best team win."

After that the game did go on in a regular manner, and the spectators were thoroughly respectful in their behavior. Whenever a Maplewood player did an unusually clever piece of work McLane and the stonecutters led the cheering for him.

The leaders of the hoodlums did not dare return to the field, and the most of those who belonged in Rockford got away on the first trolley car after they were driven off the ball ground.

It was a thoroughly exciting game and particularly interesting because of the fact that Bold was compelled to retire from the box and Jack Cole filled his place. When Jack succeeded in striking out two batters in the first inning he pitched and led the third man to lift an easy foul that dropped into the hands of Billy Bradley, John Cole nearly yelled himself black in the face.

"That's my Jack!" he shrieked, waving his old hat in the air and dancing around. "That's the boy Benton Hammerswell chucked off his team! Jest you watch him now and see what he can do pitching when he has good support! He'll show you something!"

Jack could not complain of his support. From the very first it was gilt-edged. Occasionally he was batted hard, but the fielding behind him held the enemy in check.

Still, as the game progressed and Maplewood held a fair lead, it seemed that the trickery and ruffianism at the beginning had accomplished Hammerswell's dishonest design.

In the eighth inning, however, by a bunching of hits, the islanders drew close to Maplewood. When they were retired they were only one score behind the home team, Maplewood having made seven runs and Fairhaven six.

Cole seemed to rise to the occasion. Again his pitching was of the highest order, and not a Maplewood man reached first.

In the first of the ninth inning Fairhaven succeeded in getting one man round the bases and tying the score.

It was necessary to play an extra inning, and the tenth opened amid the greatest excitement on the part of the witnesses.

Fairhaven didn't score in her half.

After striking out two men, Cole put a swift one over and it was driven to the fence. It looked like a home run, but by an amazing throw Jolliby caught the runner at the plate, and the tenth ended with the score still tied.

Then Dick called his players close around him for an instant and tried to fill them with his own indomitable spirit.

The result was electrifying.

Batter after batter fell on Raymer's curves, and before the hitting terminated and Fairhaven was retired three runs had been secured.

As Jack Cole entered the box Dick paused before him a moment, placing both hands on his shoulders and looking him in the eyes, and said:

"Now is your opportunity to prove what you can do. You won't fail. This is your day, Cole, and you're a winner."

Somehow those words filled Cole with confidence he had never felt before. Although he was not aware of it, he had deserved a little of Dick Merriwell's praise. Again his pitching was marvelous. The best hitters of the opposing team went down before him in order, and as he struck out the third man, Brick McLane and the stonecutters who accompanied him gave a yell that might have been heard a mile away.

Trickery and ruffianism had met well-merited defeat. Hammerswell's behavior had won him nothing but the scorn and contempt of all honest persons who knew him.

After the game it was learned that Fairhaven was tied with Rockford for first place in the Trolley League.

CHAPTER XVI

THE RETURN OF GRIMES.

The night was still and muggy. It was the night of the day scheduled for the first Maplewood-Fairhaven game, but because of the fog the Maplewood team had been unable to reach the island.

Long after most of the guests at the Maple Heights Hotel had retired, a solitary man paced up and down on the lawn in front of the building.

There was no moon, and the stars, which occasionally peeped through openings in the hazy clouds, gave forth a faint nebulous light by which objects near at hand could be seen only with indistinctness.

In the valley the village slept, with not a solitary light gleaming from a window.

The lonely man on the lawn was puffing at a cigar. At intervals he seemed to forget his cigar and finally it went out.

The last guest had left the hotel veranda and disappeared within when the man realized his cigar was extinguished and threw the stump away. In a moment he brought forth another weed, tore off the end with his teeth, and paused near a clump of shrubbery to strike a match.

The glow of the match, shaded in the hollow of his hands as he held it to the end of his cigar, distinctly revealed the features of Benton Hammerswell. The man's face bore a haggard, careworn expression.

There was a rustle amid the shrubbery.

With a start Hammerswell dropped the blazing match and clapped his hand on his hip pocket. He had reached for his revolver, but it was not there.

"Forgot I'd lost it," he muttered, falling back a step.

Forth from the shrubbery advanced the dark figure of a man.

"Who are you?" demanded Hammerswell.

"I guess you know me," answered a voice. "I've been watching for you. Wasn't sure it was you till I saw your face by the light of that match."

Hammerswell was startled and astounded by the voice.

"Is it you, Luke Grimes?" he demanded.

"Hit it first guess," was the retort.

"Well, what in blazes are you doing here? I supposed you were well on your way to San Francisco."

"Think likely you did," retorted Grimes. "You reckoned I wouldn't darst come back here. That's why you broke your promise ter me. That's why you didn't send me the money you promised me when I reached Montreal. I waited fer it two days, and then I decided to come back here and git it myself."

"You insane idiot!" snarled Hammerswell, in a low tone. "You're right in thinking I didn't fancy you would be crazy enough to return here. If you're seen and recognized you will be arrested instantly."

"I guess that's straight," confessed Grimes coolly. "But if you didn't want that to happen it was up to you to keep your promise. Don't be feeling in your pockets. I've got a gun myself."

"Don't worry," said Hammerswell, pulling out his handkerchief and mopping his face. "I've no pistol. It was stolen from my room to-day."

"Mebbe that's so," chuckled Grimes; "and then agin' mebbe it ain't. You're such a liar no man can believe you. I'll watch ye, and don't yer forgit that. If you start any shooting I'll join in. I'm pretty desperate, Hammerswell, and you can't snuff me out without getting your dose in return."

"Oh, dry up!" growled the manager of the Maplewood team. "I'm not a lunatic, if you are. I'm not anxious to face a murder charge."

"Jest what I thought," nodded Grimes, again chuckling villainously. "That's why I came back here. You know that I know something about you that might put you where you'd have to face a murder charge."

"'Sh! Stop that fool talk! There's a rustic seat over yonder. Come over and sit down."

Side by side they walked toward the rustic seat, which stood near another cluster of shrubbery.

Barely had they seated themselves there when forth from the same cedars near the spot where they had met crept a form resembling a huge dog, but which was in truth a human being on hands and knees. Slowly and silently this figure moved across the open space, once or twice stopping and lying flat on his stomach as he fancied one of the men had turned in his direction. At last he reached the shelter of the shrubbery not far from the bench. There he remained crouching and listening.

"Why didn't you keep your word and send the money?" Grimes was saying. "I had your promise."

"But I didn't have the money to send," declared Hammerswell. "I told you once before that this baseball business has put me on the rocks. I am down to the bottom of my pile now. You were crazy enough to demand an exorbitant sum."

"Only a thousand dollars."

"Only a thousand!" snapped Benton.

"Yes; that was the price you promised Hop Sullivan to close his mouth."

"But I didn't pay it. I closed it in another way."

"That's right," said Grimes, "and I saw you do it. I was there on High Bluff at midnight when you met Sullivan. I saw yer give him a package containing nothing but strips of brown paper. Then, while he was tearing it open, I saw yer shift your position so that he stood between you and the edge of the bluff. Jest as he ripped the package open and found it didn't contain a dollar you jumped on him and pushed him over into the river. You knew he couldn't swim. The river runs swift there, and the falls is close below. He went over, and of course he was drowned. Have they ever found his body?"

Twice Hammerswell had attempted to check his companion, and now he burst forth into a volley of low-spoken curses.

"No need of talking to me of that!" he snarled. "Yes, they found Sullivan's body two days ago. He's buried, and his tongue is silenced forever."

"But mine ain't," reminded Grimes. "It'll take money ter close me up. I knew you wouldn't like much ter see me arrested if I came back here. I might be sent to the jug for my doings, but you'd git a life term, if yer neck wasn't stretched. It ain't healthy for no man ter fool with me the way you have."

"Now look here," said Hammerswell, facing his companion on the bench, "it's best that you should know the absolute truth. I can't pay you that money because I haven't got it. All my money is gone, with the exception of what I've bet on the final game to be played to-morrow. Even if I win I can't give you a thousand. Five hundred would be the limit. I must win, and I believe I shall. I have risked everything on the result. We play two games in Fairhaven."

"How does this baseball business stand?" asked Grimes. "You oughter be on top after all your schemes and plans. I suppose you are."

"No. Maplewood and Fairhaven are tied in second position, having played forty-four games each, winning twenty-two of them. Rockford and Seaslope have played forty-five games each. Rockford is on top, as she has won twenty-three and lost twenty-two. Seaslope is at the bottom, having won twenty-two and lost twenty-three. Rockford and Seaslope have only one game more to play. If Rockford wins she will hold first place, although Maplewood may tie her. To do so we must win both games from Fairhaven. If Rockford loses and we win both games we'll go into first position, while Fairhaven will go plumb to the bottom."

"But what if Rockford loses and Fairhaven wins both games?" asked Hammerswell's companion.

"It won't happen!" savagely declared Hammerswell. "It can't happen!"

"But what if it does?" persisted the other man.

"Why, Fairhaven would win the pennant. She'd have twenty-four games to her credit."

"Where would Maplewood land?" asked Grimes, with a touch of maliciousness in his voice.

"At the bottom," confessed Hammerswell.

"And you'd be bu'sted?"

"Wiped out! I wouldn't have a dollar left. I've drawn all my money from the bank and bet it in two ways. I have found suckers who were willing to bet even money that Fairhaven will win first position, or at least will be tied for first place after the games to-morrow. I have also found others who were confident Maplewood will land at the bottom, and so I've risked everything on those two chances. I can't lose on both bets. There's not one chance in a hundred that I shall."

"If that's the case," said Grimes, "you oughter have some boodle in your clothes to-morrer night."

"I will have some," nodded Benton; "but at the most it will not be enough to make good my losses this summer or come anywhere near it."

"Well, I ain't goin' to be hard on you, seeing you've had such bad luck, but you'll have to fork over five hundred. I'll split my price in two and take that amount. Don't try to monkey with me if you win, Hammerswell. I'm going to be on Fairhaven Island to-morrer."

"How do you expect to get there without being seen and recognized?"

"Leave that ter me. I'll git there."

"Stay away," urged Benton. "I'll make an appointment and meet you somewhere on the mainland to-morrow night."

"Oh, no, you don't! I know you too well. I know how you keep your app'intments and your promises. I will be on hand after the game, and I'll keep track of you, Hammerswell, till you fork over. You can bet your life on that!"

In vain Hammerswell urged his companion not to attempt such a thing. Grimes was determined and would not yield.

"Don't worry," he said. "I won't git nabbed. I'll take care of that. Now I guess I'd better be jogging. I've had good luck ter-night in seein' you all quiet by your lonesome self, and I am satisfied. But don't forgit what I know! Don't forgit what I can tell! Don't forgit I saw you throw Sullivan inter the river! Don't forgit it's murder you will face if I peach on you! Good night!"

The speaker rose and backed off, keeping his eyes on the man he did not trust. Having retreated some distance in this manner, he turned suddenly and disappeared behind the shrubbery.

Hammerswell had risen to his feet. He stood there for several moments. Finally he savagely muttered:

"I'll find a way to fool that yelping cur! If I win to-morrow—and I must—I'll get out of these parts in a hurry. I'll disappear, and then Luke Grimes may amuse himself by trying to find me. Confound it all! he set my nerves on edge talking about Sullivan. People around here think Sullivan was drowned by accident. This Grimes is the only person living who knows the truth and can do me harm."

He turned and walked slowly toward the hotel, passing within four feet of the dark figure huddled close to the cedars near the rustic hedge.

When Hammerswell had mounted the steps of the hotel and disappeared within, this figure moved and sat up.

"Ha! ha," laughed a low, triumphant voice. "So you think Grimes is the only person aware of your crime! You're soon to learn you are mistaken! You're soon to find out that the black truth is known to Chester Arlington!"

CHAPTER XVII

A HAUNTED MAN.

After retiring to his room in the hotel, Benton Hammerswell found himself in a condition that was almost certain to banish slumber for some time from his eyes. Flinging off his coat and removing his collar and necktie, he brought forth from a closet a bottle of whisky and some glasses. Having taken a heavy drink, he lighted a fresh cigar and paced the floor of his room.

"Blazes take it!" he muttered, "why didn't Grimes wait a day or two longer before coming here? Had he done so, he would have had his trip for his pains. Confound him, he has set my nerves on edge! He's the only person who can prove anything serious against me, and as long as he lives I'll never be wholly safe. Of course I may dodge him for a time, but he's liable to turn up anywhere I go. If I could silence him in the same way I silenced Sullivan!"

Somehow these words caused to rise before his mental vision a vivid picture of the meeting on High Bluff. He saw Hop Sullivan standing at the edge of the bluff, eagerly tearing open a package that was supposed to contain a thousand dollars in banknotes. He saw the moon dive through a flotilla of clouds and burst forth to shine brightly just as Sullivan ripped the package open. Again he heard the man's snarl of disappointment on discovering the contents of that package. Then followed the deadly impulse that caused him to leap forward and thrust Sullivan over the brink of High Bluff with a terrible push.

He saw the doomed wretch whirl over in the air and heard the splash that rose from Rapid River as the man's body struck it. Then once more the moon veiled her face in horror behind a heavy cloud.

Hammerswell remembered how he had dropped on hands

and knees at the edge of the bluff and stared downward into the chasm through which the swirling river hurried toward the falls below. He remembered all too plainly that, as the tiny cloud passed from the face of the moon, he caught a glimpse of a white, ghastly face rising for a moment in the current, saw two helpless hands upflung, and then saw nothing more save the triumphant water that had quenched a human life.

But the memory of what followed was distressing and harassing. When he rose to his feet, muttering his satisfaction over his frightful deed, Luke Grimes had confronted him on that spot. Through it all Grimes had been hidden near at hand, where he could hear and see what transpired. Grimes was armed with a pistol, and, fearing the man who had destroyed Sullivan, he kept it cocked and ready in his hand. Hammerswell remembered how he had been compelled to acquiesce to the terms proposed by the engineer. He had maintained his determination to deceive Grimes, leading the fellow at last to agree to a scheme by which Merriwell was to be put out of baseball. The engineer promised to break Dick's arm.

Then came the trip of Grimes to Fairhaven Island and the burning of the naphtha launch on which he crossed from the mainland. His life had been saved by Dick and Brad Buckhart.

On the island the engineer was recognized as the fellow who had once made a vicious attack on young Merriwell, and when he attempted to escape the villagers arose in a mob and pursued him. He was captured and dragged beneath a tree, with a noose about his neck and a rope flung over a stout limb.

Only by the swift work of Dick Merriwell and his comrades was Grimes saved. He was turned over to an officer and locked up.

On arriving at Fairhaven that day Hammerswell was informed of all that had taken place, and he lost not a moment in hastening to the lockup.

In a manner never satisfactorily explained, Luke Grimes escaped from the lockup while Benton Hammerswell was talking to the guard.

The fugitive was hotly pursued, but made his way out of town to the north, where he was cornered in a swamp and finally found himself stuck fast in the mire.

While Grimes was in this helpless condition, Hammerswell discovered him and, under pretense of offering assistance, crept nearer, club in hand, to beat down the poor wretch.

But Dick Merriwell's ability as a trailer enabled him to follow Grimes, and Dick reached the spot just in time to baffle Hammerswell.

Later, Grimes had been aided in escaping, and since that day no one in that vicinity, with the exception of Benton Hammerswell, had seen the fugitive engineer. Hammerswell saw him and gave him some money, urging him to hasten away to Canada, inducing him to start immediately by promising to send him a thousand dollars, which was to reach him at an address in Montreal.

At the time of making this promise the chief rascal had entertained no intention of forwarding the money. Thinking Grimes was badly frightened and would not dare return after going away, he had felt satisfied he would thus get rid of the fellow.

Now here was Grimes back again and threatening to make further trouble.

"I am a bad man to crowd!" Hammerswell snarled when he had finished thinking this matter over. "How infernally hot it is!"

With this exclamation, he flung wide open one of the windows of his room, which had hitherto been but partly raised.

This window opened onto the flat roof of the hotel veranda. Benton sat down near it, smoking a cigar and fanning himself with a fan he had picked up.

"Little sleep for me to-night," he growled. "Of course I know I'm not going to be beaten on all my bets to-morrow, still I'm nervous. I have the team to win both those games, with proper pitching. Yes, and I have the pitchers to win. They arrived in Rockford to-day. No one but myself knows of it. Slocum and Bretton are a pair to draw to. Slocum might be in the American League if he wished to play professional baseball, and he could command his own salary. Bretton has a record that makes him well known—too well known. I'll run both these fellows in under fake names, in order not to let Fairhaven know what she's up against. My team is onto both their pitchers. Even Merriwell can be batted at times, and the boys will go after him red-hot to-morrow.

"No, it's impossible that I should lose all my bets, and it's quite likely I'll win them all. If Rockford defeats Seaslope, Fairhaven must win both games in order to be tied for first place. It's hardly possible Rockford will lose. Being at the head now, she'll fight fiercely to keep that position. If she wins to-morrow and we take one of the two games from Fairhaven, I'll win all my bets. In order for me to lose, Rockford must be defeated and Fairhaven must take both games from Maplewood. As far as that matter goes, there's no reason why I shouldn't roll into bed and sleep like a baby. Ah! but it's impossible for me to sleep that way any more! The time is past when I can sleep straight through the night without my rest being broken. Ever since my encounter with Sullivan I've been troubled by bad dreams.

"When they told me about finding him, when I knew he had been brought back here to Maplewood, when I saw the wretched little funeral procession as he was being taken to the grave, it all added to the cursed disturbance that is breaking me up and making me afraid of my own shadow. Hang it! I used to have nerve enough. Now I awake in the night and seem to see Sullivan's eyes fastened on me! I see his white face in the darkness of my room! I started up last night and saw in yonder corner his arms upflung, just as I saw them last when he went down into the current of Rapid River. Resting on my elbow, I remained staring at those upheld arms until I found that it was nothing but the legs of my own trousers hanging over the back of a chair. Just the same I could not sleep until daylight came creeping in at my window. There's a nasty feeling troubling me to-night. I am a-quiver all over. I need another drink. I'll have another drink."

He rose quickly and poured out a brimming glass of liquor, which he dashed off as if it had been so much water.

"If I get enough of that into my skin I may be able to sleep," he growled. "Got to keep these windows open. Don't like it, but I'd smother with them closed. Confound the luck! I'd like to know what became of my revolver! Missed it to-day for the first time. If I had it I'd put it under my pillow to-night."

He searched the room, but did not find the weapon for which he was looking.

After another drink, he finished undressing and slipped on a suit of pajamas. Wearing this suit, he sat by the window, his light extinguished, until he had finished his cigar.

Once as he sat there, from far, far away in the night there came a low, awesome sound that was not unlike a human cry of pain and horror. It came from the direction of the little village cemetery, and Benton Hammerswell felt his entire body grow cold. To his excited fancy it seemed that this eerie cry had been sent forth by the spirit of Hop Sullivan, which could know no rest until Sullivan's murder had been avenged.

Although he listened breathlessly for a long time after that, and his cigar went out in his fingers, the sound was not repeated. The night was awesomely still, without even a breath of air stirring.

"Just my fool imagination," he whispered. "Another drink and I will get to bed."

After retiring he turned and twisted for nearly an hour. At last he fell into troubled slumber.

How long he slept he did not know. In the night he was awakened by a horrible sensation, as if he were smothering.

With a choking sound, he started up. Somehow he seemed to feel a person near him. He fancied he was not alone in that room.

"Who's there?" he cried.

Then, to his unspeakable distress and agitation, a low, hollow voice answered:

"I'm here—I, the spirit of the man you murdered!"

Out of the gloom advanced a white, ghostly figure.

Uttering a shriek, Hammerswell leaped erect. As his feet touched the floor something fluttered over him. Instantly he was entangled in the folds of a blanket that had been cast over his head. Then a power that seemed something more than human hurled him to the floor.

It was some seconds before the man succeeded in freeing himself from the folds of the blanket. When he finally did so, he sat up and looked around, fully expecting to again behold that ghostly figure.

He seemed to be quite alone.

"Is it gone?" he chokingly whispered, fearing that once more it would confront him.

Having risen weakly to his feet, he found with shaking fingers the matches and struck one of them. As the flame blazed up, the match fell to the floor. Three matches he struck before he succeeded in holding one of them. Lifting the blazing match above his head, he stared around into all the corners, but saw nothing of an alarming nature. At last he succeeded in lighting a lamp, and with this in his hand he searched the room.

Save for the blanket lying in the middle of the floor, there was no sign of his ghostly visitor.

"But I heard the voice!" he muttered. "I saw the thing! I felt its power! I am a haunted man!"

CHAPTER XVIII

FAIRHAVEN READY.

oward night the heavy fog that had rested like a pall over Fairhaven Island all day lifted and retreated toward the open sea. At sunset the sky was bespangled with dainty clouds, which were tinted a hundred beautiful shades of such colors as no artist can reproduce. Although on the mainland it was muggy and hot, out there on Fairhaven Island there was a gentle breeze, and twilight drew on softly and silently.

After supper, Dick and his friends sat chatting on the veranda of the Central Hotel. Garrett was there, and Bart Hodge was comfortably deposited in a big rocking-chair. Singleton sprawled on a seat, and taken altogether the lads presented a picture of ease and laziness.

"Dern my picter!" Tubbs suddenly squealed. "I bet a good squash pie that something besides the fog kept old Hammerswell from bringing his team over here to-day. Said while there was such a fog he couldn't get the bo't he'd engaged to make the trip, but I don't believe it."

"You're tut-tut-too wise!" exclaimed Chip Jolliby. "What dud-dud-dud-dud-do you believe?"

"I bet, by Jim, that there was another reason why he didn't come! I bet he's going to have new players."

At this many of the boys laughed.

"He's had too many new players already," declared Earl Gardner. "That's what's kept him down. He kept shifting his team round early in the season, and it's a wonder he did as well as he did. Since getting that bunch from the Northeastern League he's made no changes and had better success. It will be a hot finish, no matter how it comes out. Why, if Maplewood could win both games to-morrow she'd take first place! If she loses both games she'll go to the bottom. I tell you that's the way to have things stand near the end of the baseball season. It keeps up the excitement."

Dick had been writing and figuring on a slip of paper. While thus engaged he was making out the standing of the various teams in the league, and this he now passed round for the boys to inspect.

"You will see, fellows," he said, "that only twelve points separate the bottom team from the one at the top. That's close enough to make it a heap exciting, as Buckhart would remark."

"Hit's halmost too close for comfort, don't you know," observed Billy Bradley. "Hif we lose both games to-morrow—hoh, my!"

"We won't lose them both," declared Buckhart, suddenly starting up and swinging his fist in the air. "We'll die right on the field before we'll lose them both."

"It's up to us, boys," said Dick, "to win both those games. It's the only way we can be sure that Rockford will not beat us out to-morrow. If we win both of them, even though Rockford takes a fall out of Seaslope, we'll be tied for first place. If we win both of them and Seaslope happens to defeat Rockford, we'll have the pennant to-morrow night."

"Oh, how sad that would make me feel!" cried Ted Smart.

Then he dodged as Chip Jolliby swung a backhand blow at him with his long arm.

"Is it a sure thing," inquired Owen Bold, "that we are to play two games to-morrow? Has Maplewood agreed to it?"

"It's a sure thing," nodded Dick. "I talked to Hammerswell myself by phone, and he has agreed to wind up by playing both games to-morrow afternoon. How's your wing, Owen?"

"I think it's back in shape," was the answer. "This fog to-day was rather bad for it, but I have it protected. I am caring for it as if it were a baby. Never bothered about my arm before, but this climate is too much for it. I am going to let it out to-morrow, if I never pitch another game. Your brother sent me down here to help you win the pennant, and I should hate to have him hear that you had lost it through my weakness on the slab in the last game I pitched for you."

"I wish Frank could be here to see those games!" exclaimed Bart Hodge. "I know he wanted to. If you can win out, Dick, we'll wire him a cheerful message to-morrow night."

"We're going to win if it's in us to do so," asserted young Merriwell. "If we can tie with Rockford for first place, we will fight it out by playing an extra game to decide things."

"Oh, my!" said Ted Smart, "what a calm, quiet sort of a game that would be! I don't believe any one would come out to see it! We'd have to play to empty benches!"

"There will be no empty benches to-morrow," said Dick. "Let's roll in now and get plenty of sleep."

The Fairhaven team retired that night earlier than any previous night during the season.

CHAPTER XIX

WHY ARLINGTON CAME.

arly the following morning, as the lobstermen were rowing off to their traps, a little naphtha launch came down the channel, rounded Crown Point, and entered Fairhaven harbor.

The boat contained two persons. One seemed to be a passenger, and he was recognized by Brick McLane, who was rowing out of the harbor in his big dory.

"Now I wonder what's up?" muttered McLane. "That chap setting all quiet in the bo't is one of them Maplewood fellers. He's the one who was captain of the Maplewood team before old Hammerswell got his new bunch together. Lemme see, what's his name? Oh, yes, it's Arlington—Chester Arlington. Seems ter me I heerd that he came down this way with Merriwell and the boys over here on the island. Yes, I did hear so. He came with them to Maplewood, and, arter old Hammerswell refused to accept the team, he deserted and stayed right here in Maplewood. He's a kind of a traitor, and Dick and t'other fellers over here don't think but precious little of him. What is he a-coming over here for at this hour? Must be something in the wind. Old Hammerswell is hot to win the games to-day, and he's as full of tricks as an egg is full of meat. Mebbe he sent this chap here to play some sort of a trick. Perhaps I ought to let my traps go to-day and turn back. Somehow I kinder think Dick ought ter know this Arlington feller is on the island."

The more McLane thought about this matter the more troubled he became. He visited some of his traps and took out a few lobsters, but wonderment over the surprising appearance of Arlington finally led him to give up making the entire round, and he rowed back to Fairhaven, sending the dory along with lusty strokes.

Arriving at the wharf, Brick covered his lobsters with some wet sacking and left them in his boat while he hurried through town and up to the Central Hotel.

In front of the hotel was a large oak tree, and as he approached McLane was surprised to see Dick Merriwell and Chester Arlington standing beneath that tree engaged in conversation.

"He don't need no warning from me," muttered the lobsterman as he turned back. "He knows all about it now. I might have pulled all my traps and saved myself some trouble."

Dick had been not a little surprised on walking into the office of the hotel after breakfast to find himself face to face with Arlington, who was smoking a cigarette and lounging near the desk.

Instantly on seeing Merriwell, Chester turned and stepped toward him.

"Hello, Dick," he said. "I was waiting for you to finish breakfast."

"Waiting for me?" exclaimed Dick, without seeking to repress his surprise. "What are you doing over here, Arlington?"

Chet glanced around.

"Can't talk here very well," he said. "I wish you'd come outside. I want to tell you something."

Dick hesitated, for the thought of having anything to do with this chap, who had treated him in such a contemptible manner, was far from agreeable.

"Better come," urged Chester. "You'll be glad to know what I'm going to tell you. It'll be a good thing for you."

"What sort of a trick are you up to now?" demanded Merriwell, piercing the other lad with his keen eyes.

"No trick at all," protested Chester. "Why should you suppose that I'm always up to some sort of a trick?"

"Why shouldn't I suppose so? Your record is enough to make anybody suppose such a thing."

"Oh, I don't know. I presume there are fellows who have worse records."

"In reform schools and penitentiaries," said Dick grimly.

Arlington's face flushed, and he seemed on the verge of a burst of anger, but this he succeeded in repressing.

"You're pretty hard on me," he muttered.

"No harder than you deserve. You must acknowledge that I have been easy with you in the past—far easier than any other fellow would have been. Patience and forbearance ceased to be a virtue when you betrayed me in such a contemptible manner after coming down here with us."

"But you don't understand about that, Merriwell. I came down here to play ball, as I have told you before. When you fellows got no chance in Maplewood, I stayed there to get onto the Maplewood team, not having an idea that you would come over here and get into the league."

"After we had been treated in a most contemptible manner at Maplewood, you took up with the man who treated us thus. You have played on his team, knowing all the time that he was up to every sort of crooked game and underhand trick to down your schoolmates. No, Arlington, as long as I remember your behavior this summer, I can never again have the slightest confidence in you—I can't even hope for your reformation."

"Well, won't you come outside where I can tell you why I'm here this morning? I'm not going to beg you to come, but I think you'd better do so."

"Go ahead," said Dick. "I'll hear what you have to say."

He followed Chester from the hotel, and they paused beneath the oak tree, where they were seen a few moments later by McLane.

"I have quit Hammerswell," said Chester. "I have been through with him for some time, but I remained in Maplewood for a particular reason. A few minutes ago you accused me of sticking by the Maplewood team when I knew Hammerswell was plotting and scheming to down Fairhaven. He never told me much of anything about his plots. I was captain of the team. As long as he kept me in that position I stuck by him. After a while I began to find out some things about his plans and plots, and I was anxious to learn still more. That led me to stay there. I thought if I could get onto his secrets I could make him cough up some good money, and I'll need money this fall if I return to Fardale. Mother used to furnish me with the cash, but she's in a sanitarium now, and I'll not be liable to get too much dough from the old man. That's why I stuck in Maplewood and did my best to find out things about Hammerswell. I thought I might squeeze him a little while I had a chance."

"In other words," said Dick, "you contemplated blackmailing him."

"I don't like the way you put it!" exclaimed Chester shortly. "I've found out all the things I want to know, but little good they'll do me. Hammerswell is busted. If he should be defeated in both games here on the island to-day he wouldn't have enough money to take him out of the county. He's bet all the money he could rake and scrape on the result of the games to-day. He's going to spring a surprise on you in the shape of new pitchers. You want to be ready for them. I know the kind of luck you have, Merriwell, and I have felt lately that you would land on top. The more I thought about it the firmer became my convictions that you couldn't be defeated. To-night Hammerswell will be strapped, and, therefore, my knowledge of his crookedness will be useless in the way of twisting money out of him."

Dick was listening quietly, his dark eyes watching Arlington with a steady stare that made Chester uneasy.

"Go on," urged Merriwell.

"Last night," said Arlington, "I learned something about Hammerswell that made me decide right away that he ought to be sent to the jug. Bad as I knew him to be before that, I never fancied he had committed murder."

"Murder!" breathed Dick, lifting his eyebrows.

"Just that," nodded Chet, "and nothing else. I was lying on the grass in front of the hotel last night, smoking a cigarette and thinking. Pretty soon a man came sneaking up, dodging from one clump of shrubbery to another. His movements interested me, and I watched him. He didn't observe me, and I took care he should not. I followed him, and saw him hide behind the shrubbery until Benton Hammerswell, smoking a cigar, approached the spot. Then the man I had followed stepped out and spoke to Hammerswell. It was Luke Grimes, the assistant engineer of the Lady May, a chap I fancy you have good cause to remember, Merriwell."

"I should say so!" nodded Dick, "but I thought detectives had chased Grimes as far as the Canadian border and then lost track of him."

"So they did, I presume. He has been up to Montreal, but is back again. Hammerswell promised to send him money, which he would receive in Montreal. The money was not sent, and Grimes came back to demand it. I was within ten feet of them last night as they sat on the rustic seat and talked the thing over. What I heard made my blood run cold. Grimes has a hold on Hammerswell, and he attempted to put on the screws. You know Hop Sullivan was paid by Hammerswell to hold up the trolley car between Rockford and Maplewood one day and run off your new pitcher, Owen Bold. Sullivan was captured, but escaped. It seems that he demanded money from Hammerswell, and they met by appointment one night on High Bluff, near Rapid River. Hammerswell pushed Sullivan into the river, and Sullivan was drowned. Grimes saw the act, and, therefore, he has Hammerswell in the hollow of his hand. I found all this out last night as I listened."

"Are you speaking the truth, Arlington?" demanded Dick.

"Why should I lie to you?" asked Chester. "It would do me no good. Of course, I am speaking the truth. Grimes received no money from Hammerswell because Hammerswell had none to give. But Grimes swore he would be on this island to-night when the ball games were finished, ready to collect from Hammerswell. I decided to let you know about this. You think I'm a pretty cheap dog, Merriwell; but you can see I'm giving you an opportunity to crush this man Hammerswell, who has tried so many times to crush you. If you can succeed in having Grimes captured, you will be able to compel Hammerswell to face a murder charge. And he will be convicted, too."

In spite of the fact that Chester Arlington was speaking the truth, his manner seemed uncertain, and Merriwell could not help doubting him. Through it all Dick was wondering what new trick it was that his enemies were seeking to play on him.

Chester saw the expression of doubt on Merriwell's face, and in exasperation he cried:

"You think I'm lying to you now! You don't take any stock in me, do you?"

"I confess that I do not," was the answer. "Knowing how natural it is for you to lie and deceive, I can't believe you, Arlington. What your reason can be in coming to me like this I can't understand, but I fancy you have some hidden object."

"All right!" snarled Chester angrily. "Fancy what you please! I don't care a rap! I've given you your opportunity to get revenge on Benton Hammerswell, and now you may do anything you choose."

Having said this, Chester coolly lighted a fresh cigarette, after which he turned and walked away.

At the first store he reached he made inquiry for the town officials, and was given directions for finding Mayor Cobb.

Cyrus Cobb was at home when Arlington appeared, and he listened with great incredulity to the boy's story of Benton Hammerswell's crime.

"You dreamed it, young man—you dreamed it!" exclaimed Cobb. "Why, such things do not happen around here! I have seen boys like you before. I've seen boys who tried to kick up excitement by telling wild and improbable yarns."

Instantly Arlington's rage flamed up.

"I have seen old fools like you before!" he snarled. "They call you the mayor of this little one-horse town, do they? Well, you look it! You're a great man for the place!"

At first Cobb had been astounded, but now his face flushed, and he shook his finger at Chet.

"You insulting young rascal!" he exclaimed. "How dare you use such language to me?"

"Bah!" said the boy, shrugging his shoulders. "Who's afraid of you? I played on the Maplewood baseball team, and I know Benton Hammerswell. I told you the truth about him."

"Yes, yes," said Mr. Cobb, "you did play on that ball team— that's right! You're not on it now, are ye?"

"No."

"Yes, yes; mad with Hammerswell, I take it? Sore because he threw you off the team? Want to make trouble for him, I see. That's your game, boy! That's your reason for coming to me and telling me such preposterous yarns! Look here, you young reprobate, you had better take yourself out of Fairhaven as quick as you can! We don't want such chaps on the island!"

"Oh, I'll get off your old island!" snarled Chester. "Certainly there are more chumps to the square yard on this island than I ever beheld before, and you're the king of them all. Good morning!"

Although the village mayor felt like rushing after the insulting chap and giving him a good caning, he contented himself in glaring at Chet's back until he disappeared.

CHAPTER XX

ON BOARD THE "SACHEM."

he sun had swung into the western sky. Under full steam the big white yacht Sachem was headed toward the northeast. The yacht was owned by Henry Crossgrove, the steel magnate, and on board was gathered a large party of his friends, several of whom were enjoying the sunshine and the sea breeze on the main deck.

Of those on deck, five persons are especially interesting to us. The handsome chap in the yachting costume who frequently bent over a beautiful girl seated at his side and spoke with her in low tones was Frank Merriwell, Dick's brother. The girl was Inza Burrage.

Not far away, in a little triangular group, were Bruce Browning and Harry Rattleton, Frank's old Yale comrades, and Elsie Bellwood.

It was no mere chance that had brought them together. Frank had planned it, but in the first place his purpose had been to proceed by rail to Rockford and cross on one of the regular boats to Fairhaven Island. In Boston, after having gathered his party ready for the start, Merry encountered Henry Crossgrove, and happened to mention he contemplated making the trip.

Immediately Crossgrove informed Frank that his yacht lay in the harbor, and, as he was bound toward waters in the vicinity of Fairhaven, he would hoist anchor without delay. Frank was ready to accept the steel man's hospitality on the Sachem.

"You and I have had some dealings in the past, Mr. Merriwell," said Crossgrove, "and I deem it a privilege to have you and your friends as guests."

"But I must arrive in Fairhaven to-morrow in time to witness a game of baseball in the afternoon," said Frank. "My brother is down there running a ball team, and the game to-morrow finishes the season. I wouldn't miss it for anything, Mr. Crossgrove. Do you think you can land us there all right?"

"Without question I will have you in Fairhaven in time for that ball game," nodded the millionaire. "It will be a much more comfortable and satisfactory way of making the trip. By rail, at this season, it's hot, and dusty, and disagreeable. Come, come, Merriwell, my boy, I won't take no for an answer."

"Then it'll be yes," laughed Frank.

In this manner it was arranged, and Frank and his friends were on the Sachem when the yacht steamed out of Boston harbor at evening.

The trip had proved most enjoyable, but now Frank seemed somewhat worried and restless. As he stood near the rail he frequently glanced at his watch.

Inza noticed this, and in a low tone she said:

"It will be too bad, Frank, if you don't get there in time. I know how much you want to see the game."

"Hush!" said Merry, forcing a slight smile. "If we don't arrive in time for the game, we'll not let Crossgrove know how disappointed we are. He's a fine gentleman and a thoroughbred, and I wouldn't wish him to think for a moment that he had disappointed us through his generous hospitality."

"I say," cried Harry Rattleton, "isn't it great to be on the sounding bee—I mean the bounding sea? Why, even the air out here is full of wind!"

"So are you," grunted Browning, who was lazily sprawled on a comfortable chair and puffing away at a brierwood pipe. "The hot air you've been giving us for the past hour is getting a little tiresome, Rattles. Can't you close your face and let me rest?"

"Why don't you do your neeping slights—I mean your sleeping nights?" inquired Harry. "I don't believe you ever wake up any more. You've been in a trance for the last few hours."

"On the occasion when I last met him before our meeting in Boston yesterday morning," said Merriwell, "he was pretty wide-awake. It was at a little railroad town down in the Southwest. Hodge, Wiley, and I were passing through that town when we saw a chap beset by a dozen burly ruffians. Evidently they were trying to lynch him. He was a big fellow, and he knocked them right and left with tremendous blows. It was Hodge who recognized him, I believe. Bruce Browning was the fellow, and he was very wide-awake on that occasion."

"That's right," grunted Browning, "but you haven't told the story quite straight, Merry. It was Barney Mulloy the ruffians were after. I sailed in to give him a hand, and then you folks chipped in just in time to help us both out. By George, Merry, I thought you'd dropped right down from the skies! Say, that's a great country down there. Mulloy is down there now, running our mine. He's a dandy, that Irishman! He's the whitest, squarest, most reliable fellow I ever saw—present company excepted. We've not had your luck, Merriwell; but I believe we have a valuable claim down there, and we'll make a dollar out of it some day. You and Hodge were mighty fortunate."

"There's no question about that," agreed Frank instantly. "Still, we've had to fight for our rights. It was a hard old fight to hold the Phantom Mine, but we held it. Hodge seemed anxious to sell in case we could get the price. That's what brought us to Chicago. The syndicate that had made us the offer balked, and the deal seemed to be as good as off. I saw the people in the syndicate fancied we were very anxious to sell. Then I let Hodge come on here, while I remained in the city and worked the wires a little. We agreed before Bart left that we would take a smaller sum than our original price, but after he departed I made up my mind that the way to work the thing was to go up on the price, instead of making a drop. Then I struck a lofty pose and let the syndicate run after me. I gave them the impression that I was on the verge of pulling out for New York to talk with other parties. They came round and attempted to do some dickering. They were willing at last to split the difference, but then I commenced to rub it in. I told them that I had decided that our original price was altogether too low. We had a hundred and fifty thousand dollars' worth of ore on the dump. It was in plain sight. In our shaft any man could see prospects that proved the lode one of the richest in Arizona. We had decided to advance our original price just fifty thousand dollars. They could take it or leave it. We were utterly indifferent."

Frank laughed a little over the remembrance of that transaction. "And they took it?"

"Not right away," said Merry. "They seemed indignant, and accused me of all sorts of craziness. They agreed to give the first price demanded. I said, 'Nay, nay; it's fifty thousand more if you want the Phantom.' Then they said, 'All right, Mr. Merriwell, we don't want your old mine; your price is ridiculous.' Says I, 'Good day, gentlemen.' They departed, but within two hours one of them came back. It seems that he had been authorized to pay my increase of fifty thousand if there was no other way to get the property. The moment I saw him I decided on a new price. After he had talked with me a few moments and found I had not reduced my figures any, he announced that the syndicate was ready to buy on my terms, and he was there to close the deal. Then I informed him that since my last quotation on the price, I had been figuring the thing over and had decided that it was folly to sell so low. I had advanced the price fifty thousand more."

Merry laughed heartily as he recalled the incident.

"Ugh!" grunted Browning. "You always did have plenty of nerve, Frank."

"You should have seen my visitor," chuckled Merry. "He came near falling in a fit. I surely thought he was done for. Then he rose up and frothed, and made a lot of wild talk. He said it was an imposition. I had named a price in the first place, and they had agreed to it.

"I reminded him that they had not agreed to it in the first place. Since naming that price I had figured the matter over a little and had gone up on my terms. I was still figuring. As I made this statement I turned to a sheet of paper at my side and began to figure. Well, you should have seen that man jump on me. He was scared blue. I believe he expected me to shove her up another fifty thousand right away. He pushed a check at me to bind the bargain, and accepted my terms then and there."

"Well, you're a dim jandy—I mean a jim dandy," spluttered Rattleton. "I'd never have the nerve to raise the price on anything fifty thousand at a jump."

"The property is worth it, and those men knew it," said Frank. "Only for the fact that I have the Queen Mystery and the San Pablo to look after, and they keep me very busy, I should not have been so willing to sell. Hodge will be somewhat surprised when he finds out what has happened. The building of a railroad in Mexico that will connect the San Pablo with the outer world is going to take up much of my time and attention in the future. The San Pablo is marvelously rich, or it would not pay me to pack ore more than two hundred miles over a rough and sterile country to the largest railroad, and thence ship it north to smelters in Arizona. I am intensely interested in this railroad scheme, and Hodge has become interested and enthused himself. The San Pablo is not the only mine down in that region. Others will be opened, and Hodge is anxious to be on the ground."

As he said this Frank covertly watched the face of Elsie Bellwood, and saw a shadow fall upon it. Instantly his heart relented, and he exclaimed:

"Cheer up, Elsie; I was talking to amuse myself more than anything else. Bart has told me he should seek some business in the

East, if you urged it."

"But you, Frank—you are going right away into Mexico?" questioned Elsie.

"It's absolutely necessary," nodded Merry gravely. "I can't get out of it, even should I wish to."

At this moment Henry Crossgrove, stout and florid, came toward them, mopping his face with his handkerchief.

"The captain tells me we will reach Fairhaven Island within an hour," he said. "I hope that will enable you to see the whole of the baseball game, Merriwell. Sorry we are not there now."

"Oh, it's all right," smiled Frank. "If we miss the first of the game, we may arrive in time to see the finish. We've had a delightful little cruise, Mr. Crossgrove, and we'll not soon forget your hospitality."

CHAPTER XXI

ARLINGTON COWS HAMMERSWELL.

It was the beginning of the ninth inning of the first game in Fairhaven and the home team was one score ahead.

The visitors had made a gallant fight for the game which was not yet ended. Indeed, Maplewood had not given up, as soon became apparent.

On previous occasions crowds had gathered on that field, but never before in the history of Fairhaven had there been such a wonderful turnout to witness a game of baseball. Not only was every seat taken, but on each side of the ground ropes had been stretched far down past first and third bases in order to keep those standing from crowding onto the field. Even then it was necessary to employ four officers to hold the spectators back and prevent them from pushing into the outfield.

Through all the game the stonecutters had whooped and cheered to their satisfaction. Although they were boisterous, they were not ungentlemanly in their language. Indeed, they were rather generous in their applause whenever Maplewood made a brilliant play. For all of that, they were intensely loyal, and, to the last one of them, were eager and anxious for Fairhaven to win.

At intervals the voice of Brick McLane could be heard above the others, but sometimes it was quite drowned.

High on the top of the bleachers, clinging to a post of the fence, was old Gideon Sniffmore, who occasionally waved his crooked cane in the air and shrieked until his face grew purple. All through the game he had remained standing there, apparently quite oblivious to his rheumatism, and once or twice, when he relinquished his hold on the post and flourished both arms in the air, he was in absolute danger of falling and breaking his neck.

"We've got um now, by codfish!" he shrieked as Owen Bold struck out a man.

This made the second man out.

There were two runners on the bases, one having reached first through an error and the other securing a pass to the initial bag on four balls.

"It's all over!" roared Brick McLane as the next batter stepped out. "Fairhaven wins the first game!"

Then Bold shot a speedy one, shoulder high, across the inside corner of the plate.

The batter stepped back a bit and met the ball fairly. It was a terrific clout.

Chip Jolliby went flying over the low rail which served as centre-field fence and splashed into the frog pond in search of the ball. He had seen it strike, and his heart was in his mouth for fear he could not find it amid the tall grass and weeds.

However, Chip secured it and turned with it dripping wet, in his hand, seeing the Maplewood player who had hit it already dashing over third base.

Standing out there at that great distance, Jolliby made one of the most amazing throws of his whole baseball career. He was ankle deep in the mire, yet he lined the ball straight to the plate, and Buckhart put it onto the man who was endeavoring to slide home.

This astounding throw caused the crowd to roar again, although almost every spectator realized what had been accomplished by the hit.

The batter had driven in two runs, which placed Maplewood ahead, the score being eight to seven.

"We've got them now!" muttered Benton Hammerswell, in relief. "Bretton will hold them right where they are. At the very best, they can take but one of these two games, and, therefore, I will win all my bets."

Hammerswell was leaning on a bat as he muttered this. He felt a touch on his arm and turned to see Tom Fernald.

"It was a relief to me when that fellow smashed the ball over the fence," he said. "I've been betting even money that Maplewood would carry off one of the games. Some lobsters were foolish enough to bet that Fairhaven would win both."

"Yes, we've got this game now," nodded Hammerswell. "And it's a good thing for me, too. It puts me on my feet again. I've risked all I could rake and scrape on the result of these games. Unless the improbable happens, Fairhaven will not be at the top to-night, nor will Maplewood be at the bottom."

"Have you figured the thing over?" questioned Fernald. "Have you considered all the possibilities? If Seaslope beats Rockford and Fairhaven and Maplewood divide honors here to-day, every team will be tied once more. It will be necessary to play other games in order to settle the matter."

"I know," nodded Hammerswell, with a grave smile; "but the people who bet their good money with me had not figured out that possibility. Unless Maplewood is at the bottom to-night, I shall win many of my bets. If Fairhaven is not at the top, I shall win the rest of them. In order for Fairhaven to be at the top we must lose both these games and Seaslope must beat Rockford. It's all right, Fernald; that can't happen."

A low, snarling laugh caused Hammerswell to start and turn his head. Chester Arlington was there, and he regarded the Maplewood manager with a singular look that caused the man to be seized by a strange feeling of uneasiness and apprehension.

"Don't think you have this game yet," said Arlington. "No game is won until it's ended. The best batters on Merriwell's team are up now. Look out for a Garrison finish. It takes but one run to tie the score, and two will win the game."

"Get away from me, you crook!" snapped Hammerswell. "I don't want you round me!"

He gripped the bat and half lifted it in a threatening manner.

"You'll never frighten any one with that stick," said Chester. "Put it down, Hammerswell. Don't try any funny business with me."

"If you two are going to quarrel," said Fernald, "I will just step aside."

"Oh, I'll not quarrel with this treacherous Smart Aleck," declared Hammerswell as Fernald walked away.

"You'd better not," said Chester in a low tone. "You're wise in not quarreling with me. I know too much about you. Wait, Benton Hammerswell; your time is coming, and you will get what's due you."

"I tell you to move on!" grated the enraged man. "I don't like that kind of talk, and I won't listen to it."

"You can't help listening," retorted Chester. "You know I am telling the truth when I say you are a scoundrel, a fraud, a cheat, a——"

With a muttered oath Hammerswell lifted the bat.

Chester did not shrink in the least. Looking the man straight in the eyes, he hastily said:

"Strike if you dare! Add another murder to your crimes!"

"Another murder?" whispered Hammerswell, aghast.

"Yes, another murder. You see, I know what you've done. You see, I know what happened on High Bluff one night near the hour of twelve."

"Good heavens!" choked the astounded rascal as he nervelessly lowered the bat.

"I know you are haunted by the memory of that crime," persisted Chester, in a low tone. "Your face tells the story. You fear Luke Grimes. You fear the ghost of Hop Sullivan."

Three times Hammerswell tried to speak before he could command his voice. Then of a sudden, as if struck by a thought, he panted:

"You—you were in my room last night! The window was open! Some one entered that room! Some one played the ghost! I don't believe in ghosts. You were there!"

"You're right," confessed Chester. "I was there, Hammerswell, and I gave you a fright you'll not soon forget. How did I dare come there? Why, I had your pistol in my pocket. I wasn't afraid of you. You missed the weapon, didn't you? Well, I took it. I knew you were not armed. How did I know so much about what happened on High Bluff? I heard your talk with Luke Grimes. Oh, I'm not fool enough to tell the story without the backing of Grimes, but they're looking for him, Hammerswell. He's liable to be captured at any moment. When he's taken, he'll blow on you. Now, sir, I hope you enjoy the game."

Laughing with malignant satisfaction, Arlington disdainfully turned his back on the agitated man and walked away.

140

CHAPTER XXII

WINNING THE PENNANT.

Owen Bold was the first batter to face the Maplewood pitcher in the last half of the ninth inning. After two balls had been called, Bold hit a savage liner in the direction of Connor, who was playing at short. Connor made a sidelong leap and caught the ball with his bare right hand.

It was a startling play, but it caused many of the spectators to groan with dismay.

"Robbery!" muttered Bold as he turned back toward the bench. "That was a clean hit in nine cases out of ten. He didn't know he had it."

Billy Bradley followed Bold, and he felt his nerves quiver under the strain.

"Great codfish, do hit it out!" implored Uncle Gid Sniffmore. "We've got ter have this game, boys."

Bradley responded by smashing a hot liner toward Dillard, who made a beautiful stop and snapped the ball to Hunston, on first.

Bradley was out.

There was another groan from the spectators.

"It's all over!" shouted Hunston. "We've taken a scalp, boys!"

"Not yet!" grated Brad Buckhart, as he picked out his pet bat and strode toward the plate. "I opine I'll try to put up some sort of an argument with you."

Bretton was confident now—in fact, he was too confident. Feeling sure he had the game in his hands, he gave the Texan a swift one over the outside corner.

It was just where Brad wanted it, and he lashed out a beautiful single.

An instant later there was a fearful uproar on the field, for Dick Merriwell was seen advancing toward the plate. The stonecutters thundered their applause, while bats, handkerchiefs, and flags waved everywhere.

"Enough to rattle any batter," muttered Benton Hammerswell.

The pitcher waited until the shouting crowd became quieter. Then he put over a swift inshoot, which Dick missed.

"One strike!" cried the umpire.

"Get him, Bretton—get him!" cried Hunston.

Bretton tried a wide out, and a ball was called.

Then he whistled over another one, and again Dick missed it cleanly.

Once more the crowd groaned.

At this moment several persons who had reached the ground pushed through the crowd and appeared in view back of the ropes. Three of them were lusty-lunged chaps, for they gave a Yale cheer that surprised the crowd and caused almost every one to turn in their direction.

In the greatest amazement, Bart Hodge started up from the Fairhaven bench, crying:

"Frank Merriwell! Am I dreaming?"

It was Frank, accompanied by Browning, Rattleton, Elsie, Inza, and the others from the yacht Sachem.

Now, although that Yale cheer had caused so many to look toward the newcomers, even though Dick heard it and recognized his brother's voice, the boy with the bat did not flicker an eyelash. Perhaps he was the most astounded and delighted person on that field, yet not a muscle of his face changed. With the gaze of a hawk he watched Bretton, fearing if he turned for a single instant the Maplewood pitcher would put a straight one over the base.

Perhaps never before had Dick's nerves been tested under such circumstances. Had Frank and his friends known just how this game stood and how critical it was at that moment, beyond question they would have remained silent, fearing to unnerve the boy at bat.

Bretton was a sharp chap, and he heard Hodge shouting the name of Frank Merriwell. Instantly he decided that Dick Merriwell would be somewhat unmanned, and therefore he sent over a straight ball with all the speed he could command.

Dick met it squarely on the trade-mark.

Away sailed the ball—away over centre-field fence. It was into the frog pond, and batted to the extremity, at that.

"It's a home run!" shouted Brick McLane.

Round the bases sped Brad Buckhart, and after him came the boy who had made this wonderful hit at such a critical moment.

Through the mire of the frog pond splashed the fellow in search of the ball. He found it and turned to throw it into the field. He did not possess the wonderful throwing arm of Chip Jolliby, and therefore he was compelled to throw to Dillard, the second baseman. Even had the fielder been able to line the ball to the plate, he could not have stopped the winning run, for when Dillard whirled with the sphere in his hand he saw Merriwell crossing the plate.

How Uncle Gid Sniffmore ever got down from the seats and rushed onto the field in advance of the crowd forever remained a mystery in Fairhaven. In some manner the old man made the descent, and, when those roaring stonecutters picked Dick Merriwell up and bore him triumphantly around on their shoulders, Uncle Gid marched in advance, waving his cane and dancing like a frolicsome boy.

No wonder Frank Merriwell stood with a mist in his eyes watching the spectacle. No wonder he gripped the arm of Browning, and, thrilled with satisfaction, cried in the big fellow's ear:

"That's Dick—Dick, my brother!"

It was in the fifth inning of the second game that a message from Rockford reached the ball ground in Fairhaven telling the players there that Seaslope had won her final game of the season. Having heard this report, Tom Fernald hastened round to the Maplewood bench, where Benton Hammerswell sat with the scorer and Bretton, the pitcher of the first game.

Fernald betrayed his anxiety in his face. In spite of his reputation as a "good loser," Fernald was worried and distressed now.

"Say, Hammerswell, this thing is getting pretty desperate," observed the Rockford man as he took a seat at Benton's side.

"That's right," nodded the Maplewood manager grimly. "Our boys can't seem to hit Merriwell at all. He's pitching in amazing form. The presence of his brother seems to inspire him. It's true they haven't been able to score on Slocum thus far; but twice we have prevented it by good luck rather than good playing. They have a runner on third now and only one out. I am afraid they are going to get a start right here."

"If you lose this game do you know what the result will be?" asked Fernald. "Do you know where it will land Fairhaven?"

"Why, I am not sure——"

"But I am sure. I have just heard from Rockford. Seaslope won the game to-day. Unless you take this game from Fairhaven, the team here wins the pennant and you land at the bottom. A little while ago you were confident of winning all your bets. It begins to look now as if you might lose them all."

Slowly Hammerswell removed the half-smoked cigar from his lips. It quivered a little in his fingers. Fernald saw this, and knew how the strain was telling on the Maplewood man.

"Win or lose," muttered the schemer, "I have done everything in my power to come out ahead. It's impossible to play anything underhand here to-day. This crowd wouldn't stand for it. Those stonecutters would lynch a crooked umpire, and they'd mob a player who did any dirty work on the field. I hope to win this game on its merits, but there's no telling what may happen."

"I know what will happen if you lose," said Fernald bitterly. "I will get it in the neck. I will be down to hard pan. It will be a case of hustle for me in the future. Hang it all! Hammerswell, I had a comfortable little roll when the baseball season opened this year, but it will be wiped out if you don't carry off this game."

Hammerswell laughed harshly and bitterly.

"You'll be no worse off than I will," he muttered. "We'll both be in the same boat. Ha, look at that! By George! it's good for a run. Too bad! They're going to score!"

The batter had driven a liner toward left field, and the runner on third unhesitatingly started toward the plate.

"Watch! watch!" exclaimed Fernald. "Halligan is after it."

"He can't get it," said Hammerswell.

But the next moment he sprang up with a cry of satisfaction and relief, for Halligan had leaped into the air and captured the ball with one hand.

Immediately the Maplewood left fielder threw to Lumley at third, making a double play, as the base runner was unable to get back to the bag in time.

"Great stuff!" breathed Tom Fernald, in untold relief. "That kept them from scoring."

"It did," nodded Hammerswell, sitting down again; "but once more it was a piece of luck for us. We can't depend wholly on luck."

"Push your team now," urged Fernald. "Make them get into this thing and win."

Once more Dick Merriwell walked into the box, his eye clear, his determination firm and unshaken. Connor was the first man to face him.

Young Merriwell had found Connor a difficult hitter to deceive, but he now resolved to use his cleverest curves on the Maplewood shortstop. Opening with the jump ball, he caused Connor to lift a foul over Buckhart's head, although Brad was unable to get back in time to catch it.

The Texan called for the combination ball, and Dick nodded.

Even though this remarkable curve was used, Connor again touched the ball. This time it was the slightest sort of a foul tip, but the ball was slightly deflected, and struck Buckhart on the end of his right thumb.

When Brad stooped to pick up the ball, which had fallen to the ground, he noticed that his thumb had been put out of joint and was split.

The umpire called time while Buckhart's injury was examined by a doctor, who pulled the thumb into place and dressed it.

"You can do no more catching to-day," said the doctor.

"Don't you believe it, doc!" exclaimed the plucky Texan. "I opine I will stay right under the stick and finish the game."

Nor could Buckhart be persuaded by any one to retire from the game. For all of his injury, he returned to his position.

Now, however, Dick felt that he must consider Brad's condition, and in doing this he gave Connor a ball which the fellow hit and sent flying along the ground between first and second for a single.

Halligan followed with a scratch hit, and the bases were filled when Bold permitted Lumley's hot grounder to get past him.

It was a time of great anxiety, as the game was drawing near its close, seven innings having been agreed upon in advance.

"Too bad that catcher got his bum thusted—I mean his thumb busted," spluttered Harry Rattleton. "Dick hasn't dared let his wing out since then."

Bart Hodge had joined Merriwell's party, and he now seized Merry by the arm, eagerly panting:

"What do you think, Frank—had I not better offer to go into that game? Hadn't I better take Buckhart's place? Dick can't pitch to Buckhart now. You can see he's afraid to let himself out. Don't you think I'd better go in?"

Merriwell shook his head.

"No, Hodge," he said. "Let them fight their own battle. Let them win or lose with their own team. Keep out of it."

"Oh, I am sorry you won't let Bart go!" almost sobbed Elsie Bellwood. "I know they are going to lose unless some one else goes in to catch."

"Frank is right," declared Inza. "Let Dick win or lose without assistance from outsiders."

"But everything depends on this game!" palpitated Elsie. "I just heard a man back of us say that Fairhaven would win the pennant if it could get this game. Why, it seems to me that both Frank and

Bart might go into the game to save it. These men near us have been telling how the manager of the other team paid two great pitchers to come down here and pitch this game to-day. They say he had intended to put his professional pitchers in under false names, but people found out who they were, and he gave up trying to fool any one that way. If he could do such things, why couldn't Dick have his friends help him?"

"Because I had rather he would depend on himself and his own team," said Merry. "If he loses this game, I understand that all the teams in the league will be tied, and he will have still another chance to fight for the pennant. If he wins without any of our assistance, he will deserve all the praise and glory he'll receive."

"But oh! oh!" cried Elsie, "he can't win now! Just look at that! It's a home run, Frank!"

Dillard had smashed the ball hard and fair, lifting it over the centre-field rail.

Over that rail Chip Jolliby went flying in an endeavor to get under the ball. He was not successful, but he secured it and returned it to the diamond in time to stop Dillard at third base. Nevertheless, Connor, Halligan, and Lumley had all scored.

For the first time during the game the cloud lifted from Benton Hammerswell's face. He felt Tom Fernald slap him on the shoulder, and heard Fernald laughingly cry in his ear:

"That settles it, Hammerswell! Slocum is the man to hold them down after that. Only six more Fairhaven batters to be retired and the game is yours. We will both win our bets."

"I believe we will," nodded Hammerswell.

Brad Buckhart called Dick and stepped down a little in front of the home plate to meet him.

"Look here, pard," said the Westerner, "what are you doing? You've been easing up. Are you trying to give these fellows this game? Just slam the ball over as speedy as you like. Don't worry about me. I don't give a rap if I lose that old thumb. I will hold them, never fear."

"All right," said Dick. "You will get all the speed you want after this, Brad."

"That's the stuff!" nodded Buckhart as he turned and retired to his position.

Brad did get all the speed he could handle, but he handled the ball amazingly well, considering his injury. Farrell fell before Dick's clever pitching, while Garvin was easily thrown out at first, after batting a grounder to Bradley.

Although the Maplewood players implored Slocum to get a hit

and bring Dillard home, Dick caused the pitcher to go after three sharp shoots, all of which were smothered in Buckhart's big mit.

Benton Hammerswell implored Slocum to hold Fairhaven down, and the pitcher promised to do so. He was unequal to the task, however, for with the head of the batting list up, Gardner led off with a savage swat, while Bold lifted a safe one into the field, and Bradley brought them both home with a whistler that went clean to the right-field fence.

Billy tried to stretch a handsome two-bagger into a three-base hit, and was thrown out at third.

Buckhart lifted a high foul, which was captured by Hunston.

Dick Merriwell was cheered as he walked to the plate, and he responded by getting a clean single. He then stole second on the first ball pitched, but died there, for Jolliby put up a fly that was caught.

Once more, in the first of the seventh, Dick pitched in his finest form, and before him the batters fell in order.

Fairhaven now had its final turn at bat.

With two strikes called on him, big Bob dropped the ball over the fence and easily reached third, while two fielders were searching for the sphere.

Although he might have trotted home, the big fellow stopped at third at the command of Dick, who had raced down to the coaching line.

"It would tie the score, Dick!" grunted Singleton, in astonishment.

"We will win this game right here," said Merriwell. "Stay where you are. One run will tie, but two will win. Let's worry that pitcher."

Already Slocum was worried. The fact that Singleton had remained on third had annoyed him. Nevertheless, he deceived Tubbs, who hit a weak one into the diamond and was thrown out. Smart struck out quickly, and it began to appear as if Dick had made a bad mistake in stopping Singleton at third.

Gardner came to bat, a grim look on his face. He hit a hot one to Connor, who fumbled it.

Earl was a great sprinter, and by the time Connor picked up the ball it was seen that Gardner could reach first in safety.

Then the Maplewood shortstop threw swiftly to the plate to catch Singleton, who was going home.

It was a bad throw.

The ball struck Garvin's mitt as the catcher reached for it and bounded off.

Gardner had crossed first, and he heard the coacher yelling for him to take second. Garvin leaped for the ball, caught it up, and threw to Dillard.

It was another bad throw, and the ball went into centre field.

"Third, Earl—third!" cried Dick, making signals to the runner.

Gardner kept on toward third.

Mole secured the ball, which was swiftly thrown to Lumley. It struck the ground and took a bad bound over Lumley's shoulder.

"Home!" shouted Dick as Gardner came tearing toward third.

Then the wildly excited crowd saw Earl cross third base and go scooting toward the plate.

The ball had struck a post to which the rope was tied that held the crowd back. Lumley secured it and threw to Garvin. The throw was a trifle high, and Gardner made a beautiful slide, his hand reaching the plate an instant before he was tagged by Garvin.

"Safe!" yelled the umpire.

Pandemonium broke loose, for Fairhaven had thus won the game and the pennant in the Trolley League.

There was a celebration in Fairhaven that night, and it was one long to be remembered. The whole town seemed ablaze with red fire and alive with people, who marched up and down the streets, blowing horns, ringing cow bells, shooting off pistols, and singing, and cheering. The Central Hotel was ablaze with light. In front of it speeches were delivered by several persons; but the crowd was not satisfied until Dick Merriwell appeared on the steps. They kept calling for him, and at last he was pushed forward. The moment they caught sight of him they started to cheer, but in advance of that cheering Brick McLane was heard roaring:

"There's the boy that done it! He's the kid Benton Hammerswell kicked out of Maplewood—him and his ball team that won the pennant right here for Fairhaven to-day! Where is Hammerswell now? Why didn't he wait and see the fun to-night?"

After the cheering had subsided somewhat, old Uncle Gid Sniffmore suddenly climbed to the shoulders of Abner Turner and waved his cane in the air, shrilly crying:

"Do you want ter know where Benton Hammerswell is? Well, he's what they call a dead one! He won't cut no ice round these parts arter this! Folks, I'm mighty glad I let them boys have my field! If they'll come back here next year they can have every dratted thing I own on this island!"

"Hurrah for Uncle Gid!" shouted the laughing boys.

Frank and his friends were enjoying all this. They were gathered in a little group on the veranda of the hotel. Merry felt a warm

148

hand press his, and in his ear Inza whispered:

"Aren't you proud of Dick?"

"Proud of him!" he exclaimed. "How can I help being?"

The next issue of the Rockford Star contained an account of the final games in the league series, and likewise the fielding and batting averages of all the players in the league. There was also a high eulogy of Dick Merriwell and praise for his companions, who had aided him in winning the pennant for Fairhaven. For once, at least, the Star was fair and impartial. The final standing of the teams was given as follows:

	Played.	Won.	Lost.	Per C.
Fairhaven	46	24	22	.522
Rockford	46	23	23	.500
Seaslope	46	23	23	.500
Maplewood	46	22	24	.478

Honesty and true manhood had triumphed and received their well-merited reward.

CHAPTER XXIII

ON THE "SACHEM'S" DECK.

ith Frank Merriwell's party on board, Henry Cross-grove's magnificent steam yacht finally dropped anchor in Camden Harbor on the coast of Maine.

After Dick Merriwell's victory, he and his triumphant companions of the Fairhaven team had been invited by Crossgrove to join Frank's party on the Sachem. While the winners of the pennant in the Trolley League had accepted this invitation and were taken from Fairhaven by the handsome yacht of the steel magnate, on arriving at Camden Dick and Brad Buckhart were the only ones of the victorious nine who had not dropped off at other ports and departed for their various homes.

The evening following the arrival of the yacht at Camden was a glorious one. A full moon shed its mellow light over the village that nestled at the foot of the mountains. The harbor was unrippled by a breath of air, and the mellow sweetness of passing summer lay over everything.

During the day Frank and his friends had enjoyed a buckboard ride along the turnpike road, and, therefore, both Elsie and Inza were quite content to remain on the yacht that evening when Frank announced that he must go ashore for the purpose of mailing some letters.

For a time the girls sat chatting in the moonlight, unapproached or interrupted by any one.

"It doesn't seem so very long since we were here before, Inza," said Elsie. "Do you remember all the strange things that happened then?"

"I can never forget them," declared Inza, reaching out and grasping Elsie's hand. "I can never forget your nobility and generosity, my dear friend. For my sake you tried to make Frank believe yourself shallow, fickle, and false-hearted. You deceived me, but you couldn't deceive him. He never lost confidence in you, Elsie."

"I don't think we quite knew our own minds in those days, Inza," declared Elsie. "We thought we did, but I am sure we didn't. It's all come right at last. There are no more jealousies, no more heart-burnings, and no more bitterness."

"It took us a long time to know each other, didn't it, dear?" murmured Inza. "But in one way you are more fortunate than I."

"How's that?"

"Frank must go back to Mexico. It's absolutely necessary, he says, to have a hand in the building of that railroad which will open up the country in which lies his San Pablo Mine. He has heard some things of late that make him uneasy. You know there's always a chance for trouble over any large investment in Mexico. There are rumors that another syndicate wishes to build a railroad through exactly the same territory, and that powerful influence is being brought to bear on the Mexican government by this rival concern. I am almost sorry Frank has not sought a market for his Sonora Mine. Now that Bart has no mining interests, he is at liberty to go into any business he chooses, and he may remain in the East."

"We have talked that over, Inza," said Elsie. "Already Bart has told me about this trouble Frank may have, and I have urged him to stand by Frank until it is settled. Instead of remaining in the East, Bart will return to Mexico when Frank goes."

"Oh, Elsie!" exclaimed Inza; "I know how keenly you must feel the sacrifice! You had planned something entirely different, and now——"

"And now I am ready to put my plans and hopes aside for a time. Bart knows how much he owes to Frank, and he is anxious to stand by him. If I were to ask it, he would not go back to Mexico; but I have urged him to do so."

"Just like you, Elsie!" declared Inza. "Frank may not start for some time yet. He will have considerable work in New York with the capitalists who are going to push that railroad through. You know he has a number of maps and plans of the country through which the railroad will pass. True, a survey has been made, but Frank knows that country better than the engineers who made the survey. This he has demonstrated to the capitalists, and there's to be a meeting in New York some time next week. It's impossible to say how soon after that meeting he will be obliged to leave for Mexico."

"Don't you fear to have him go down there into that wild country, Inza?"

"No, I don't fear," was the immediate answer. "I have absolute confidence in Frank."

"But the Mexicans are so treacherous. They often strike at an enemy's back."

"That's true of a certain class of Mexicans, Elsie. There are several classes of people in Mexico, you know. For instance, there are the native Indians, then the Creoles of Spanish descent or Mexican birth. Then there are the Spaniards born in Europe, and, finally, the half-breeds, or cross between the Mexicans and Indians. These half-breeds are the treacherous ones, Elsie. They are called Mestizos. They are the enemies to be watched and avoided."

"Do you believe, Inza, that they are really the most dangerous? Are they not in many cases the tools of others with more brains? Now you know there's a person on board this yacht who can't be a Mestizo, yet I am afraid of him. He is a Mexican, for he has said so."

Inza laughed a little.

"You mean Señor Porfias del Norte. He's a friend of Mr. Crossgrove."

"I don't care," said Elsie. "I don't like him. I'm afraid of him. I'm afraid of his smooth and snaky ways. I am afraid of his smile and his restless eyes."

"I am sure he is a fine-looking fellow in a way."

"In a way, perhaps," admitted Elsie. "Some might call him fine-looking, and I have no doubt he considers himself very handsome."

"Yes, I think he does," nodded Inza. "He has a way of rolling his eyes at one, and then that smile which shows his perfect teeth—I am sure he practices it before the mirror."

"It's very strange, but I can't bear to have him near me."

"It's very strange, but somehow I have taken a great interest in him. I fancy he has some underlying purpose in life, and I wonder what it is. I am consumed by a desire to read his secret and sound the depths of him."

"Well, you may spend your time reading him as much as you like," said Elsie; "but excuse me! When he comes around I vanish."

"He's a fine singer, and he plays beautifully on both the guitar and mandolin."

"I confess he's a fine singer. Had I never seen him to talk with him, I should enjoy his singing; but now the very sound of his voice gives me a little shivery feeling, and I want to stop my ears."

"Why, I never dreamed you were such a prejudiced person, Elsie! You always see the good in everybody."

"That's right, and, therefore, something tells me that when I see the bad in a person that person must be very, very bad. Inza, I can't help it, but in spite of the polish of Porfias del Norte, in spite of his politeness, his education, his entertaining manners, I feel that he is a snake, and a poisonous snake at that."

"Of course, you may be right, Elsie," said Inza; "but I have never regarded you as an acute student of human nature."

"Nor do I profess to be, but still Profias del Norte——"

"I beg your pardon," said a smooth, musical voice that made both girls start. "Are you speaking of me, ladies? I hope I don't intrude."

A slender, graceful man stepped forward with a soft footfall. He was dressed in light flannels and bowed politely, with his hat in one hand and a guitar in the other, as the two girls partly rose from their chairs.

"I beg you not to be disturbed, ladies," he said. "I was seeking a spot on deck where I might smoke and drum a little on my guitar when I happened to pass you. I fancy Iheard my name spoken."

"Yes," said Inza at once, "we were speaking of you Señor del Norte. I don't know just how it happened—perhaps it was caused by the moonlight, by the almost tropical calm and beauty of this night."

"Ah!" he said. "It is a beautiful night—a glorious night! Never have I dreamed that so far up here in the North they could have such nights. I am a child of the South, and to me the North has ever seemed cold, and sterile, and barren, and devoid of all that's beautiful and attractive. I love beautiful things. I love the flowers, the birds, the open air, the sunshine, almost everything but darkness. Somehow I don't like darkness. It oppresses me! It crowds me! In the moonlight I am happy, but let the moon go behind a cloud and I am heavy-hearted. At night I sleep always with a light within reach of my hand. Strange, isn't it?"

"Strange!" exclaimed Elsie. "Yes, it is. I have known children and women who always slept with a light burning, but it's a rare thing for a man. Isn't it possible, señor, that you have a reason for being afraid of the darkness?"

"Possibly I have," he admitted at once. "My father was murdered at midnight on a very dark night. My mother heard the blows and tried to aid him. She sprang to his assistance and grappled with his assailants. They beat her down. She was stricken unconscious to the floor. When she recovered she struck a light, and it fell on the dead body of my father, who had been stabbed nineteen distinct times. My mother never forgot it. She told me of it scores of times. No wonder I hate the darkness!"

He gave a heavy sigh and then suddenly exclaimed:

"A thousand pardons, ladies! I hope I've not disturbed you by this little story. I should not have mentioned it. It's a gruesome thing, and I don't like to think of it myself. Miss Bellwood led me into telling you about it."

"I am very interested," declared Inza immediately. "Why was your father murdered?"

"It's a very long story. I cannot tell you everything in connection with it now, but there were enemies who wished him out of the way. You know my family has been connected with revolutions and government troubles ever since the days of Miguel Hidalgo. And I may add, by the way, that the blood of the Hidalgoes runs in my veins. I can trace my family back to Aneta Hidalgo, the half-sister of the famous priest who led the first insurrection against the provincial government."

"Your family history must be very interesting, señor," said Inza. "I should love to hear something of it."

"Perhaps you may some time, señorita," he bowed. "Just now it would give me pleasure to amuse you both with the guitar, if you don't object."

"Not in the least," Inza hastened to say.

He drew up a chair and sat down.

"Wait a minute," he said. "How is the wind? There seems to be scarcely a breath. Still, I think you're to leeward of me, to use a nautical term. I will change to the opposite side, as I wish to smoke a cigarette, to which I hope you have no objections."

He made the change and sat close at Inza's right hand. In a moment, having received permission from her, he was deftly rolling a cigarette.

"It always interests me to watch an expert roll a cigarette," she laughed. "They do it so cleverly. It's like magic."

"You should see a Mexican vaquero roll one," he said. "Some of them do it with one hand while riding at full gallop on the back of a horse."

He struck a match and lighted the cigarette, at which he puffed in a manner of absolute satisfaction and content, at the same time continuing the conversation.

"Have you ever visited my country, señorita?" he asked, directing the question toward Inza.

"Never yet," she answered.

"You have missed much," he declared. "Old Mexico is the fairest land in all the world. The American who simply crosses the line and visits the northern part of Mexico comes away with a bad opinion of it. He sees deserts and a country that is both mountainous and arid. Besides that, in the north the Indians roam restlessly and create much trouble. But let the visitor go as far south as the City of Mexico—let him go beyond. Ah! the south of Mexico; it's like paradise! The climate is perfect. Down there in many places the thermometer never reaches eighty by day and never sinks below sixty by night. It's a land of peace and plenty. If a man is lazy, he need not lift his hand to work from one year's end to another."

"You say it's a land of peace and plenty," laughed Inza. "Perhaps it's a land of plenty, but I don't think it has always been a land of peace."

"By no means, señorita," he promptly confessed. "It has been a land of many troubles. In recent years, however, under our good president, there has been great advancement. Sometimes when far from home I dream of it. I hear the songs of my country."

He began strumming the guitar. The air was a soft, sweet one, and Inza listened, keenly pleased by it.

Not so Elsie. She had been growing more and more restless. Finally she leaned toward Inza, breathing in a low tone these words:

"He's going to sing. I can't stay here and listen. Excuse me, Inza, but I must go if he sings."

A moment later Del Norte began to sing, and he was not aware that Elsie Bellwood rose and slipped softly and quietly away. He sang in Spanish, his voice being remarkably clear and sympathetic.

Understanding a little Spanish, Inza soon divined that he was singing a love song. She saw him lean toward her, and felt his dark eyes upon her.

Anchored at various distances about them were other yachts, and to the girl it seemed that on board all these the people paused to listen. A small rowboat had been passing with clanking oars; but now the oars were silent and the boat was drifting, while its occupant sat perfectly still.

Finally the song ended, and Del Norte remained quite motionless, still gazing at Inza with those deep, dark eyes of his.

She laughed with pleasure and clapped her hands softly.

"Very fine, señor," she said. "You are a very fine singer. But I confess I don't know what it was all about."

"Do you wish me to tell you?" he murmured.

Suddenly she realized that they were on dangerous ground.

"I think not," she answered quickly. "I will have more pleasure in guessing at its meaning."

"Señorita, as I sang that song I thought of you and I thousands of miles away, far down in my own country. I have seen beautiful maidens in Mexico, but never one quite your equal—Inza!"

Instantly she straightened up a little, and her voice was cold and full of reproof as she said:

"Señor del Norte, only my most intimate friends call me by my Christian name. We've not yet known each other a whole week."

"I beg your pardon!" he exclaimed, with apparent humbleness and regret. "The name slipped from my lips before I knew what I was saying. It's such a beautiful name. You don't know, but all alone by myself I have repeated it over a hundred times. Of course, you can't object if I keep saying it to myself—Inza! Inza! Inza!"

"I fear, señor, that you are like most men—you fancy every girl you meet is smitten on you. You will find that American girls are not the sort who fall in love with every stranger with fine teeth, and eyes, and polished manners."

"I accept the reproof, señorita. I presume I deserve it, still I can't repress my feelings. We people from the South differ from you of the North. You are able to hide your real emotions behind a placid exterior. Just as you live in houses to keep out the cold, you train yourselves to live in bodies that hide your real natures."

Inza laughed a little.

"You're indeed a clever talker, Señor del Norte."

"Let me say a little more. Let me tell you that many times I have thought you should be one of my own blood. You are like my people in your dark eyes, your hair, your bearing, all save your cold exterior. Could you cast that off and be your true self—ah! what a wonderful change for the better! Something tells me your heart is not cold; something tells me it's warm and impulsive."

"Let's not talk of these things," said Inza. "I don't like it. I wish you would tell me more of yourself and your family, señor. Do you know you have aroused my curiosity. I confess that."

"Then, at least," he laughed, "I am not wholly unattractive and repulsive to you? Perhaps you will forgive me if I have spoken too openly. I know you are engaged to Señor Merriwell, and a splendid gentleman he is. I admire him very much. Like many progressive Americans, he is interested in business projects in my country. Perhaps, señorita, you know a great deal about his plans?"

Del Norte uttered these words in a careless manner, but somehow Inza felt as if he were trying to pump her.

"Perhaps I do," she answered.

"He is soon to return to Mexico?"

"Yes."

"He has a mine in Eastern Sonora?"

"That's right, Señor del Norte."

"I presume his title to the mine is a good one?"

"Without doubt. Frank seldom gets trapped. A little while ago a powerful mining syndicate attempted to wrest his property from him. They investigated his right to his mine in Arizona and to the one in Mexico. They engaged expert lawyers to look over the titles to both properties. As a result it was decided that his claim to the San Pablo Mine was solid and could not be shaken by process of law. They thought differently in regard to the Queen Mystery. After trying to seize it, they took the matter into the Arizona courts, where it was fought out, with the result that Frank's claim to the mine was made indisputable. Had the Consolidated Mining Association believed there was the slightest chance to shake his claim to the San Pablo they would have made more trouble than they did for him down there. Fancying he did not have that mine well protected, they employed a famous brigand to raise a force and seize it. He discovered the plot, and the attack on the mine was repulsed, the result being that the syndicate quickly gave over the attempt to get hold of it."

"Señorita," said Del Norte, "I wish to tell you something. There are very few titles to mining properties in Mexico that cannot be broken. You must know that the government of my country has undergone such vicissitudes that thousands of old claims and titles are utterly worthless. I have told you that I am perfectly frank and outspoken. You suggested a desire to hear my story. You admitted I had aroused your curiosity. Señorita, if you are truly in earnest, if you care to listen, I will tell you the story."

"It will interest me very much," she declared. "Elsie has gone in. Frank will be back soon, and you will amuse me by telling me the story to pass the time."

"Then listen," he said.

CHAPTER XXIV

SEÑOR DEL NORTE'S STORY.

I have said, señorita, that the blood of the Hidalgoes is in my veins. Perhaps you did not know that Miguel Hidalgo, the priest, was the organizer of the first conspiracy against the Spanish provincial government in Mexico. That was in the year eighteen hundred and ten. For some time my people had been saying among themselves that they could survive and flourish independent of a foreign government. There were the signs and the spirit of nationality and independence. They wished to become a nation in many respects like the United States. The influence of the Spanish government was already declining when Miguel Hidalgo started the insurrection in the province of Guanajuato. At first it was a mere speck on the horizon. At the beginning he had less than a hundred men, but his army grew swiftly until it finally became a host of a hundred thousand men. He was brave and energetic, and would have succeeded in his scheme had not he been betrayed by treacherous enemies. He fell into the hands of the Spanish viceroy and was executed.

"That did not end the matter, however. Although the patriots were broken up into small hands, another priest, by the name of Morelos, soon placed himself at their head and carried on the war. A national congress was convened, and an act was passed declaring the independence of Mexico.

"It may seem strange to you, señorita, that with a hundred thousand men Hidalgo could not accomplish his design. It may seem strange that, although as many men, and still more, flocked to the leadership of Morelos, they were unable to crush the power of Spain. I will explain why this was. The Spanish army came equipped in the best possible manner, while hundreds of the patriots were without any arms save such implements as they could manufacture themselves. Being thus poorly armed, they were unable to cope with their enemies, and in December, eighteen hundred and fifteen, Morelos was taken and shot.

"That was simply the beginning. In eighteen hundred and twenty-one one of my ancestors, the son of Aneta Hidalgo, began again the work of rousing the patriotism of my people. He was a young man, but full of fire and energy, and he stirred up enthusiasm in a most astonishing manner. In the same year came the news that the revolution had broken out in Spain, and almost immediately the agitation in my country was renewed afresh. At this juncture a great soldier arose, Colonel Don Augustine Iturbide, and under him the son of Aneta Hidalgo, Guerrero del Norte, fought with bravery and distinction. This movement drew the support of the better class of the Mexicans, and in the end the revolt was successful. The government in the provinces was quickly overthrown, and the Spanish viceroy, Don Juan O'Donoju, was cooped up in the capital. This city soon fell into the hands of the Nationals, and on August twenty-fourth, eighteen hundred and twenty-one, O'Donoju signed a treaty at Cordova by which the independence of Mexico was recognized.

"Now followed the thing that marred all the great work which had been accomplished. The patriots proclaimed the victorious Iturbide emperor, instead of forming a government similar to that of the United States, as had been first contemplated. The disappointment of Guerrero del Norte was intense, and he refused any compensation or reward from the hands of the new emperor. He retired into the northern provinces, where he gathered about him a band of desperate men, who pledged themselves never to submit to the rule of the emperor and never to lay down their arms until Mexico had become a government of the people, by the people, and for the people.

"In the course of a few months another insurrection broke out at Vera Cruz, under the leadership of Santa Anna, and Guerrero del Norte hastened with his men to place himself under the command of the new leader. Thus it happened that my ancestor took part in the struggle that followed, and was one to be highly rewarded when Santa Anna finally conquered and the Mexican republic was organized with nineteen states and five territories. Del Norte was rewarded for his services by a large land grant in Northwestern Mexico. Already he had traveled over the territory awarded him, and had discovered that it was rich in minerals. In many ways he was in advance of the people of that region, and he believed the mines on his property would make him vastly wealthy.

"Without doubt, señorita, you will know how the new government was forced to face a revolution in turn, and the chief magistrate was driven from office. Since that time there have been many changes, but the course of events finally placed General Santa Anna at the head of the new government, and he at once reaffirmed Guerrero del Norte's claim to a large tract of land in Eastern Sonora. Thus you will see that Del Norte had a double right to this property, yet since then there have been many vicissitudes and many persons have arisen desiring to secure possession of that land. The title to it finally descended into the hands of my father. He attempted to open up some of the mines, but found the region swarming with brigands and hostile Indians. On investigating, he discovered that the Indians were incited to drive away certain parties who should venture there, and the brigands were in the employ of enemies who held counterclaims to the land. These counterclaims had been granted by a chief magistrate, whose authority to make such grants no one in all Mexico now recognized. Nevertheless, my father's enemies were persistent, and misfortune placed him in such a position, that he was unable to raise the needed capital to carry out his plans.

"Finally he decided that he would seek to employ American capitalists. He concluded to interest Americans and form a syndicate that would open up the mines down there on his land. I was a very young boy then.

"On the night before my father intended leaving Tampico by steamer for the United States he was murdered, as I have before told you. The murderers sought to gain possession of his papers, but failed, as they were at that time safely locked up in a vault. These papers were placed in my hands by my mother when she died. I have them, and, at last, I have decided to carry out the plans formed by my father. For that purpose I am in this country. I came here to interest capitalists who will join me in opening up the region that belongs to me and in developing the mines down there. In pursuance of my purpose I became acquainted with Henry Crossgrove, and was invited to join him on this cruise."

Del Norte paused a moment, and then added:

"I am very glad it happened so, even if I had not succeeded in interesting Señor Crossgrove. I am very happy, for it has been a delightful cruise, and I have met you—you! Pardon, señorita; I can't help it! I tell you frankly that I always speak what comes into my heart. I can't repress it. I can't hold it in check. I am very, very sorry you ever met Señor Merriwell. Wait, señorita; I know it's now too late for me to speak. My tongue must forever remain silent. Some day when I form the syndicate in which many rich men are now interested—some day when I have taken possession of all my land and my mines—some day when the railroad we shall build runs through my property I will be a very rich man. In that time, señorita, it would give me untold pleasure to have one like you to share my success and my riches. Ah! even wealth will not give me perfect happiness without that one. When I think of that my heart is heavy and sad. When I think that in a few days more we must part, perhaps never to meet again, there are tears in my eyes."

Inza did not attempt to repress a laugh.

"Señor del Norte," she said, "you will meet some one ready enough to share your wealth with you. The American girl is looking out for the main chance. Just convince her that you have the money and she's yours—or, rather, you will be hers, for she generally proposes to take charge of affairs."

"You can't make me believe, señorita, that you have so little romance in you," he protested. "Do you not feel it—does not the night thrill you? And is it possible you have no regret because we are to part so soon? Ah, well! I will simply smile, though my heart is torn with anguish. I will try to hide my secret, but now—now let me say—adios!"

Ere she suspected his purpose he had seized her hand and pressed it to his burning lips.

Instantly she sprang erect.

"Señor del Norte, you are impudent!" she exclaimed. "If Frank were here——"

"He is here," said a quiet voice as Frank Merriwell himself stepped forward.

So interested had Del Norte become in Inza, and so interested had she been in his story, that neither of them had observed the approach of the little boat that brought Frank back to the yacht. As they were sitting on the port side, and he came aboard on the starboard side, neither of them became aware of his presence until he spoke.

For a single instant Porfias del Norte seemed startled. Then he bowed with courtly grace, his guitar in his left hand, saying:

"At last you have returned, Señor Merriwell. The señorita was lonely without you, and I sought to interest her with music, song, and chat."

Inza felt that Frank heartily disliked Del Norte, and she saw in Merry's manner a trace of suspicion and doubt. He glanced searchingly at her, and then once more turned to survey the suave, smiling Mexican.

"You're a very interesting person, Señor del Norte," he said, in a cold tone of voice. "From what I have seen of you I fancy you are a great admirer of the ladies."

Del Norte laughed softly and pleasantly.

"My dear Merriwell," he said, with a touch of polite familiarity, "all the men of my country admire the ladies. It's as natural for them as it is to breathe."

"Quite so," nodded Frank. "But you know there is such a thing as too much adoration. An admirer who is both obnoxious and persistent becomes a terrible bore in time. However, if you have amused Miss Burrage while I was absent I am pleased."

"He told me the most interesting tale, Frank," said Inza. "He told me of his family, and the history of the Del Nortes seems closely interwoven with that of Mexico's struggle for liberty."

"I fancied you were startled by something, Inza, just as I appeared," said Merry in a low tone. "Was I mistaken?"

"If you could hear Señor del Norte's story I believe it might startle you, Frank," she answered evasively.

It was not Inza's intention or desire to deceive Merry, but she knew how quickly her lover would administer reproof and chastisement to Del Norte for his conduct in case she revealed what had happened. Not wishing to bring about an encounter on board the Sachem, she thought it best to evade revealing the truth at that time.

The girl now urged Merriwell to listen to Del Norte's story, and once more asked the Mexican to go over it.

It's possible that Del Norte was relieved when he discovered she had no intention of telling Frank what had taken place. He seated himself once more, after Inza had resumed her chair, and invited Frank to draw up and be comfortable.

"See how the moonlight turns the water to silver," he said, stretching out his hand toward the shimmering waves of the harbor. "See the town nestling there at the foot of the dark mountain. Look yonder on the top of the nearer and smaller mountain. Up there you can behold a star, but it's a light in the window of the hotel. To-morrow we are to go up there. Señor Crossgrove has arranged it. We may climb the mountain on foot or be taken up in carriages, just as we choose. They say we will be entertained up there and be given a fine dinner, if we wish it. Ah, how surprised my countrymen would be could they look on this beautiful scene away up here in the so-called barren North! But they tell me this land is buried deep in snow in the winter, while my own land is blooming with flowers and is sweet with fragrance. It's only for a very short time in summer or in early fall that the inhabitants here really enjoy life."

"That's where you make a mistake, señor," said Merry. "They enjoy life the whole year round."

"How can it be?" asked the Mexican unbelievingly. "They must work like slaves during the pleasant weather in order to protect themselves from hunger and cold through the bitter winters. Thus while they work at the most beautiful time of the year they lose all the pleasure they might have; and in the winter they are compelled to huddle by their fireside. To me the people here are much like slaves. They know nothing of the real enjoyment of life."

"On the contrary," denied Frank, "they enjoy life more fully than most people. To them labor is enjoyment. They are ambitious, and not only do they labor that they might eat, and drink, and be clothed and housed, but they labor to accomplish something that will make the world better and brighter. It's from this frozen North that the most ambitious, most energetic, most brainy men go forth into the world. By this I do not mean that it's from the State of Maine alone, or even from the New England States, that such men go forth. It's from the entire North, the temperate portion of the country. The people of the far South are inclined to be slothful. It's in the atmosphere. The climate affects them. If they have ambitions, they say to-morrow we will begin; but for them to-morrow never comes."

"Still," persisted Del Norte, "I can't see how any one who is forced to labor may possibly be happy. To me it's like slavery."

"Nor can you comprehend, I presume," said Merry, "that the people of the North labor from choice. It's a fact that many rich men and many rich men's sons labor because they love to work— they feel they must work. It's in their blood to do, to accomplish, to be something. But we have strayed away from our subject, Señor del Norte. You have been telling Miss Burrage an interesting tale of yourself and your family, and you promised to repeat it for me."

"Ah! yes, so I did," murmured the Mexican as he rolled a fresh cigarette. "I have thought for some time that I would tell you that story, Señor Merriwell. I know you are interested in Mexico."

He struck a match and lighted a cigarette, at which he puffed a moment in silent meditation, his head bowed. It was a shapely head, with dark hair, in which there was the slightest wavy curl.

His profile as shown by the moonlight of the far North seemed to carry with it the warm atmosphere of the tropics. Still, there was about it something sad and poetic.

Finally he began speaking, and once more he went over the story as told to Inza. At times he turned his dark eyes toward Frank, and watched the young American keenly, as if seeking to know the effect of the narrative upon him.

"A most interesting tale, señor," said Merriwell when it was finished. "It is indeed too bad that the grant of land accorded your family should have been made at such a time and by President Pedraza, whose power was only temporary and passing, and whose acts have been recognized by few of his followers in office as legitimate."

Del Norte laughed softly.

"But you have forgotten, my dear Señor Merriwell, that the grant of President Pedraza was reaffirmed by President Santa Anna."

It was Frank's turn to laugh.

"It happens, Señor del Norte," he retorted, "that I know a little something of Mexican history. It happens very strangely that I know something of this very affair about which you have been speaking. I have found it necessary on my own account to look into the legality of many old land grants in Mexico. President Pedraza had the misfortune to be overthrown by Santa Anna, who previously overthrew Don Augustine Iturbide. In this new uprising of Santa Anna, Guerrero del Norte must have been actively concerned in order to win favor of the victor. Santa Anna conquered and was made president.

"It was about this time, señor, that the people in what now is known as Texas became uneasy and restless. The central government of Mexico was changed under Santa Anna. The constitution of eighteen hundred and twenty-four was abolished and a new form of government, and more substantial, was produced. Although the office of president was retained, the executive powers were extended in a manner that constituted a virtual dictatorship. Now, Santa Anna was no man to rule by love. He was harsh, and cruel, and vindictive. Texas refused to recognize his authority and bow beneath his iron hand. Then came the uprising of the Texans and the war which followed in the rebellious province. Santa Anna himself headed the army and attempted to crush the rebellion by ruthless butchery. When captured, the Texans were not treated as prisoners of war, but as traitors and spies, and were in many cases murdered in cold blood. The name of Santa Anna is held in the greatest detestation by the people of Texas. He sought to crush the Texans, but he himself met defeat in the battle of San Jacinto, where he was captured. In this manner Texas won her independence, and for a time Santa Anna had no hand in the government of Mexico.

"During this time there were revolutions, and counter revolutions, and broils, and turmoils unmentionable. The country was in a state of disquietude and unrest, and no man knew that what he to-day called his own would not belong to his neighbor on the morrow. Old laws were changed and favors granted to citizens were annulled. It was during this time, señor, that Guerrero del Norte was himself proclaimed an outlaw and a price was placed upon his head."

Porfias del Norte gave a slight start at this declaration, cast his cigarette over the side, where it struck with a sizzling sound in the water, and folded his arms.

"Am I not right, señor?" asked Frank, facing him squarely.

"It's possible you are right," admitted the Mexican. "In those days the man who one day was a patriot the next day was declared a brigand. Your knowledge is very wonderful, señor. It gives me great surprise."

In Del Norte's musical tones there was hidden the keenest sarcasm, which the young American did not fail to observe.

"I told you at the outset," said Merry, "that I had looked up many things in connection with Mexican history. From the fact that I possess certain interests in Eastern Sonora, I was led to investigate the career of Guerrero del Norte. I found that not only was he proclaimed an outlaw, but he became a leader of bandits. He retired to what he called his own land, a vast stretch of mountains and plains, and gathered about him a band of desperadoes and cutthroats. They did not labor, but they lived on the fruits of others. They made various raids to the south and to the north. At one time they ventured across the Rio Grande into Texas, but were driven back without success and with great loss of life. Guerrero, the chief, was himself seriously wounded. From this time until his death I believe he remained practically an outlaw and a bandit."

"Wait a minute, señor," urged Del Norte. "Have you forgotten that in eighteen hundred and fifty-three, for the fifth time, Santa Anna was made president of Mexico? You must remember that General Santa Anna had reasons for feeling most friendly toward Guerrero."

"Perhaps that is true," nodded Merry; "but by this time the life Guerrero had been leading had taken such a hold upon him that he could not abandon it. He had become a lover of brigandage. He chose to remain a bandit and a plunderer to the end of his days, and thus did he remain. Señor del Norte, I happen to know that in the end the grant of land made to Guerrero was revoked and annulled and a price placed on the head of your bandit ancestor. These are facts. You can't deny them."

Once more the Mexican laughed, but this time there was a trace of annoyance in the sound.

"I must again confess," he said, "that Señor Merriwell's knowledge of Mexican history and my own affairs is most astounding. It seems strange indeed that he should know so very many things about my family."

"It's not so strange, Señor del Norte, when you consider that at the present time I have a mine in Eastern Sonora located on territory given to Guerrero in his land grant."

"Ha!" cried Porfias. "Then your mine is on that land? I thought as much! I was confident it must be! Señor, I am very sorry, but that mine belongs to me!"

"You never made a greater mistake in your life," said Merry quietly. "Before spending any great sum of money in opening up that mine, señor, I took pains to investigate thoroughly my right to the property. That's how I came to know so much about the history of your family. I found in the City of Mexico a record of the old land grant made to Guerrero by Pedraza. I found a record of its affirmation by President Santa Anna. I also found a record of its annulment at a later period by President Santa Anna. For your sake, Señor del Norte, I am sorry; but for my own I am glad that you have not the remotest right to one inch of that land."

"We shall see!" cried the Mexican, his eyes flashing. "You think, like all Americans, that possession is nine points of the law. Well, it may be; but again I say we shall see. You have money. You are seeking to interest capitalists in opening up that country with a railroad. Ah! Señor Merriwell, I am not idle. It's not always my way to disclose my plans, but, feeling sure of my ground, I tell you now that your railroad will never be built. Instead of that, it's I who will build the railroad. It's I who will reap the reward to be taken from that rich country. I shall not fight you with violence, for the day of violence in Mexico ought to be past. I shall fight you with the hand of the law."

"Very well," said Frank. "You may fancy that I am not aware that at the present time you are doing everything in your power to induce the Mexican government to reaffirm that old land grant. I happen to know all about that. Señor del Norte, every move you make in Mexico is known to me. I have men on the ground who are ready to meet those moves and baffle them. President Diaz is a just and honorable man. He is also a wise man and cannot be bamboozled. Your efforts will be vain, Señor del Norte."

"We shall see! we shall see!" muttered the Mexican, all the music gone from his voice. "It was a strange chance that threw us together on this yacht, Señor Merriwell, but I am very glad it happened. Although we met here as friends, we know now that we are enemies, and I promise you, my dear gringo, that I will keep you busy. You have boasted of the energy and ambition of the men of the North; you shall see something of the energy and ambition of the men of the South. I will give you no rest, señor. If you become tired, beware lest while your eyes are closed I gain a step on you. Beware lest when you awake you find your vaunted possessions have passed from you and are in my grasp. Oh, it shall be a noble struggle! Ha! ha! ha!"

The laugh of the Mexican sent a chill through the body of the listening girl. Instantly she started up, grasping Frank's arm.

"Come!" she said. "I am cold. Escort me to the cabin, please."

Del Norte rose, bowing most profoundly and most gracefully.

"Good night, señorita," he breathed. "May your dreams be as sweet as the dreamer. Good night, Señor Merriwell; but beware lest you dream and awake to regret it!"

CHAPTER XXV

SEÑOR HAGAN.

In spite of Del Norte's menacing words, Frank slept well that night.

In the morning the Mexican met Merry with the politest manner possible and with the blandest smile. Indeed, his air was one of cordiality, and apparently he declined to be snubbed when Frank gave him something like the cold shoulder.

After breakfast Del Norte was set ashore at Fishmarket Wharf, and he presented an air of tropical comfort as he slowly sauntered into town attired in spotless white garments.

Proceeding to the post office, he had paused to purchase a paper at the news stand in the building when a hand touched him on the arm and he glanced up to see at his side a thick-set, florid-faced man, who was perspiring freely.

"Ah, Señor Hagan!" exclaimed Porfias, at once turning and grasping the hand of the stout man. "It's pleased I am to see you here. I received your letter telling me how the good work is progressing, and it interested me exceedingly. You are doing well."

"There are some things I didn't care to write about, Del Norte," said the man addressed as Hagan. "That's why I told you I would find you down this way somewhere and have a little chat with you. I traced the Sachem to this place, arriving here last night. Not wishing to arouse suspicions of a certain party on board the Sachem, I decided to wait and watch for an opportunity to see you. Had the Sachem departed before I could obtain such an opportunity, I should have followed it to its next port."

"You were exceedingly cautious, señor."

Observing that the smooth-faced, youthful attendant at the news stand was regarding them with some curiosity, Hagan at once proposed to his companion that they should step outside.

"Never knew they had such devilish hot weather up here at this time of year," he growled, mopping his perspiring face with his handkerchief as they reached the sidewalk. "Let's walk up the street beneath the shade of those tall elms. We can chat as we walk without danger of being overheard. That youngster has a sharp nose, a keen pair of eyes, and ears altogether too good to suit me."

"These confounded gringos seem to hear and see everything," said Del Norte.

"That's all right," nodded Hagan; "but they can't get ahead of the Irish, Del Norte, old man."

"It's the truth you speak, señor," nodded the Mexican. "I have observed its truthfulness, and that was why I sought one to assist me in my plans who had in his veins good Irish blood."

"You made no mistake on that point when you dropped on me," said Hagan. "I am Irish to the core. But let me tell you, my friend, we're going to be kept mighty busy if we get ahead of this Yankee, Merriwell. He is a hustler. He has a faculty of setting things in motion so that they keep on moving while he seems to forget them. Apparently just now he is enjoying an outing on a yacht, yet before he stepped foot on the Sachem he had started a movement that is progressing with astonishing rapidity. I refer to the scheme for opening Eastern Sonora with a railroad. The syndicate is being organized, the capital pledged, and everything is making ready to push the project. Del Norte, I want you to answer me one question frankly and squarely."

"You shall have the answer, Señor Hagan. What is the question?"

"Are you absolutely confident you can induce the Mexican government to reaffirm that old land grant?"

"I am absolutely confident, señor. There is not the remotest doubt of my ability to accomplish this. I have friends who are powerful with their influence and who stand close to President Diaz. Of course, they can't push this thing through with a rush, for he might suspect something was not right if they seemed too eager. They are biding their time, and when the right moment comes President Diaz will reaffirm that grant of land."

"Unless," said Hagan, as they walked slowly along the sidewalk—"unless he favors this American syndicate organized by Merriwell. Del Norte, the operations of that syndicate must be checked. They are moving altogether too rapidly. That's why I came here to see you. Before it became known that a project for building a railroad through Central Sonora to tap the Sonora line had been conceived, the men first concerned in the syndicate sent engineers down there and made a survey. They worked swiftly and quietly. Frank Merriwell paid a large part of the expense of this survey, and he has the result of it in his own possession. He has the papers. I believe he has them with him now."

"What makes you think so?" asked Del Norte quickly.

"I think he brought them along with the idea that he might interest Henry Crossgrove."

"Perhaps it's right you are."

"Yes, I believe I am right, Del Norte. That's why I took the trouble to come 'way down here. I didn't wish to write anything that might fall into the hands of the wrong people and make trouble for us, but I have a plan I desire to whisper in your ear. Lend me your ear, Del Norte, and I will do the whispering act."

"It's aloud you may talk, señor, if you modulate your voice, without fear of being overheard. We will walk up and down here in front of this church as you talk. No one may come near us to listen."

"It's not a great deal I wish to say, Del Norte; but if by any means we can get our hands on that document it would give us a big advantage over the enemy. They would lose the plan, and we would secure it. If it pleased us we could push our work by their own survey just as soon as we were given the privilege to begin by the Mexican government. Thus, you see, Del Norte, we would save a pretty penny and give the enemy a solar-plexus blow."

The dark eyes of the Mexican were gleaming now, and there was a strange, crafty smile on his lips.

"You are right, Señor Hagan; but it may not be with any great ease that one could secure those papers. This Merriwell is cautious, and I fancy he guards them constantly."

"From what I have seen of you, Del Norte, me man," said Hagan, "you're the boy to get ahead of a chap like Merriwell. You're slick and smooth as they make 'em, and if you set about it I will guarantee you will find out where those papers are carried in less than two days. It then remains for you to get possession of them without detection. Get ashore with them, and mail them to our headquarters in New York. Once they are in the hands of the post office authorities you are all right. Then you can laugh defiance in the teeth of Frank Merriwell."

"Quite so," nodded the Mexican. "But I should hate to do the laughing as openly as you propose, Señor Hagan. They say this Merriwell sometimes strikes, and strikes hard. I don't care to have him strike me. But let me tell you he must guard himself every moment, or I may find my opportunity to strike him. I have now a double reason for hating him."

"A double reason?" said Hagan. "Why, you Mexicans are queer. I don't hate the boy. I rather admire him. All the same, I shall take great satisfaction in downing him as hard as I can."

"I have not told you one reason why I hate him. I will tell you: On board that yacht is the most beautiful American girl it has ever been my pleasure to behold. She is the affianced of this American. Is it strange I should hate him for his good fortune when I tell you that I love her?"

"Come, come, Del Norte!" exclaimed Hagan, "don't get mixed up in a love affair just now. You have something else on your hands if you are going to get ahead of Frank Merriwell."

"To-day," said Del Norte, "this afternoon we go up yonder upon the mountain. Señorita Inza will go with us. Up there, as you may see, are many steep precipices. Would it be strange, indeed, if sometime to-day Señor Merriwell should slip and fall over one of those precipices? They tell me that a girl once fell from the higher mountain and was killed. A cross stands at the top of the cliff over which she fell. Ha! ha! ha! I wonder if they would put up a cross on the smaller mountain should Señor Merriwell fall to his death from a high cliff?"

Hagan gave a little shrug with his thick shoulders.

"Why, hang you, Del Norte!" he exclaimed. "I believe you would commit murder if you had a first-class opportunity and you could get an enemy out of the way by it!"

"I don't like the word murder, Señor Hagan. It has a very bad sound to the ear. I have not spoken of such a thing. I said this smart American might slip and fall. Of course I would have nothing to do with it. Oh, no! Of course I would try to save him as he was going over. I would spring to clutch him. I would be horrified by the terrible disaster. I would weep and tear my hair, and offer Señorita Inza my sympathy and consolation. I would tell her how grand and noble I thought the poor youth and how deeply I regretted his untimely death."

"Say, you're the limit!" growled Hagan. "Better be careful, man. Murder will out, you know."

"Not always—not when cleverly done," retorted Del Norte. "Thousands of murders have remained a mystery for all time. It's only the fools and bunglers who are caught. They are in the vast majority, and therefore it comes that most people believe murder can't be concealed. Let a man of brains commit the deed, and in almost every instance he covers his tracks so beautifully, so completely, that the mystery remains unsolved forever. In most cases, you know, a murder proclaims it is such upon its face. When it can be made to look like suicide or accident, then suspicions are lulled and investigations are lax. Don't worry about me, Señor Hagan. I am altogether too wise to be caught. You have proposed to me a plan of securing certain papers. How much easier this plan may be carried out if the possessor of those papers should meet with a sudden and terrible death! It would create consternation among his companions and friends. For the time being they would think of nothing else. His valuables would be forgotten. If the desired papers were removed they would not be missed for some time. Ah! you see, Señor Hagan—you see?"

"By the sod of old Erin, I see that you're one of the slickest devils I have ever had the luck to encounter! Why, you talk of murders with a ring of music in your voice. You smile as sweetly as a child when you discuss such things. Look here, Del Norte, if the time ever comes when I think you have anything against me, confound your soul! I will not wait for you to get at me, but I will shoot you in cold blood. I will take no chances with you unless I am plumb anxious to die."

Again the Mexican laughed softly.

"That time will never come, Señor Hagan. There should be no cause for it, so do not worry. Leave everything to me. You are anxious to secure those papers, and I promise you we will have them before two more days have passed. With Merriwell himself out of the way, all our troubles will be ended. His mine shall become ours. I will make you rich, my Irish comrade. You shall be what they now call a money king."

Then, strangely enough, following close the look of anticipated triumph on Del Norte's face came a shadow of sadness that was softly pathetic. The corners of his mouth drooped a little, and there seemed to be a faint mist in his dark eyes.

"But I," he murmured—"though I possess millions I shall never be satisfied unless some day I claim as my own the beautiful Señorita Inza."

CHAPTER XXVI

CLIMBING THE MOUNTAIN.

arly that afternoon two parties from the Sachem started for the top of Mount Battie. One party, including
Mrs. Crossgrove and the captain's daughter, decided
to make the ascent by teams.

It was Inza who proposed to Frank and Frank's friends that they
should take the footpath up the southern side of the mountain.

Near two o'clock they started, having induced Browning to accompany them, much to Merry's secret satisfaction.

"If I find any one is lying to me about this old trail up the mountain," said the big fellow, as with his coat on his arm he came puffing after the others, "I will certainly deal out retribution in large
quantities. Inza says the path is perfectly delightful. Frank says
it's a simple climb. Hodge says it's almost too easy. While others
have told me it's a simpler matter climbing up the footpath than
riding up the road. In fact, I have received the impression that it's
just about as easy to climb the mountain by this footpath as it is to
slide down hill on a toboggan."

A little later, when they had struck the first steep ascent and
were climbing a path where loose stones abounded and frequently rolled beneath their feet, Bruce began to growl, and gurgle, and
make strange sounds in his throat. Looking back, they could see
him with his face flushed and perspiring, and his eyes glaring
ominously.

"What's the matter, Bruce?" cried Inza laughingly.

"No matter! no matter!" he declared, with a touch of savageness
in his voice.

"But I fancied there must be from the strange sounds coming
up to my ears. I fancied a whole pack of wild animals were at our
heels."

Again Browning made one of those singular growling gurglings, and then, as a rock rolled beneath his feet and he nearly fell down, he paused and cried:

"Where's Frank Merriwell? Let him come back here just a minute. I want to show him something."

"Can't stop, Bruce," laughingly called Merry. "It's altogether too much trouble."

"Hang you!" panted Browning. "I always regarded you as a man of veracity. I took you to be a second George Washington. But let me tell you now, sir, that my opinion has changed. You have Cap'n Wiley, Baron Munchausen, and old Ananias whipped to a finish. Easy climbing up this path! Simple thing sauntering up this path! Delightful promenade up this path! Can almost go to sleep walking up this path! Yah-h-h-h!"

The shouts of laughter these words invoked did not seem to soothe Browning's feelings or cool him down in the slightest degree.

"Laugh, confound you—laugh!" he shouted. "There will be a settlement with somebody! Say, we're pretty near the top, aren't we?"

"Yes, pretty near the top," said Frank. "We'll be there in a short time. Come ahead, Bruce."

"You wait till we do get to the top," growled Bruce threateningly as he resumed the climb after his amused companions.

In a short time Browning found most of the party assembled on a flat ledge where there was an open view of the village below, the country beyond it, and the bay and islands.

"Ah!" exclaimed Bruce, in great relief. "Reached the top at last! By George, that was a climb!"

"The top?" said Elsie Bellwood. "Why, this isn't the top of the mountain!"

"W-h-a-t?" roared the big fellow in astonishment.

Then he glanced upward and saw the precipitous slopes above him, with the path winding in and out amid the rocks and bushes and showing itself only at intervals. For some moments he stood with his mouth open, seemingly thunderstruck.

"Well, I'm a liar if I ever saw a mountain grow before!" he muttered. "This one has grown about three thousand feet taller than it was when we started to climb it. Jumping jingoes! you don't mean to tell me we've got to scratch gravel all the way up that declivity, do you? Why, look at those cliffs! Look at those smooth rocks! We'll never get up there in a thousand years."

Dick Merriwell and Brad Buckhart had been admiring the view. The Texan nudged his friend with his elbow, chuckling in a low tone:

"I sure opined Bob Singleton was some lazy, but this gent certainly has him beaten to a custard."

"It's not half as lad as it books—I mean it's not half as bad as it looks," said Harry Rattleton.

"That's right," agreed Frank. "You know at a distance a thing looks small and insignificant many times, but in this case, being close under the mountain makes it look more precipitous and difficult than it really is."

"Oh, yes! oh, yes!" grated Browning, glaring at Merry. "You're a fine talker, you are! I have heard you talk before. You told me it was such a delightful thing to jog up the side of this mountain by this old footpath. It was such a simple matter that one might fall asleep while walking up the path! If there's anything that exasperates me, it's a liar! If there's anything I have no use for, it's a liar! Fabricators are dangerous. They should be abolished, and here's where I think I will abolish one."

As he said this he clinched his fist, turned it over and over, and examined it as if making a critical inspection; and then, with it shaking ominously, he advanced toward Frank, who was standing close to the edge of the rock.

"What are you going to do?" asked Inza.

"I am going to kill him," said Bruce, in a deliberate manner. "I am going to throw him clean over the village and into the harbor out yonder. I will throw him out so far he'll never be able to swim ashore."

"Oh, please—please don't, for my sake!" entreated Inza, with mock terror. "Spare him and give him a chance to repent of his sins!"

"Well, for your sake I will spare him," said Bruce. "You spoke just in time. He owes you his life. Say, children, let's not climb the mountain to-day. Let's rest here a while, call it a full day, and go back."

They laughed at him mockingly, and finally he flung himself down with a hopeless groan.

"I think I will go back, anyhow," he said. "I don't think I'd ever survive the rest of this climb."

"But you can't go back, Bruce," said Elsie. "We won't let you go back. We want you with us. We want you to provide amusement for us."

"Oh, so that's it?" he exclaimed, with another pretended burst of anger. "So you want me to come along and make a holy show of myself, do you? You think I am better than a three-ring circus, I suppose! You think I am better than a cage of monkeys, I suppose! I have heard you laughing and saying things to one another in low tones. I am onto the whole of you. You're a heartless lot of heathens! You enjoy human suffering! You have no sympathy or tenderness in your marble hearts! Pretty soon I will get mad and tell you just what I think of you."

"Don't do it," entreated Henry Rattleton. "You might knock our sherves—that is, shock our nerves."

Having admired the view spread beneath them and refreshed themselves by a rest on the ledge, they finally prepared to start again. It was then found that, with his arms curled beneath his head, Browning was fast asleep. Frank gave the big chap a nudge with the toe of his boot.

"Come, come, Browning," he cried; "it's your move."

"Gimme half the bed," grunted Browning, rolling over on his side and apparently preparing to continue his nap.

Merry was compelled to shake him violently, and, protesting against such usage, the lazy chap finally sat up.

"Why, it's morning!" he said, in apparent surprise, as he rubbed his eyes. "Hey? Why, this is the funniest bedroom I ever slept in. What? That's the biggest window on record. Thunder! Where am I, anyhow?"

At last he was wide-awake, and when Frank told him where he was, and that some of the party had already resumed the ascent. Bruce seemed on the verge of shedding tears.

"Have I got to do it?" he asked. "Why don't they run a tramway up this old mountain? Why don't they have a car to take people up this blazing mountain? It's an outrage to have a path up such a steep place! There ought to be a law against having such a path!"

"Better stick by us, Bruce," said Frank. "You remember how many loose stones there were in that path. If you attempt to go back by yourself those stones may give you a fall that will break your arms or legs or finish you completely. The rest of the way the path is comparatively solid."

"Oh, don't talk to me! Don't you tell me anything! I wouldn't believe you under oath!"

However, Browning decided to follow them, and soon he was again panting, and puffing, and growling as he plodded up the path.

After leaving the ledge, this path wound in and out beyond some small trees and high bushes where there was considerable shade; but finally it came out upon the bare rocks, and the complaints of the lazy chap in the rear became more violent, although less frequent. Once he sat down, and finally refused to move another foot. It was necessary that Inza and Frank should offer him further encouragement to urge him on.

"Get ahead of us, Bruce," said Merry. "The others are away up yonder. You can see that both Dick and Brad have passed out of sight over the shoulder of the mountain."

"How high did you tell me this mountain was?" asked Browning.

"Oh, about one thousand feet, more or less."

"More or less!" roared the exasperated giant. "That was just the way you said it, doggone you! You said one thousand feet, more or less. It's more, all right! It's five thousand more! If I haven't climbed five thousand feet already, I haven't climbed an inch!"

After a time they succeeded in getting him started again, but when they came to a turn of the path that ran over some smooth and slippery ledges the big fellow lost his footing, fell sprawling, and lay grasping a cleft in the rock, while he grunted out his declaration that he was on the verge of dropping the full distance to the foot of the mountain and ending his earthly career in that manner.

"Come on, Bruce," said Frank. "You can't fall very far if you try. You might roll down a rod or so and bruise yourself, but there's no great peril here."

"How can I believe a liar like him?" muttered Browning, still clinging to the cleft and declining to budge. "One thousand feet, more or less! Just wait until I get on level ground again! I'll give him something he'll enjoy—more or less!"

"Oh, Bruce," laughed Inza; "if I had a camera now! You would make such a beautiful picture! Your pose is so graceful!"

"I sup-pose so," punned the big fellow.

"Here! here!" cried Frank. "Punning is a worse crime than lying, and you're lying and punning both."

"You're another!" said Bruce, as he slowly pulled himself up to his hands and knees and began crawling cautiously along the ridge in the ledge.

This was not the only spot over which it was difficult to urge Browning, but finally the dangerous ledges were left behind, and they passed over the shoulder of the mountain.

By that time Browning had forgotten his threats or was too exhausted to attempt to carry them out.

Those who had reached the top in advance were found waiting, and soon the entire party was collected. They then made their way through the cedars and low bushes toward the hotel.

To the surprise of all, they failed to find at the hotel their friends who had chosen to go up by team.

On the veranda, however, a man sat smoking a cigarette and enjoying the beautiful sea view. It was Porfias del Norte.

As he saw them, Del Norte rose and waved his hand, bowing with the grace of a dancing master and smiling with the sweetness of a beautiful woman.

"Hail to the mighty mountain climbers!" he cried, in a musical voice. "I welcome you as kindred spirits. I, too, climbed the mountain by that path. I found it toil, yet it was toil well rewarded."

"You climbed by that path?" said Bart Hodge, regarding Del Norte in surprise. "Why, I didn't suppose you ever exerted yourself to such an extent, señor. It seems utterly improbable that you should do so. What could have been your object?"

"Yes, what could have been your object?" muttered Browning. "I was fooled into it. You must have had an object."

"They told me how beautiful the scenes were my eyes could behold while climbing the mountain that way. I am a lover of beauty. I adore nature. A hundred times I paused while making the ascent and turned to look back. Down almost directly beneath me lay the beautiful village of Camden, with its snug little harbor, with the blue bay and the purple islands beyond, and then with such a grand stretch of country and the village of Rockport yonder, smoke rising from its limekilns. The winding, brown roads, the fields, the grass, and away down there another place, which they call Rockland, also with its smoking kilns. And toward the west were other mountains, rugged, and wooded, and broken. Then over all was this deep blue sky—this sweet blue sky! And the sunshine warmed me, and the sweet airs thrilled me. Oh, yes, I was well repaid—well repaid for my climb."

"Señor del Norte," said Inza, "you seem to have the soul of a poet."

"I have," he answered, bowing again to her. "It's the poet's heart that beats in my bosom."

"All the same, señor," said Bart Hodge, "I decline to believe you climbed the path solely for the love of the beauty your eyes can behold from it. You had another object."

The Mexican lifted his delicate dark eyebrows with an expression of surprise.

"If that is true," he said, "I myself do not know what the object was. There is a wagon road on the western side of the mountain, and I could have ridden from the foot to this hotel. I didn't do so."

"Which makes me believe all the more," said Hodge, "that you had some powerful incitant to climb that path."

"Either that or you're the blamedest fool I ever met!" said Browning, as he collapsed on a chair and began weakly fanning himself.

CHAPTER XXVII

ELSIE'S DREAM.

he others came in due time. They had enjoyed a short drive on the turnpike, which explained their delay in reaching the top of the mountain.

Crossgrove was in high spirits. He had sent word in advance that his party would arrive at the hotel and wished supper there. Everything had been made ready for them, and they proceeded to enjoy themselves on the broad veranda, from which they could look 'way over the island-besprinkled bay. With the aid of a field glass they could see the outer islands, beyond which lay the open ocean. They could also see the mountains, at the foot of which nestled Bar Harbor.

Del Norte seemed to take delight in pointing out the particularly striking or attractive features of the view. He descanted upon each feature. His language was indeed poetical in many instances. From one group to another he passed, apparently in highest spirits and the most genial humor. Always he was the soul of courtesy and politeness.

But a score of times Inza Burrage detected him watching her or flashing her a strange, quick glance.

She was standing alone by the rail at the edge of the veranda when she heard a soft step and felt a presence at her side.

"You seem enchanted, señorita," said Del Norte, in a low tone. "I do not wonder. Yet, do you know, for all the beauties I see spread out before me there is something in the scene that reminds me of death."

"Death?"

She shrank away involuntarily, looking at him with startled eyes.

"Yes," he said, "that is what I meant to say. After climbing the path I made a little exploration. I found certain precipices over which it would be almost certain death for one to fall. I keep thinking of these precipices. Strange I cannot forget them."

"But we see none of them from here, so why should the scene remind you of death?"

"You see none of them distinctly, but there's one down yonder, señorita. You might walk out to the verge of it without going so very far. But it was not of these things I meant to speak when I said the scene reminded me of death. I was thinking what it must look like in the bleak winter. I was thinking how repellant this must be when buried deep under snow and ice. And I thank my fate that I was not born to such a land. I thank my fate that I am a child of the sweet land of Mexico, where flowers bloom and birds sing the whole year round. I say I thank my fate that this fortune was mine, but even as I say it I curse my fate that a great misfortune is also mine."

"A misfortune, señor?"

"Yes, the greatest that may be known to a man with a poet's soul like mine. The greatest that may come to him whose heart burns always with living fire as my heart burns within me."

"How strangely you talk!"

"I suppose it does seem strange to you, Señorita Inza."

"I don't think I understand you."

"Possibly not. Still, I fancied I had said enough so you couldn't fail to understand me. Last night as we sat on the deck of the Sachem, with the placid harbor spread around us and the mellow moonlight turning its waves to silver, I couldn't choke back the things which came to my lips. Perhaps I was rash. Perhaps I was foolish. I couldn't help it. You must know, señorita—you must know how I love you!"

"Stop!" she commanded, in a low, intense tone. "Let me give you a warning now. I had no chance last night, for Frank came."

In Spanish Del Norte muttered something that was strangely like a curse.

"Yes, he came," said the man. "I have not forgotten; nor have I forgotten, señorita, that you did not tell him just what had happened. You did not tell him I kissed your hand. That made me think that perhaps my case was not hopeless. That made me think perhaps you looked with a little favor upon me."

"You quite mistook the reason why I did not tell him," she declared, still repressing her voice. "I did not dare."

"Did not dare?"

"No."

"Why?"

"Because I know him."

"And you mean by that—just what, señorita?"

"Frank knows that you know we are engaged. Had I told him of your presumption he would have made trouble for you. I am sure he would have punished you for it. And I don't wish you and Frank to engage in an encounter—at least, while you are both guests of Mr. Crossgrove on the Sachem."

"I am willing that you should tell him, señorita," declared the Mexican, with a touch of passion. "If you don't, I may yet tell him myself."

"If you do you will make the mistake of your life—you will surely regret it. Be warned, Portias del Norte. I know Frank Merriwell, and you do not. Keep away from me if you are inclined to forget your place and talk folly. Save your protestations of love for some one else."

"Impossible! impossible!" he breathed. "When I see you my soul pants to speak. I feel a yearning that makes me willing to face any peril. I have dreamed strange dreams since we met, señorita. I have dreamed of my home far away in Mexico, and of you in it as my bride."

"If you speak one word more of this," said Inza, "I shall leave you, and I shall be gravely offended. I am in earnest, Señor del Norte. It's the height of folly for you to entertain such thoughts. I do not care in the slightest about you, and never could care."

"You say so; but I know—ah, I know! Were he out of the way it would be different."

"Not a bit different. You interest me, but you are not the sort of man for whom I could bear the slightest touch of love. I wish you to understand this in order that you may put aside your foolish thoughts."

"Never! never!" he whispered. "I can't put them aside! I refuse to put them aside, even as they refuse to be cast aside. You do not know what change time might bring to your heart. Don't go, señorita—please don't! I will say no more. Do you know I can't help thinking—I can't help thinking! Even though my lips are silent, my heart shall speak to you. You shall see the undying passion of my soul in my face and in my eyes. You shall hear it in my voice when I talk of common things. And the time may come—the time will come when you will yield to it, even as the branch yields to the caress of the vine that twines about it."

For some time Elsie Bellwood had been watching Inza and her companion, and now Elsie approached them.

Del Norte saw her and quickly said in a low tone:

"Here comes the girl with the sunny hair and the flower-like eyes. She doesn't like me."

He laughed softly, and added:

"They never like me unless I make love to them. You're not that way, señorita. You are much different from all the women I have ever met. Yes, I will be silent—never fear. She shall not hear or know—unless you tell her."

"Where is Frank, Inza?" asked Elsie as she came up.

"I don't know," was the answer. "He strolled away a little while ago."

"Bart has been asking for him."

Elsie came close to her friend and grasped Inza's hand.

"Let's see if we can find him," she invited. "Perhaps Señor del Norte will excuse you."

"Oh, don't let me detain you," bowed the Mexican. "It has been my pleasure to chat a few moments with you, and I will easily find others, although they may be less entertaining."

As Elsie and Inza moved away, the former said:

"I don't like the way he was talking to you, Inza, and I fancied you didn't like it, either. I saw something in your manner—your movements—that made me think he was saying things he should not. What was he saying?"

"Oh, nothing more than a lot of foolishness," Inza laughed. "He's a clever talker."

"Altogether too clever," said Elsie. "He's just what I said he was, a snake. There are beautiful snakes, you know, and Porfias del Norte is of that variety."

"I am not in the least afraid of him," laughed Inza. "The most beautiful snakes are usually perfectly harmless. The venomous kind are hideous and repulsive."

"Still I fear you underrate the danger of having anything to do with that man. When I saw you with him a chill ran over me. When I saw him bend toward you, speaking swiftly, with that strange look on his face and in his eyes, my blood was cold in my body. Inza, do beware of him. Bart dislikes him quite as much as I do. Bart says he is one who strikes at an enemy's back."

"That's not strange coming from Bart," said Inza, "for he is one who always forms violent prejudices. But it does seem strange that you should feel so strongly about Porfias del Norte. I think you must have absorbed it from Bart."

"No! no! I felt it the first time I saw the man. I didn't know what Bart thought until I said something about him. Last night I dreamed of him. I suppose it was because he came upon us so softly and suddenly while we were chatting on the deck of the Sachem. You know I couldn't bear to listen when he started to sing, but after I left you I was sorry I did so. In the night I dreamed that I saw you asleep, with a great cluster of crimson flowers on your bosom. I remained still in order that I might not awaken you. I could see your bosom rising and falling as you breathed. Suddenly I saw a hideously deformed creature creeping into the room where you lay. It was like a man, yet like a beast. I can't describe it. But a terrible horror came upon me as I watched.

"I knew you were in frightful peril, yet my tongue lay silent in my mouth and I could not cry out to you. I tried to shriek to arouse you, but not a sound would my lips utter. Nearer and nearer moved the hideous creature until it stood directly over you. Then, for the first time, I saw its head, and beheld that it was the head of a man. It turned for a moment in my direction, and its face was that of Porfias del Norte, smiling his terrible smile that is so fascinating and yet so full of something deadly. He picked up the crimson flowers and breathed upon them. Then he replaced them on your breast and slowly retreated, smiling all the while. As I watched, those flowers suddenly sprang into life. They became moving things, and to my nostrils came a soft yet terrible odor that made me faint and sick.

"I saw those flowers with their writhing vines twist around your arms and about your neck. The blossoms clustered thick about your face, while the twining vines grew tight about your throat, and I knew they were strangling you. Then I managed to break the spell upon me and utter a shriek that awoke me. I was shaking all over, and it was daylight before I again closed my eyes in sleep. Oh, Inza, I now feel doubly sure that this man, Del Norte, will bring some terrible catastrophe upon you! It will be in the form of something beautiful, but it may destroy you."

Elsie was pale and breathless as she finished.

Inza gave her a hug and laughed at her folly, but in her heart the dark-eyed girl felt strangely impressed by Elsie's dream.

CHAPTER XXVIII

THE STRUGGLE ON THE CLIFF.

he supper was wholly satisfactory. It was enjoyed by every person, the host having spread himself on this occasion.

While the shades of evening were gathering at the foot of the mountain they sat over their coffee in the cool dining room of the hotel and chatted.

Now, for a wonder, the Mexican was strangely silent. On his face there lay a soft shadow and his eyes seemed full of dreamy, faraway sadness. Even when Frank told a humorous story that set all the others in a shout of laughter, Del Norte remained absorbed and silent, not even smiling slightly.

Ere the party rose from the table the Mexican got up, excused himself, and strolled out. He was not on the broad veranda when the others left the dining room and took their seats outside.

Some of the male members of the party smoked, Browning declining a cigar and asking leave to light his pipe, which was freely granted, as he had taken a seat to the leeward of the others.

Creeping along with surprising closeness to the shore, they saw below them one of the huge white steamers which ply between Boston and Bangor. At that distance, as it rounded the point and swung into the little harbor, it looked like a toy boat. The sound of its hoarse whistle came up to their ears, mellowed and made musical by the distance.

Twilight was on the harbor, and the steamer was glowing with lights when it crept out once more and continued on its course. Already at a bound scores of electric lights had gleamed forth down at the foot of the mountain. The town was illumined.

"Señor del Norte should be here," said Crossgrove. "I wonder where he is."

The stars came out one by one, growing clearer and plainer as the last remnant of day was smothered by the advancing night.

"Yes, Señor del Norte should be here," said the captain's daughter. "Look yonder to the east. See that glow of light. The moon will rise soon."

There was little talk, and that in low tones, as the huge, round moon came pushing up in the east and flooded the bay with its light. It was so cool that the ladies gladly accepted the wraps brought them by some of the men. Still, it was not cold enough to be disagreeable. The air was clear and winelike. But the beauty of the night took hold of them one and all.

For some time Inza had been strangely silent and moody. In vain Frank had tried to arouse her. She protested that nothing was the matter, yet finally she arose and left the veranda without asking him to join her. He watched her with a restless feeling, and finally called after her, asking where she was going.

"Come on and you will find out," she answered, with a short laugh. "See if you can catch me."

The others watched the pursuit with languid interest. They saw Inza flit from bush to bush, from rock to rock, with Merry laughingly pursuing. Before long both had vanished, but still, for a few minutes, their voices were to be heard.

Inza was successful in avoiding Frank for some time. Once he thought he had her safely overtaken, only to find she was not crouching in a shadow of a bush where he fancied she must be. At last he paused in perplexity, realizing he had lost all trace of her.

"Inza!" he called. "Where are you?"

All around him were stunted cedars, and rocks, and shadows.

A sudden fear came upon him. What if something had happened to her? Once more he called her name.

Out of the shadows something came, moving swiftly, and a moment later a bareheaded, panting man dashed up and seized Frank's arm.

"Merciful heavens, señor!" cried the familiar voice of Del Norte, "who was the lady? I caught barely a glimpse of her! It's the most frightful thing! We must hasten to find her, for she may be yet alive."

"What's that?" hastily demanded Merry, grasping the Mexican in turn. "What are you talking about, Del Norte?"

"Why did she do it?" moaned the Mexican, releasing his hold on Frank to wring his hands. "She seemed distracted. She seemed crazy. I saw her flit along, but didn't dream she meant to leap from the precipice."

With sudden fear, Merry gave the panting man a shake.

"What are you talking about, you crazy imbecile?" he demanded. "It was Inza Burrage you saw!"

"Merciful saints!" moaned the Mexican, seeming ready to collapse with horror. "The beautiful Señorita Inza? And I saw her plunge over the precipice to her death! A moment before I was looking from the brink myself into the black treetops down below. The shadows are deep and dark down there."

"Take me to the spot!" cried Frank.

"Hasten, then!" palpitated the Mexican. "I will show you where it happened. Oh, the beautiful señorita! She has gone to her death! Not even a cry did she utter! What a frightful thing, Señor Merriwell!"

Frank followed the Mexican, who quickly led him to the verge of a high cliff, over which he declared the girl had rushed without pause and without sound of any sort.

Frank bent forward and peered over. Beneath him the bluff dropped almost straight down. Far below in the shadows he could see the tops of many trees growing thickly.

A sudden feeling of doubt and uncertainty swept over him. It seemed utterly preposterous that Inza in gay spirits should rush blindly over that precipice. Had she done such a thing by accident or miscalculation, surely she would have uttered a cry as she fell. Like a flash he whirled on Del Norte, and he was barely in time to save his own life, for he discovered the Mexican in the act of thrusting him over the brink of the precipice.

Quick as thought, Merry clutched Del Norte's wrists and clung to them.

"You dog!" he said, in a low tone, as they both tottered on the very edge of the cliff. "If I go, you go with me."

"Fiends take you!" hissed the vindictive and treacherous Mexican. "Why did you turn? One second more and you would have found yourself falling to your death!"

Even as he panted these words, the wretch tried to squirm clear of Merry's clutch and send him over the brink. He was like an eel in his writhings, yet Frank managed to hold fast to him.

"If I go, you go, too!" palpitated the young American.

"You shall not escape!" hissed the other, his dark eyes glaring in the moonlight.

"Then say your prayers, Porfias del Norte, for your end comes with mine!"

Frank felt that it was useless to shout for help. Long before any one on the veranda could answer the cry and reach the spot, the encounter would be over and one or the other would be victorious.

The moon was well up by this time, and its bright light fell full upon the two men battling for their very lives at the brink of that frightful precipice. All around them the world appeared calm, and still, and at peace. They alone of all human creatures, it seemed, were aroused by beastlike passions, seeking to destroy each other.

Del Norte had approached Merry in such a manner that Frank was at a decided disadvantage. He was swaying over the very brink of the cliff when he clutched the Mexican's wrist. Being somewhat heavier than his antagonist, there was danger that Frank's weight would drag them both to their doom.

Beneath Merriwell's foot a portion of the ledge crumbled and gave way.

"Let go!" suddenly urged the Mexican, taking a grip on the collar of the youth. "Let go and I will hold you. I don't mean to push you over. It's all a joke, señor. Look out! The ground is slipping beneath your feet!"

In this manner the Mexican did his best to deceive Frank, and a moment later the two men were locked in each other's arms, each seeking to hurl the other prostrate.

"May the fiends take you!" panted Del Norte. "What evil spirit saved you from my hands? You turned just in time."

"The blood of Guerrero, the bandit, runs strong in your veins," said Merry. "You dare not fight the battle out between us in the courts, but you seek by murder to secure your ends."

"I shall yet triumph!" snarled the Mexican. "Even though you escape to-night, my time will come."

Then Merry crushed him down and hurled him heavily to the ground.

"Tell the truth, you treacherous dog!" commanded Frank, with his hands at the fallen man's throat. "Did you see Inza Burrage?"

"Yes, I saw her."

"Where did she go?"

"She fled past me as I stood in the shadow of some bushes."

"You lied when you said she fell over the precipice?"

"It was a little stratagem of mine, Señor Merriwell; that's all. She didn't fall over the precipice. No! no! Had she done so my heart would have been broken! I should have been crushed by the frightful horror of it. Oh, I am not afraid of you, dog of a gringo! You have me down, but to your face I tell you that I love her and she shall yet be mine! Now, do your worst!"

"You poor fool!" laughed Frank harshly. "You're not worth

kicking over the cliff! Don't deceive yourself with foolish dreams. And let me give you this warning: Keep away from Inza Burrage if you value your life!"

"Bah! You speak boldly now, for you have conquered by your brute strength. It's not the strength of the brute that wins in the end; it's the brains of the wise man. You think you're wise and crafty, but in the end you shall know that Porfias del Norte is a thousand times your superior."

With an exclamation of scorn and disdain, Frank rose to his feet.

He turned to move away, but as he did so Del Norte, who had risen to his knees, suddenly clutched Merry by both legs and once more sought to hurl him over the cliff.

Only by dropping, quickly doubling himself at the hips and clutching the Mexican about the shoulders, did Frank prevent the treacherous scoundrel from accomplishing his dastardly design.

Taken thus at a disadvantage, it was not strange Merry could not prevent his enemy from rising to an upright position. Then once more the Mexican exerted all his strength to hurl Merry over the brink. To the right and to the left they swayed. Once they staggered to within a foot of the edge.

Frank sought to break the other man's hold, and this he finally accomplished just as Del Norte made an upward surge and thrust out a foot in an effort to trip the American.

The Mexican's heel struck something, and a moment later, with a shrill cry of horror, he found himself tottering at the edge of the bluff.

Merry leaped forward with one hand outstretched in an effort to grasp the fellow and save him from that fall.

Too late!

Beneath Porfias del Norte's feet the ledge crumbled, and, with another cry of despair, the miserable wretch dropped from view, turning over and over as he fell.

It happened that Inza Burrage, who had concealed herself some distance away, being directed by the sound of voices during the struggle, had approached the cliff just in time to witness Del Norte fall. To her horrified eyes it seemed that Frank sprang forward with hand outthrust and hurled the wretched Mexican over the precipice. She stopped in her tracks, turned to stone by what she had witnessed.

Merry stood for a moment or two as if horrified. As he dropped on his hands and knees and peered over the brink, he heard a crashing sound amid the treetops far, far below.

"They will find a dead Mexican down there!" he muttered.

CHAPTER XXIX

IN THE HANDS OF DEL NORTE.

ard," said Brad Buckhart, edging his chair close to Dick as they sat on the veranda of the hotel, "this yere business is a whole lot like a Sunday-school picnic to me. I sure am getting some weary of it. I don't want to kick any, but it seems to me you're not having a hilarious old time yourself."

"Oh, I am enjoying it all right," answered Dick.

"Still don't you feel a heap like a misfit in this crowd? If it were our bunch it would be different. We don't seem to pair up any. There's Rattleton, he's satisfied to sit and look on, and Browning is too lazy to be disturbed over anything, while the rest of the party kind of pair up and go it first-rate. I don't want to make a holler, but I'd some prefer to be down on the Sachem about now, and I think we can add to the bliss of the others if we vamoose."

"Well, if you're anxious to go——" began Dick.

"Not exactly anxious, but I am tired of keeping still. We won't break up the congregation any if we pull out by our own selves, partner."

"All right," said Dick, "we will do so. I fancy we'll have no trouble in following the wagon road down the mountain."

Young Merriwell told Rattleton of their decision, and asked him to inform Frank when Merry returned to the hotel.

A few moments later Dick and Brad set out, taking the wagon road. At intervals they passed through dark strips of timber, where the moonlight failed to penetrate. There were other spots where it shone through in patches upon the winding road.

"Don't suppose there are any panthers or catamounts?" said the Texan.

"It's quite improbable," answered Dick. "There are few wild creatures in this vicinity."

"Seems a whole lot strange to me. You know out in Texas we kind of reckon Maine as being made up of woods, and bears, and creatures of that sort. Down here I find lots of folks think Texas is all prairie, and cattle, and cowboys. I didn't get back home this summer, but I've had a mighty fine vacation, Dick. I will never forget it. Pard, we certain did a big thing by landing the pennant in the Trolley League. When I think it over now, I don't wonder any at all that the people in the league laughed at us a heap and fancied we would finish at the bottom. They didn't know us, though. We were out for scalps, and we took 'em. Those last two games in Fairhaven were corkers. How old Hammerswell did fight to lug off one of those games! They say he went clean busted by losing them both."

"That's right," said Dick. "I understand he didn't have a dollar left in the world when the season was ended."

"Money wouldn't have been much good to him."

"Possibly you're right, Brad, for if Arlington told the truth, Hammerswell stood in the shadow of a murder charge. For he it was who hurled Sullivan into Rapid River and thus caused Sullivan's death by drowning."

"Don't talk to me about Chet Arlington!" exclaimed Brad growlingly. "Don't mention that coyote to me! The sound of his name makes my fur stand. Pard, do you reckon he'll have the nerve to show his nose at Fardale after what he's done this summer?"

"It wouldn't surprise me to find him there."

"Why, dern his pesky hide! he went plum back on us the very day we landed in Maplewood. He turned traitor. Then he had the crust to crawl around you and try to excuse himself."

"He has plenty of crust," agreed Dick. "It's his cheek that keeps him up in the world."

"When do you plan to start for Fardale?" asked the Texan.

"In a day or two. I wish to be with Frank as long as possible. I have thought he may be ready to go on to New York by the time we have to start for school."

"Well, I don't know, but I'll be glad to get back to the old school," confessed the Texan. "There will be doings this fall. I suppose you will jog out the bunch and commence football practice just as soon as we strike there?"

"I will not waste time about it. The more practice we get the better it will be."

"We ought to have a hot old team this year, partner."

"I think we'll have a good one. Frank wants to come on to Fardale for a few days, but he's afraid he can't do it. He's going to have his hands full directly with that railroad business."

"How would you like to go down there into Mexico with him

and see the railroad pushed through?"

"I should like it," confessed Dick; "but there's nothing of the sort for me. It's school for me now."

"I don't take much to greasers. They are a-plenty treacherous. Now there's that smooth, smiling chap, Del Norte—he don't hit me at all fine. He's too slick and oily for my fancy. Oh, we see lots of them down on the Rio Pecos. You know we're some near the Mexican border. I have had dealings with the varmints, and you can never depend on them to any great extent. They are not all bad, but a Texan never takes stock in any of them. He can't afford to. Where you find one that's white all the way through, you find a hundred who will eat your bread and stick you between the shoulder blades. I reckon old Del Norte is one of those."

"I myself don't like Del Norte," confessed Dick. "I have seen him watching Inza in a way I didn't fancy. He had better be careful or Frank will teach him a lesson if he gets too forward in that direction."

"What is he doing on the Sachem, anyhow? I heard him talking yesterday with Mr. Crossgrove about mines and a railroad and one thing and another. I believe he's a promoter."

"I think he's a schemer of some sort. There's not much doubt about that."

Having reached the foot of the mountain and the main road, the boys turned toward town and Dick began singing "Fair Fardale." Brad joined in, and the rocks and cliffs of the mountainside reverberated with the melody of the beautiful song.

At length they passed the cemetery at the foot of the mountain and came into the village.

"How will we get off to the yacht, partner?" asked the Texan.

"Oh, we can find some one to set us off, I think," said Dick. "If not we will signal, and one of the sailors will row ashore for us."

Arriving at Fishmarket Wharf, they were just in time to see a boy row in with a small boat.

"Hello!" said Dick. "Do you want to make fifty cents?"

"Sure thing," was the reply. "Just made a dollar, and fifty more will keep it from being lonesome. What can I do?"

"Set us off to the yacht Sachem."

"Hey?" exclaimed the boy, with a slight show of surprise. "Are you in a great hurry?"

"No."

"Don't want me to rip things in getting you on board, I suppose?"

"No; you may take your time. We have the whole night before

us."

"Well, I didn't know," muttered the boy, a touch of disappointment in his voice. "I thought mebbe you was in the same hurry t'other chap was. He gave me a dollar to hump myself and put him off to the Sachem."

"To the Sachem?" questioned Dick.

"Sure thing."

"I wonder who it was."

"Didn't ask his name," said the boy; "but I guess he just got through some sort of an accident. His hat was gone and his clothes were all torn, and his cheek was scratched and cut. Is there a doctor on the Sachem? Mebbe he wanted the doctor to patch him up."

"This is some interesting, pard," said Buckhart, as they settled in the boat and the boy pushed off. "I wonder who the chap was."

"What did he look like?" asked Dick, directing his question toward the rower.

"Well, from what I saw he was kind of slim and had dark eyes and hair, and a little pointed mustache."

"That description fits Porfias del Norte right well," said Buckhart; "but it can't be the greaser, for he's up yonder on the mountain."

"No, it can't be Del Norte," agreed Dick. "We will find out very soon who it was, for yonder lies the Sachem."

As they swung in at the side of the yacht a sailor appeared and watched them come aboard.

Dick questioned the sailor, and both boys were greatly astonished when they were told that the man who had just preceded them was none other than Porfias del Norte.

"He had a bad fall on the mountain, sir," said the sailor. "His clothes were torn, and he was cut and bruised. Said he slipped and fell over a steep ledge."

"Hey there!" called the boy from the boat. "When do I get that fifty cents? You fellers clean forgot me."

"I will pay him, Dick," said Buckhart.

Brad paused to pay the boy, but Dick turned at once toward the main saloon of the magnificent yacht.

The singular and unexpected return of Del Norte had filled the boy with wonderment and speculation.

The Sachem was large enough to have a number of staterooms, and Dick turned at once toward the one occupied by Frank and himself.

To his surprise through the keyhole of the door to this room he saw a gleam of light.

"What's this?" he exclaimed, in a low tone. "There's a light in that room!"

Softly stepping to the door, he stooped and peered through the keyhole.

Some one was in the room, for he saw the person moving, but the room was very small, and the person was so near the door that Dick could not tell who it was.

Immediately the boy seized the knob of the door and flung it open.

Porfias del Norte himself, still wearing his torn clothing, was standing beside the berths, on the upper one of which sat a small iron box. This box had been opened, and in the hands of Del Norte was an outspread paper that looked like a map.

Instantly Dick realized that the Mexican was rifling Frank's private papers. In some manner Del Norte had opened the iron box, and now he was going through the papers to find the valuable ones he desired.

The opening of the door caused the rascal to wheel instantly, uttering a suppressed exclamation.

"What are you doing?" cried Dick, lifting a hand and pointing an accusing finger at the Mexican.

For a moment the rascal was taken aback. Then he swiftly folded the paper and thrust it into his trousers pocket.

"I beg your pardon, young señor," smiled Del Norte, seemingly to recover his ease. "You startled me a trifle when you opened the door so suddenly."

"What are you doing, you scoundrel?" cried the boy. "Give up that paper!"

"What paper?" asked the man, with pretended innocence.

"The one you thrust into your pocket."

"Oh, it belongs to me. Why, what's the matter with you? You seem greatly agitated. Has anything happened to excite you?"

"I should say something had!" said Dick. "How dared you enter this room?"

"This room? Why, I have a right in my own room, have I not?"

"But this is not your room."

"Not my room?"

"You know it's not. This room is the one occupied by my brother and myself. How dared you enter it?"

"Is it possible I have made a mistake?" exclaimed Del Norte, lifting his eyebrows and looking very much surprised. "Why, I really believe I have! I trust you will pardon me."

He made a move as if to leave the room.

"Stop!" cried Dick, planting himself squarely in the doorway. "You have made a serious mistake, Porfias del Norte. Now I know why you were in such great haste to reach the Sachem. You had a key by which you entered this room. You had another key by which you opened my brother's strong box. You have stolen a paper from that box, but you must put it back. If you refuse——"

Del Norte exposed his beautiful teeth as he laughed in the boy's face.

"If I do not," he purred, "if I do not put it back, what will you do, señor?"

"I will make you!" cried Dick.

The Mexican laughed.

"Why, you child! You can't make any one do anything! Get out of my way!"

With a stride he attempted to pass Dick. A moment later the boy grappled with him, and a struggle began in the saloon of the Sachem.

"Poor fool!" snarled Del Norte, "what do you think? Do you fancy you can interfere with me? Why, I will crush you!"

"I hardly think you will!" grated Dick, as he back-locked the man and hurled him to the floor.

Although Dick had thrown Del Norte with comparative ease, the Mexican was like an eel in the grasp of the boy. As Dick attempted to pin the fellow down, he realized that he had failed and that the Mexican had squirmed from beneath him.

Together they arose. Dick hastened, in order that the man might not get the advantage.

By this time the look on the face of Del Norte, as revealed by the lamplight shining from the open door of the stateroom, was one of savage ferocity. All his smiling and sweetness had vanished, and his eyes glared with a deadly light. His small white teeth were keen and pantherish beyond his curling lips, which were stretched tightly over them.

"Poor fool!" he once more snarled. "It's your brother who nearly destroyed me to-night! We fought up there on the mountain, and he pushed me over the precipice! I fell through the air, feeling that my hour had come! The horror of it is something that never touched me before. I believed I would be killed when I struck, but I landed in the treetops, and I was saved! Though my clothes were torn and I was bruised and battered, not even one bone was broken!"

He panted forth these words as they were again struggling for the mastery.

"I hate your brother!" he grated. "It will give me pleasure can I kill you here and now! That much revenge on him will I have!"

"But you can't do it," said Dick, as he again wound his leg round those of the man and started to hurl him to the floor.

As he was falling, Del Norte caught at the edge of the table, which enabled him to turn while coming down. He had clung to Dick, and this turn had flung the boy sidewise, Dick's head striking a chair with great violence.

A moment later Porfias del Norte was kneeling astride Dick Merriwell, with his hands on the boy's throat. As if from a great distance, the boy heard the scoundrel saying:

"It's my time, and this is my revenge on your brother! Now you die!"

CHAPTER XXX

THE ESCAPE.

Frank Merriwell rose from the edge of the precipice and turned away. He stopped in astonishment, uttering an exclamation, for not fifteen feet away stood Inza Burrage, her face ghastly white in the moonlight and her eyes regarding him with an expression of horror.

"Inza!" he exclaimed.

She shrank from him.

"I saw you do it!" she panted.

"You saw?"

"Yes."

"Saw what?"

"I saw it all! I saw you hurl him over the precipice!"

"But I didn't hurl him over, Inza."

"I saw it!" she palpitated. "Oh, Frank, what made you do it?"

"Inza, I tell you I did not! He attempted to hurl me over. He led me here, saying you had fallen over this very precipice. Then I bent over the brink and looked downward. He sprang upon me. We had a struggle."

"And you ended it when you pushed him to his death!"

"Can't you believe me, Inza? Your eyes deceived you. I didn't push him. He tore away from me, and I saw him reeling on the very verge of the cliff. I saw he must fall, and I sprang to grasp him. I was too late, for almost as soon as my fingers touched him he fell."

She was silent now, looking intently at Frank.

"It must be true," she muttered; "but it seemed to me that you gave him a push. Frank, I know you never speak anything but the truth. Even had you pushed him over I would have kept your secret."

"I haven't a doubt of it, Inza," he said. "But I have hardly descended to such measures in disposing of an enemy. I regret exceedingly that this thing happened, for it spoils the trip up the mountain. We must go down without delay and search for Del Norte's body. Let's return to the hotel."

She was trembling as she took his arm.

"I suppose that Mexican attacked me in order to get me out of the way, which would enable him to carry out his schemes in Mexico," said Merry.

"There was another reason," confessed Inza.

"Another reason?"

"Yes."

"What was it?"

She hesitated.

"I will tell you the truth, Frank," she finally said. "It's best that you should know. I didn't tell you before because I didn't wish you to have trouble with Del Norte while we were guests of Mr. Crossgrove on the Sachem. It was my intention to let you know everything the moment we left the yacht. Del Norte has twice tried to make love to me. Last night on board the yacht he kissed my hand. Perhaps I was foolish to give him the opportunity, but he interested me with his story, and he seized the occasion to kiss my hand before I fancied he would attempt such a thing. To-night, on the hotel veranda, he made an effort to resume his love-making, but I gave him a warning which silenced him. Had he offered to annoy me again, even though it must have caused trouble between you, I should have told you everything. He swore to me that he would some day get the best of you, Frank, and make me love him."

"And this is what it has come to," muttered Merry. "Well, the treacherous dog brought it on himself."

When they reached the veranda and told what had happened there was consternation in the party. Merry did not tell the entire truth. He concealed the fact that a struggle had taken place on the brink of the precipice.

Without delay Henry Crossgrove ordered the team hitched up, and in a short time the party left the hotel, the men descending on foot.

Frank led them all, with Hodge close beside him. As they hastened down the road, Merry told Bart in low tones exactly what had taken place.

"I knew it!" said Hodge. "I knew the kind of thing he was! Are you going to lead the searching party, Frank?"

"Yes. I think it best to notify the authorities and secure lanterns.

Without the aid of lanterns we will be handicapped in our search down there amid the dark woods near the foot of the mountain."

They had reached the outskirts of the village when a carriage approached at a rapid pace. To their surprise they were hailed by the voice of Dick Merriwell.

"Hello, Dick!" exclaimed Frank. "Is that you?"

An instant later Dick and Brad sprang out.

"We were just making for the top of the mountain," explained young Merriwell. "We have something on board the Sachem that will interest you."

"What is it?" questioned Frank.

"A slick rascal who broke into our stateroom, opened your strong box, and attempted to get away with one of the papers."

"Who was it?" cried Merry.

"Porfias del Norte."

"Dick, you're dreaming!" almost shouted Frank, as he caught his brother by the shoulder. "Porfias del Norte lies dead up there on the mountainside. He fell over a precipice."

"Porfias del Norte lies tied hand and foot in the saloon of the Sachem," said Dick. "You can thank my friend Buckhart for it, too. I caught Del Norte as he was trying to get away with the paper, and we had a little racket in the saloon. I downed him once, but he squirmed away from me. The second time, as he was falling, he caught hold of the table, which threw me to one side, and my head struck against a chair. I was stunned, and Del Norte proceeded to choke me, with the intention of finishing me. Just then Brad sailed in and landed on Del Norte's shoulders with one spring. We handled him all right, and left him tied hand and foot, with one of the sailors keeping watch at the head of the companionway."

"This is wonderful! This is astounding!" gasped Henry Crossgrove. "I didn't think it of the man."

"It is astounding," nodded Merry. "It's astounding that he should escape death after falling over that precipice."

"He was some tattered and battered," put in Buckhart. "His clothes were ripped and his face and hands scratched and cut."

"He must have landed fairly in a treetop and escaped in that manner," said Frank. "Boys, you have done well. Let's hurry to the Sachem and take a look at our captive."

No time was lost in getting off to the yacht. They found the sailor apparently still on guard at the head of the companionway. He was sitting in a bowed position, and when they approached him he was seen to be fast asleep.

Henry Crossgrove was exasperated.

"This chap shall receive his walking papers as soon as I can speak to the captain," he declared.

Dick led the way into the saloon, with the others close behind him. When he opened the door and looked in a cry of astonishment and dismay escaped his lips.

On the floor lay the cords with which Del Norte had been bound. In some manner the slippery Mexican had released himself, and he had lost not a moment in sneaking up the companionway and past the sleeping guard. He was gone, having in some manner escaped unobserved from the yacht. It was supposed he had dropped overboard and swum to another yacht near by, where he secured a rowboat and put ashore. The boat was found drifting the following morning.

"Too bad he got away," muttered Bart Hodge. "Perhaps he has learned his lesson and will not bother the Merriwells in future."

"On the contrary," said Frank, "I think I shall see more of Porfias del Norte before much time has elapsed. I fancy the struggle between that man and myself has just begun."

THE END.